Red Sky
In Mourning

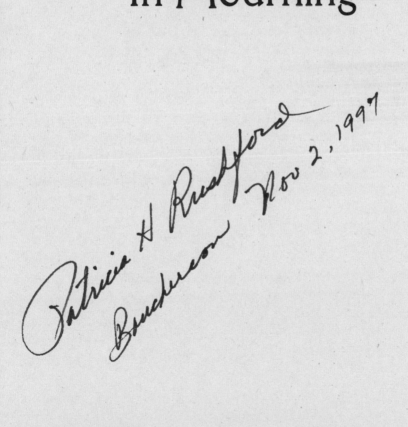

PATRICIA H. RUSHFORD

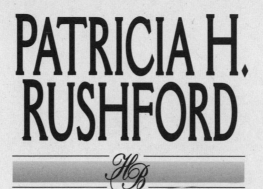

HELEN BRADLEY MYSTERIES

Red Sky
In Mourning

BETHANY HOUSE PUBLISHERS
MINNEAPOLIS, MINNESOTA 55438

Published by Bethany House Publishers
A Ministry of Bethany Fellowship, Inc.
11300 Hampshire Avenue South
Minneapolis, Minnesota 55438

Printed in the United States of America.

Library of Congress Cataloging-in-Publication Data

Rushford, Patricia H.
    Red sky in mourning / by Patricia H. Rushford.
        p. cm.—(Helen Bradley mysteries ; 2)
      ISBN 1-55661-731-3 (pbk.)
      I. Title. II. Series: Rushford, Patricia H. Helen Bradley mysteries ; 2.
PS3568.U7274R43   1997
813'.54—dc21   97-21117
                                                CIP

To the Willapa Bay Writers,
the real Long Beach Peninsula,
and the people who make up
"The Lost Corner."

Helen Bradley Mystery Series

Now I Lay Me Down to Sleep
Red Sky in Mourning

Jennie McGrady Mystery Series

Too Many Secrets
Silent Witness
Pursued
Deceived
Without a Trace
Dying to Win
Betrayed
In Too Deep
Over the Edge
From the Ashes

PATRICIA RUSHFORD is an award-winning writer, speaker, and teacher who has published numerous articles, and over twenty-five books, including *What Kids Need Most in a Mom*, *The Jack and Jill Syndrome: Healing for Broken Children*, and *Have You Hugged Your Teenager Today?* She is a registered nurse and has a master's degree in counseling from Western Evangelical Seminary. She and her husband, Ron, live in Washington State and have two grown children, six grandchildren, and lots of nephews and nieces.

Pat has been reading mysteries for as long as she can remember and is delighted to be writing a series of her own. She is a member of Mystery Writers of America, Sisters in Crime, and several other writing organizations. She is also co-director of Writer's Weekend at the Beach.

One

Helen Bradley lowered her book, *How to Murder the Man of Your Dreams*, and peered at the man of her dreams and husband of ten weeks, Jason Bradley. At least J.B. had been her dream man until recently. Now aspects of their relationship lapsed at times from dreams to near nightmares.

Not that she was reading the book with murder on her mind. Helen doubted she'd have to resort to killing him, but she needed to do something—and fast. Off work for three weeks and facing retirement, J.B. was driving her to the brink. She'd be leaving soon to do research for a book, but knowing J.B., he'd want to go along.

The big Irishman paced from the entry through the living room to the kitchen and back again. The house, a roomy, remodeled Cape Cod, overlooked the Oregon coast in Bay Village, just south of Lincoln City. It had once seemed too large for her. Now it bordered on cozy—a little too cozy.

"Darling . . ." Helen marked her place and set the book on the coffee table with the front cover down so he couldn't see the title. "Would you like to walk on the beach?"

He stopped. His blue gaze seemed as unfocused as his life had become. "A walk?" He blinked away the confused look and smiled. "Aye, that would be nice." Glancing out at the gunmetal gray sky, he added, "But 'tis a bit soupy out there."

Helen chuckled and unfolded her lanky frame from the plush cushions of her favorite chair. She wrapped her arms around his firm and still muscular torso. "In case you hadn't noticed, we're at the beach."

"I thought you wanted to get some writing done this morning."

"I did." Helen hesitated. With her husband stalking through the house like a caged lion, she'd managed to write about three words an hour. "Can't concentrate," she admitted but couldn't bring herself to tell him why. Instead she stretched up to kiss him. "You'll love walking in the rain—especially with the gale winds in your face—clears the sinuses."

"Clogs 'em, you mean." Nevertheless, J.B. followed her to the entryway, where they donned hooded yellow rain slickers. Minutes later they braced themselves against a chilly August wind and made their way to the trail that would eventually lead past the rocks to the sandy beach at Fogarty Creek State Park.

In the silence that stretched between them, Helen wondered what she was going to do about J.B. Only a few weeks before she'd encouraged him to take the early retirement the government had offered. J.B. deserved it. He'd spent most of his life working as a special agent. First in Great Britain, then for the last thirty years in the United States. When he wasn't off on some secret mission for the State Department, he worked for the FBI.

J.B.'s last mission for Uncle Sam had taken him to the Middle East, where he headed up a special task force to rescue five prisoners who'd been held by guerrilla forces since the Gulf War. He'd been hailed a hero by the president and awarded a medal. They also offered him a substantial retirement package. He'd surprised her by taking it. Helen had been pleased at first, but she realized now that retirement could be hazardous to one's health.

Helen had heard tales about retired husbands getting underfoot, but she thought J.B. would be different. Surely he'd find ways to keep busy.

He hadn't. Somehow fishing and writing his memoirs in a journal weren't enough.

Helen sighed as he cradled her hand in his. She loved him

too much to hurt him, but if she didn't get rid of him for a couple weeks, she'd be forced to retire herself. Which was not an option at this point. She'd just signed a contract to write her first book. True, it was an assignment. And she'd be finishing a project someone else had started, but it was a book just the same, and she wanted very much to write it—and she needed the time alone.

"We need to talk." Helen squeezed J.B.'s hand.

"You don't need to say it, luv. I can see it in your eyes. You've grown weary of me."

Helen gasped. Had she been that transparent? "How can you say that? I love you."

"I don't blame you," he went on as if he hadn't heard her objection. "I'm poor company—even for myself. I don't know what I'm going to do. I thought I wanted to retire, and now . . . you were right, you know."

"About what?"

"My being addicted to danger. 'Tis true, I'm afraid, but I've no idea what to do about it."

Tears stung her eyes. *Helen Bradley*, she scolded, *you've been so concerned about yourself, you didn't even stop to think about how he might be feeling. You of all people should understand.*

Helen had retired from active duty with the Portland Police Bureau ten years earlier—shortly after her first husband's death. Ian McGrady and J.B. were two of a kind, both dedicated to ridding the world of evil. In fact, the men had been best friends since their military academy days in England. Ian's final mission had taken him to the Middle East, where a terrorist group bombed the government building in which he'd been working. Little wonder, then, she'd welcomed J.B.'s retirement.

She understood his difficult transition. Heaven knew it hadn't been easy for her either. Following a time of mourning for Ian, Helen had eventually turned to a career in writing. And thanks to J.B., she'd satisfied her own addiction to danger by working on occasion as an undercover agent. She'd done her share of pacing before taking up the pen.

Through the persistent encouragement of her daughter, Kate,

Helen had taken a cruise and written an article about it. Then, after querying several in-flight magazines, sold it for the not-too-shabby sum of $1,000. She hoped J.B. would find something he enjoyed as well.

"At any rate," J.B. was saying when she tuned back in, "I've got some serious thinking to do, and I thought perhaps it might be best if I left."

Helen grabbed his arm, yanking him around to face her. "You're leaving me?"

"Only for a short while. Look at the bright side, luv. I'll be out of your way, and you'll be able to concentrate on that book of yours. That is what you've been wanting, isn't it?"

"How did you. . . ?"

"I know you better than you think, lass." J.B. offered her a wry smile. "I saw the book you were reading."

"Oh." Heat rose to her cheeks.

"Thought I'd best leave before you decided to do away with me permanently." His teasing tone lifted the cloud that had been hanging between them.

"As if I could."

"Why didn't you tell me straightaway you needed me out of your hair?"

"Didn't want to hurt your feelings. I was afraid you'd think I didn't love you."

"I might have at that." He held up his hand to silence her. "I know. You told me more than once before we married that you'd be needing uninterrupted time to work now and then. I'd forgotten that until today."

Helen eased her arms around his neck, her dark blue gaze meeting his. "You're right. I do need space. And you need time to make plans for the future."

"True. As much as I enjoy fishing, it gets tiring after a bit. I've thought about bringing the boat down—docking it here in Bay Village and perhaps developing a charter business. Might be interesting."

"That's a wonderful idea."

J.B.'s boat was a twenty-seven-foot cabin cruiser. He'd

dubbed her the *Hallie B.* "Hallie" was Greek for *thinking of the sea*, and "B" stood for Bradley.

J.B. brushed his lips across hers and made a halfhearted attempt to smile. "You're lucky to have your writing."

"Yes. And speaking of that, I need to go up the coast to the Long Beach Peninsula for at least a week—maybe two."

"Ah, to research the guidebook. Have you started it yet?"

"No—I wanted to finish up a couple travel articles first and get them turned in."

"Did you ever find out why the original author didn't finish the book?"

Helen frowned. "No, but I intend to. Maybe it's my insatiable curiosity or my imagination, but I have the strongest notion my editor wasn't telling me everything. I put in a call to my contact person on the Peninsula—Emily Merritt. She runs the bed and breakfast where I'll be staying. Hopefully she'll be able to fill me in on the details."

"When do you plan to go?"

"I'm not sure—tomorrow maybe."

"So soon?"

"Or Sunday if you'd rather. And you?"

"Sunday would be good. I'd like to get settled in the condo before I go in to the office."

The condo in Portland had been J.B.'s home before they'd married. Since they made so many trips to the city to visit family and travel in and out of the Portland airport, they'd kept it.

"You're going back to work?" Helen asked.

"I—" He gave her a sheepish grin. "I'd like to. And I might be talked into doing an occasional job. But that may not be an option. For now, I'm going in to clean out files and tie up some loose ends."

"Sunday it is, then." Helen bit her lower lip, feeling a sudden sadness. Love was a crazy thing. It could fill you with ecstasy one moment and break your heart the next. At that moment her love for J.B. twisted her insides so tight her stomach hurt. In a day or two they'd be apart again. As much as she needed her space to work, she wanted to be with him. None of it made much sense, and she told him so.

J.B. wrapped an arm around her shoulders and turned her around. "I know just the thing to make us both feel better." He grinned down at her and winked. "I'll build us a cozy fire while you make us some tea." J.B. didn't have to divulge what he planned after that—his eyes said it all.

❖   ❖   ❖

Emily Merritt called at nine o'clock that evening. J.B. and Helen had just returned from having a late dinner at the Tidal Raves, their favorite restaurant in Depoe Bay.

"Sorry I couldn't call sooner," Emily said. "Had guests that kept me busy all day. What can I do for you?" Her voice sounded scratchy, as though it had been used consistently for a very long time.

"Thanks for calling back. My publisher gave me your name. I'll be writing the guidebook about the Peninsula."

"Humph. I know who you are. Publisher already made reservations for you." Emily didn't sound too happy about the arrangement.

"I suppose I could stay elsewhere if you'd rather," Helen said.

"No need to do that. Room's already been paid for."

"Good. I was hoping you could direct me to the woman who was previously writing the book—I'd like to—"

"Can't do that. Isabelle won't be talking to anyone."

"I don't understand. I was told I could get her notes. Perhaps you could ask her—"

"What exactly did the publisher tell you about Isabelle, Mrs. Bradley?" Emily asked.

"Nothing really—only that she had been commissioned to write the book and couldn't finish it. I assumed it was because of illness."

"She wasn't sick. They probably didn't want to tell you the truth for fear you'd think the book is jinxed."

Helen rubbed her forehead. "What truth? What are you talking about?"

"Isabelle is dead. And you mark my words—it was working on the guidebook that killed her."

Two

Sunshine followed Helen as she made her way north along the Oregon Coast. Despite the forecast for rain, she'd trusted the blue skies and put the top down on her vintage Thunderbird convertible. Several times along the way she stopped to admire the view. Though Helen saw the ocean nearly every day, she never tired of it. Today the glimpses of gemstone blue water and white rows of waves raised her spirits and promised adventure.

Once she crossed the Astoria-Megler bridge into Washington, Helen stopped to photograph the historic St. Mary's church. About a mile later she pulled in at the entrance of Fort Columbia State Park and was disappointed to see it had already closed for the day. Just as well, she reminded herself. If she kept stopping, it would be midnight before she got to her destination. "There'll be plenty of time to explore in detail over the next two weeks," she told herself as she turned the car around and continued northwest. Besides, she needed to talk with Emily and learn more about the mysterious death of the guidebook's original author, Isabelle Dupont.

Jamie Lindstrom, Helen's editor at Tour and Travel Publications, had apologized for the short notice but hadn't bothered to mention the fact that Isabelle had died—and under suspicious circumstances. All Jamie said was, "The writer we had lined up didn't work out, and since you live so close . . ."

"Didn't work out indeed," Helen mumbled. Emily Merritt hadn't been too helpful either. All Helen managed to find out was that Isabelle had drowned in the boat basin at the Port of Ilwaco. Helen was not about to let the matter rest.

She glanced at her watch. It wouldn't be long now. With lunch, rest stops, and view breaks, the three-and-a-half-hour drive had taken nearly five hours.

It was five-thirty when Helen finally spotted the carved wooden sign directing her to Bayshore Bed and Breakfast. Helen made a sharp right, then wondered if she'd read the sign correctly. Tall shrubs and trees lined both sides of a rutted gravel road that seemed to go on forever.

She'd driven close to a quarter of a mile when the woods gave way to a lovely manicured lawn and gardens still displaying colorful dahlias, marigolds, Lobelia, and morning glories. It was the house, however, that captured Helen's heart. The magnificent three-story Victorian with its turrets and bay windows looked like something out of a fairy tale. Beyond the house and gardens lay the serene tidelands of Willapa Bay.

Helen parked near the entrance and stepped out of her car. The door to the house swung open. A white-haired woman in a blue flannel shirt and jeans strode across the porch and down the stairs, her cotton white curls barely moving in the wind.

"You Helen?" The voice was unmistakably Emily's.

Helen nodded, feeling a bit out of kilter. The woman and the house didn't seem to match. "Sorry I'm late."

"No problem. Just be the two of us for dinner tonight. Rest of the guests left round noon. Decided not to start fixin' dinner till you showed up."

"Did you expect me to change my mind?"

"Anyone with a lick of sense would have." Emily pointed to the trunk. "Got any luggage?"

"Lots, but I can get it." Helen unlocked the back and grunted as she pulled the heaviest suitcase out.

Emily whistled. "Thought you were only staying for a couple weeks, not moving in permanently."

Helen chuckled. "That's what my husband said. It's not that much, really—only the two suitcases for my personal things. The rest is my office—laptop computer, printer, paper."

Emily grabbed two suitcases and headed for the stairs.

"Wait, you shouldn't be . . ." Helen's protest died under Emily's sharp blue gaze. The woman was apparently used to fetching and hauling and didn't need pampering.

An hour later Emily rang the dinner bell. Helen tucked the last of her empty boxes into the closet and straightened. Rubbing the kink out of her lower back, she surveyed what was to be her home for the next two weeks. "I could get used to this," she murmured. The room had been beautifully decorated, perhaps by Emily herself. Helen sensed a touch of elegance behind the woman's harsh exterior. She loved the big brass bed and the muted rose and green accents against a cream background.

Helen had set up her office in the turret, from which she had an unobstructed view of the bay. The main room also offered a view, and Helen imagined herself waking up to it every morning. A large wardrobe held her clothes, and a graceful claw-foot tub compelled her to take a long hot bath. But the bell clanged again leaving no doubt as to Emily's impatience with her tardy guest. The bath would have to wait.

Helen hurried down the winding staircase to the dining room. The long formal table, though lovely with its ivory lace tablecloth and floral centerpiece, had not been set. Helen wandered past it and followed the light and the unmistakable aroma of fresh bread to the kitchen. Emily was already seated at a small wooden table set for two.

"Hope you don't mind eating in here. Isabelle and I usually did when we didn't have guests to tend to." She'd changed clothes, exchanging the jeans and flannel shirt for a denim skirt and an oversized white blouse, caught around the waist with a silver belt. On her feet she wore a pair of Birkenstocks.

"I don't mind at all." Helen pulled out a chair. "It's much cozier."

"Good, then you won't mind serving yourself either. I made us some clam chowder and salad. And rolls." Emily passed the cloth-covered basket.

"This is perfect."

"Mind if I ask a blessing? Try to make a habit of it. Isabelle and I used to take turns."

Pretending not to notice the catch in Emily's voice, Helen nodded and bowed her head. When Emily had finished saying grace, Helen silently added a prayer of her own, that God would ease Emily's heartache over the loss of what must have been a very close friend. "Isabelle lived here with you, then?" Helen asked.

Emily nodded and promptly changed the subject, going on to talk about the gardening that needed doing.

After dinner, Helen helped Emily clear the table. She'd have helped with dishes as well if Emily hadn't ordered her out of the kitchen.

"Kitchen's not big enough for the both of us. If you want to make yourself useful, you can tend to the fire in the parlor. I'll fix a pot of chamomile tea. When I'm finished in here, we can talk. Figure there's some things you ought to know if you're going ahead with this fool idea."

Bypassing the numerous couches and chairs, Helen headed for the fireplace and piled three split logs and some kindling on a heavy iron grate, then stuffed in newspaper. Once the fire was lit, she sank into the nearest chair to watch the flames, wishing J.B. could be with her, and at the same time glad he wasn't. They'd be together again soon enough. J.B. would be coming to join her for the weekend. She closed her eyes and let her mind drift to the guidebook and to Isabelle. What had happened to Isabelle?

"You asleep?" Emily set a tray on a nearby coffee table.

"Not quite. I was getting close, though." As Helen straightened, her gaze drifted to an enormous orange tabby who'd followed Emily in and was now approaching Helen with a wary who-are-you-and-what-are-you-doing-in-my-kingdom look.

Helen leaned forward and extended her hand. "Hi, kitty," she cooed.

"That's Ginger. Isabelle's cat." Emily lowered her slightly overweight body into the chair beside Helen's. "I don't have much use for her myself. But I haven't the heart to turn her away."

"Meow." Ginger ignored Helen's hand and jumped into Emily's lap, turned around three times, then settled into a ball. Emily's arthritic fingers stroked her golden fur. The cat's loud purring rendered Emily's denial of ownership null and void.

"She's a nuisance. You might want to leave your door ajar— in case she decides to make her rounds. With you using Isabelle's room, she's likely to want to come in and check things out. Won't harm anything. She'll meow up a storm if she can't get in."

Noting the weariness in the older woman's eyes, Helen poured tea and offered Emily a cup.

"Thanks." Emily took a sip, then asked, "What time will you be wanting breakfast in the morning?"

"You don't need to trouble yourself. I'll be happy to—"

"Isabelle liked to work for a couple hours before eating. 'Course she had to have her coffee first thing."

"That will work out fine. Except—if it's no bother I'd just as soon drink tea—Earl Grey if you have it."

A smile curved Emily's thin lips. "I do."

They spent the next few minutes in companionable silence. Helen found the cat's steady purr relaxing.

"How long have you had the bed and breakfast?" Helen asked.

"Well, now, that depends. It's been a bed and breakfast for ten years. But it's been in the family since 1882. My grandfather built it and passed it along to his son. Isabelle and I were both born here."

"Really. So you're sisters?"

"Cousins actually, but we grew up together."

"I wondered about the connection."

"Our mothers were sisters. My family lived here so my mother could look after her parents. I just kept the tradition going."

"And Isabelle?"

"Her family lived in Portland but came down to the Peninsula nearly every weekend. After Isabelle's husband died she moved in here with me. Said she liked the peace and quiet—ideal for writing. It was her idea to turn the place into a bed and breakfast. Idea was we'd be able to make enough to keep the place up."

"What will you do now?"

"Keep it, I imagine. May need to hire someone to come in and help one of these days."

Helen scrutinized her. "You've been taking care of this place alone?"

"It's not that bad most of the time. Weekends are worse."

Sipping at the soothing hot tea, Helen felt a distant camaraderie with Isabelle. "How long had Isabelle been writing?"

"Took it up when her kids were small. She figured it was one career where she could work and stay home at the same time."

"What happened to her, Emily?"

"I told you. She drowned."

"Yes, but you indicated it was because of the book."

"Not the book exactly. She was writing about all the things a person could do at the south end of the Peninsula. Isabelle called me round eight the night she disappeared. I'd never heard her so excited. 'It's a long story,' she said, 'and you are not going to believe what I found. Can't talk now. I'm meeting Danny in a few minutes. I should be home in an hour.' Isabelle never showed up for that meeting and she never came home. Chuck Frazier found her under the dock two days later when he came in from a fishing trip. Guess he was backing into his slip when he spotted her body."

"How awful." Helen paused a moment reflecting on the tragedy. "You mentioned her meeting someone named Danny. Who is that?"

"Dan Merritt—my brother's boy. He's the sheriff here in Pacific County. I think she must have stumbled onto something illegal—otherwise why call Danny?"

"Was there an investigation into Isabelle's death?"

"Humph—if you could call it that. Coroner said she must have tripped on a rope and fallen off the dock. She had a skull fracture. They're guessing she fell into the water and got trapped under the dock. Accidental death."

Helen drained her cup and set it down. "Apparently you don't think so."

"Don't matter much what I think. I'm an old woman. What do I know?"

"What *do* you know? Please tell me."

Emily's wounded gaze disappeared behind parchment lids, then reappeared. "Suppose it could've been an accident, but I suspicion there's more to it. From the way she sounded, she uncovered something big—maybe drug dealers or something. Whoever it was might have killed her before she could get to the sheriff."

Emily heaved a sigh and stood up. "Don't figure it does much good to talk about it. It's not like you could do anything. Only reason I'm telling you is that if it wasn't an accident and if you go stirring up the same waters—who's to say you wouldn't end up just like her?"

Three

Helen awoke with a start. The light from the hall tumbled into her room. Something soft and furry brushed against her arm. In the seconds it took to realize where she was and what was on her bed, Helen's heart had careened into overdrive.

"Ginger!"

The cat scrambled off the bed.

One hand on her chest, Helen tossed the covers aside and padded to the open door. Ginger sat just inside, licking a paw and acting as though she'd accomplished her task and now it was time to clean up.

"Are you staying in or going out?"

Ginger ignored her.

"Suit yourself." Helen closed the door, leaving just enough room for the cat's paw to slip through and open it again when the time came. Going back to bed, she caught a movement and turned to stare at the ghostly apparition reflected in the window.

She gasped, then shook her head when she realized it was only her white brushed cotton nightgown. Helen sank back onto the bed. She was bordering on paranoia. There was nothing out there to fear—at least she hoped not. Prone to premonition, Helen couldn't escape the feeling that something unpleasant was about to happen. Best, however, not to dwell on it. She'd know what it was all about soon enough.

Helen pulled her thoughts back to the moment and focused on the still, clear night. Moonlight poured through the shadeless windows, creating replicas of the lace curtains on the opposite wall. The full moon hung high in the sky, yellow and bright as a child's drawing.

For a moment she wished she could capture it on canvas. Unfortunately, she didn't paint. Her mother had, but those genes had bypassed Helen and gone directly to her daughter, Kate.

"Kate. Dear Kate," Helen whispered, her lips curled in a half smile as she thought about their strained relationship. Kate meant well, but like a lot of grown daughters, she had gotten a bit too bossy of late. Imagine telling Helen to slow down. "As if I could." *Or wanted to.*

Not that Kate hadn't had cause for concern. Helen did have a knack for getting into difficult situations. She'd taken a bullet while looking into a murder case a few weeks earlier. Helen rubbed her stiff right shoulder. The injury had slowed her down for a time and reminded her of how fragile life could be. Maybe that was why she felt such a strong urge to keep going—to maintain her independence and ignore Kate's admonitions to take it easy.

Kate had been none too happy with her for getting involved in what turned out to be a multiple murder investigation. And here she was, faced with another possible murder. She could imagine what Kate would say if she knew about Isabelle.

Ah, but she was getting ahead of herself. The authorities had called Isabelle's death an accident.

Helen turned on the bedside lamp and glanced at her watch. Not quite midnight. "So much for a good night's sleep."

"Meow." Ginger scurried in and curled herself around Helen's ankles.

"What's this? An apology?" Helen bent down to rub Ginger's ears and neck. Standing again, she made her way to the desk, where she'd set the papers Emily had given her before they'd gone to bed. The files contained Isabelle's notes on the guidebook and apparently several articles she'd started. One was on pollution, another on the fading fishing industry, and still another on increasing drug use on the Peninsula.

26

Helen picked up the thick file folders and after bunching pillows against the antique headboard settled back to read. Ginger coiled herself against Helen's hip.

Isabelle had collected a variety of brochures advertising some of the businesses and events on the Peninsula. Helen looked at a few fliers on charter fishing, then moved on to a yellow note pad outlining the book. Isabelle had started at the south end and listed places to see and things to do, beginning at the Astoria-Megler Bridge to Baker Bay, west to the Port of Ilwaco and the Coast Guard station. After that the notes were sketchy. On another sheet Isabelle had written "Contacts" and on another "Places I need to visit."

Isabelle had compiled an extensive list, beginning with the fisheries department in Astoria, then under Chinook she'd listed a potter, and the Chinook Indian tribal office to get records on early Indian villages and culture. She also listed the Sanctuary Restaurant and several others in that area. Helen moved down the page, focusing on those people and places in and around Ilwaco, where Isabelle had died—or been killed. Next to each name she'd written a brief description and phone number. How many of these people had Isabelle interviewed? Who was the last one to see her alive?

The first listing for Ilwaco was *Chuck and Shells Frazier— Shells: owner of Shells' Place. Chef. Chuck: runs* Mariner III. *Commercial fisherman.*

Beneath the Fraziers, Isabelle had listed *Mike Trenton: runs the* Merry Maid, *a forty-foot charter out of Ilwaco,* then *Hank and Bill Carlson:* Klipspringer—*mostly commercial these days.*

The following entry, while listed with the commercial fishermen, seemed out of place: *Scott Mandrel: new to Peninsula. Chinook Indian. Claims ancestors lived here. Owns Pisces International. Has been buying up property and small commercial fishing businesses in the area. Curious.*

Isabelle had starred the next name: *Adam Jorgenson: Coast Guard, Cape D.*

"Adam Jorgenson," Helen murmured aloud. "It couldn't be." She leaned back against the pillows, remembering the Adam

Jorgenson she knew. Like her son, Jason, he'd be thirty-eight now. Adam and Jason had gone to high school together, and for several years he had been like a second son. He kept in touch for a time, but Helen hadn't heard anything for—how long? Ten years?

She reached to her side to pet the purring feline. Despite her excitement at seeing Adam—if he was indeed the same Adam—she could hardly keep her eyes open. She gathered the papers, set them on the bedside stand, and snapped off the light. Her last thoughts before drifting off were not on the guidebook she was supposed to be writing but on Isabelle.

Tomorrow she'd try to retrace the writer's steps. She'd call Adam first, then arrange to meet others on the list. She also wanted to talk to Sheriff Dan Merritt to find out where the investigation into Isabelle's death stood.

✤   ✤   ✤

By morning a bright warm sun had replaced the moon. A perfect morning for a run. Helen was just putting on her tennis shoes when Emily knocked on her door and entered with a tray of hot tea and two cups.

"Get much work done this morning?" Setting the tray on a round cloth-covered table, Emily poured already brewed tea.

"Not yet. I read through some of Isabelle's notes last night. Thought I'd drive to Ilwaco today and talk to these people." Helen handed Emily the list. "Do you know any of them?"

"I do, except for this Mandrel fellow and the coastie. The rest of 'em are all locals. Known their families for years."

"Coastie?"

"Nickname for the Coast Guard folks." She sniffed. "If you're thinking of asking them about Isabelle, you can forget it."

Helen joined Emily at the small table, puzzled about her response. "Well, I was thinking I'd work it into the conversation. You seem convinced last night that Isabelle met with foul play. Perhaps talking to the people she had contact with might help solve the puzzle."

Emily sighed. "Dan's already talked to most of them. They weren't much help."

Helen nodded. "I may hit a dead end too. But since I have to do some research for the book, I may as well see what I can find out."

"Suit yourself." Emily poured the tea. "Just be careful. No point in asking for trouble."

⚜   ⚜   ⚜

After a brisk walk around the grounds, a modified workout, and a run to the main road and back, Helen ate breakfast, then made a call to the Coast Guard station. Adam was delighted to hear from her and would give her as much time as she needed. Helen gathered her supplies—camera, film, binoculars, note pad, and pens—and Isabelle's files on the guidebook and stuffed them into a black leather backpack.

The bag had been a gift from J.B. A stroke of genius. It had a number of pouches—perfect, J.B. had assured her, for a photo-journalist, which in a way she was. She often sent a photo layout with her articles for the travel magazines, and she planned to do the same for the guidebook.

Eager to be off, Helen bid Emily a hasty good-bye, put the top down on her T-bird, and climbed in.

"Better take this with you." Emily approached with a wicker basket and set it on the backseat. "Some nice picnic spots out that way. Enough there for you and your coastie friend."

"What a nice thing to do." Helen thanked her, wishing she could wipe away the worry from the older woman's eyes. Once out on the main road, she breathed a sigh of relief. Until that moment she hadn't realized how Emily's fears had blanketed her as well. She hauled in another deep breath and let the wind blow away the lingering oppression.

Helen drove south on Sandridge Road and followed the signs to Ilwaco. Once there, she took the winding road through the hills, past Beard's Hollow and the North Head Lighthouse, then on to Fort Canby State Park. There she followed the signs up the hill and left to the Coast Guard station. Excitement rose at the thought of exploring the area in detail. She wouldn't right now, of course. First she'd talk to Adam. During their phone conversation he'd said he remembered Isabelle and had given her a tour of the Coast Guard facilities. Helen was eager to find out what their conversation and the tour entailed.

Following Adam's instructions, Helen ignored the *Keep Out: Authorized Personnel Only* signs and drove into the restricted area, parking in the lot near the neatly painted white buildings. The red trim went well with the background of evergreens. A sign over the main entrance read USCG. Cape Disappointment. Beneath that was the phrase "Pacific Graveyard Guardians."

Adam emerged from a two-story building and was halfway down the stairs before she could pull the key out of the ignition.

Adam Jorgenson hadn't changed much. His hair had gone from flaxen to ash blond. His light skin, flushed cheeks, and wide grin made him look about twenty. The uniform, a light blue short sleeved shirt and navy slacks, contributed to his youthful appearance. Helen waved and stepped out of the car. "Adam! It's good to see you." She wrapped her arms around the tall, muscular Swede, returning his exuberant welcome.

"I couldn't believe it when you called, Mrs. McGrady." Adam released her and took a step back. "Oh," he frowned. "That's not your name anymore."

"It's Bradley." Helen retrieved her backpack and hooked a strap over her left shoulder.

"Sorry, I should be able to remember that. I sure remember J.B. Jason was named after him, wasn't he?"

"That's right. J.B. was Ian's best friend—mine too. We met in Ireland. Not long after Ian died, J.B. and I struck up our friendship again, and this summer he proposed."

Adam settled his arm across Helen's shoulders and steered her toward the building he'd come out of and up the steps to his office. "I'm glad. Must have been pretty lonely for you after losing Ian. And then Jason. I . . . uh . . . I should have called you when he died. I meant to, but—"

Helen stopped him. "Jason isn't dead, Adam."

"But the plane crash. The papers said he'd been killed."

"That's what the government wanted everyone to believe. Jason had to go undercover for a while. He was working with the DEA to break up several major drug cartels in the Caribbean and South America. He couldn't even tell his family. Not even J.B. or I knew. It's a long story, but thank the Lord, he's back home now."

"Great! That's fantastic! I can't tell you how glad I am to hear that. So, is he still with the DEA or what?"

"He's working as a homicide detective in Portland. So far it seems to be working out well."

"Homicide, huh? Isn't that what you used to do?"

"Uh-huh. What goes around comes around, I suppose."

Adam shook his head. "You always were a strange family. You still chasing criminals?"

Helen smiled. "Occasionally." They spent the next few minutes in his office while she caught Adam up on her family and bragged about her four grandchildren.

"They sound like neat kids."

"Oh, that they are. Jason's oldest, Jennie, is sixteen and giving her parents fits. She's planning a career in law enforcement." Helen caught something akin to loneliness in Adam's blue eyes. "Are your parents still in Florida?"

"Dad is. Mom died last year—breast cancer."

"I'm so sorry."

Adam shrugged. "She was happy to go in the end, I think."

"Did you ever marry?"

He shook his head. "Came close a couple times."

"You should come spend Thanksgiving and Christmas with us. We've plenty of room."

"I'd like that."

Helen glanced around the tidy office, pulling her thoughts back to her mission. "Adam, when we spoke earlier you mentioned that you'd talked to Isabelle Dupont. Could you tell me more about your visit with her?"

"Better than that. I'll show you." Adam grabbed a jacket from behind his chair and slipped it on. "I told her a little about the history of the place. Coast Guard station's been here since 1875.

31.

Our Motor Lifeboat School is the only one like it in the U.S. We teach the students to perform search and rescue operations in some of the roughest surf conditions in the world. We equip them to handle just about anything they might encounter on the high seas. It's one of the busiest Coast Guard stations on the West Coast."

"Have you been here long?" Helen ducked under his arm and slipped outside when he held open the door.

"Three years. I've got four more to go before I can retire. Then I'm heading south."

"Sounds like you don't like it here."

"I like the scenery and the green. I guess I like the laid-back lifestyle too. But I'm not too crazy about the attitude some of the locals have toward us. It hasn't been easy making friends. I definitely don't like the cold winters and the wind. Speaking of which—you brought a jacket, didn't you? Once we get up to the lighthouse, you'll need it."

Helen grabbed her jacket out of the car and put the top up. As Adam reminded her, the weather conditions could change quickly on the coast. "In case you haven't heard, in the *Guinness Book of Records* Cape D is listed as the foggiest point in the contiguous U.S."

From the parking lot they took the road Helen had come in on and followed it out to the boat docks.

"This is where we keep our fleet. We have several forty-four-foot motor lifeboats, and a forty-seven-footer. Plus the fifty-two-footer." Adam pointed to a vessel bearing the name *Triumph*. "We've also got a couple surf rescue boats—a twenty-one-foot inflatable and a thirty-footer. We're equipped to handle just about any emergency that comes up out there."

Adam promised her a trip sometime during her stay. "If you want we can take you out on one boat, then do a vessel-to-vessel transfer so you can experience it firsthand. Hope you don't get seasick."

"Not usually."

From the boat basin they began the trek up the steep hill to the Cape Disappointment Lighthouse, which Adam referred to as Cape D. They'd just cleared the buildings when they passed a picnic area to the right. Helen asked about it.

"Overlooks Dead Man's Cove. We'll get a bird's-eye view of it a little farther on."

"Dead Man's Cove? Sounds ominous."

Adam smiled. "Legend has it a body washed ashore there years ago. I suspect there have been more than one over the years."

"How gruesome."

"It fits when you consider the number of shipwrecks we've had out here. This place is known as 'The Graveyard of the Pacific.' " Adam stopped at a wooden railing and pointed down at a short and inviting sandy beach tucked between two giant headlands. High cliff walls bordered a narrow inlet. "That's Dead Man's Cove."

"It's beautiful."

"Isabelle told me it was her favorite spot on the Peninsula. I'll take you down there later if you want."

"I'd love it. In fact, Emily packed a picnic lunch—that looks like the perfect place to eat it."

"Sounds great." Adam stopped again in front of a concrete bunker. "You knew this used to be part of an army fort, didn't you?"

Helen nodded. In the mid–1800s, the army constructed a number of military installations to protect the country's coastline from enemy invasion. This fort had been in use until around 1957. Many of the old concrete bunkers and batteries were still standing. "I've visited Fort Stevens on the Oregon side, but I haven't been through these."

They continued up the hill for another quarter mile, following a part concrete, part dirt and grass road to the Cape D Lighthouse. Too winded by the steep climb to ask questions, Helen followed Adam until they reached a chain link fence that ran along the cliff's edge. Adam glanced back at her, then rested his arms on top of the fence. "You okay?"

"Why wouldn't I be?" Helen panted. She eyed the concrete steps near the small square building that must have been the

Coast Guard's official watchtower but joined Adam at the fence instead. "You think a little hill like that would stop me?"

"I have to admit you surprised me. Must be in pretty good shape."

"I manage. I try to work out nearly every day."

Adam chuckled. "And you still do karate, I'll bet."

"Brown belt. But enough about me." Helen let her gaze drift over the unhindered view of the North Jetty and a stretch of beach beyond that, then south to the mouth of the Columbia river as it divided Washington from Oregon. Isabelle had no doubt stood on this very spot.

Having been raised there, Isabelle must have known the area well, yet she'd come to interview Adam. "What sort of things did you and Isabelle talk about?"

"The Coast Guard station mostly. She knew the history of the area far better than I do. She ended up teaching me some things. For example, the Coast Guard had to build two lighthouses here. This one was built first, in 1856, but ships coming from the north couldn't see it soon enough. There have been around two thousand shipwrecks—and about fifteen hundred deaths in these waters.

"Ironically, the first supply ship bringing in the beacon and the precast concrete blocks to build the lighthouse shipwrecked just off the coast, and they had to wait for another one. A second lighthouse, North Head, was built in 1898."

Adam went from one story to another, talking about the Coast Guard officers and relating the legend of how one of the wives went mad from loneliness and jumped off the cliff to her death in the surf 220 feet below. So fascinating were the stories, Helen almost forgot about her original question.

After twenty minutes, she managed to get back on track. "Sounds like Isabelle did all the talking. Did she ask you anything?"

"She wanted to know about me—how much authority I had as base commander and what experience I had as a law enforcement officer."

"And you said . . ."

"I've had intelligence training." His lips curled in a melancholy smile. "We have investigative authority over anything that happens on the base and in the water. Most cases are handled by the Marine Safety Office in Portland."

"Did she say why she was interested?"

Adam stroked his chin. "Not exactly. She asked a lot of questions about Chuck Frazier's boat."

Helen recognized the name from Isabelle's list. "He's a commercial fisherman."

"Right. His craft, the *Mariner II*, was lost a' month ago—smashed up on the rocks right below us. We got a rescue team out there within five minutes. Managed to pick up Chuck but lost the crewman. Young kid—inexperienced—wasn't wearing a life jacket. Isabelle wanted to know if I thought it was an accident."

"And was it?"

"No reason to think otherwise. Fog came in. He had engine problems. Started taking on water and drifted too close to the rocks at Peacock Spit."

"Did she talk about anything else?"

Adam rested his arms on the chain link fence and looked out over the ocean. "Drugs." He stepped away from the fence. "She asked if we'd ever caught anyone smuggling drugs into the area. Thought Dead Man's Cove would be the perfect place."

"And have you?"

"Nope. Things are pretty quiet around here as far as I can tell. Oh, we've had the occasional kid hauled in for possession, but nothing major. And trust me, Dead Man's Cove is not the perfect place. Getting a boat of any size through that inlet without it breaking up on the rocks would be close to impossible. Besides, it's too close to the Coast Guard station. A person would have to be crazy to try it." He ran a hand along the brim of his hat before putting it on. "The port's another story. The Department of Fisheries routinely boards boats and checks cargo, but some contraband could still slip through. In hindsight maybe I should have taken Isabelle's comments more seriously."

"According to Emily Merritt, the authorities consider Isabelle's death an accidental drowning. Do you know anything about that?"

"That's what the paper reported. Dan hasn't said much about the case, but I think he's still working on it."

"Dan . . . sounds like you know him fairly well."

"I know him."

Apparently not wanting to talk more about Dan, Adam escorted Helen into the observation room and introduced her to the petty officer on duty. The young woman looked up from her clipboard and smiled.

"Anything exciting happening out there?" Adam hunched over to look through a large telescope.

"Pretty quiet today," Lowe reported. "We had to go pick up a guy in a twelve-footer. He nearly capsized going over the bar."

Adam sighed and turned to Helen. "Some people never learn. Had one man try to take a rowboat out this summer. What some people will do to catch a few fish." He turned back to Lowe. "Many out today?"

"Most of the charters went out this morning—a few commercials and some private boats. Looks like a good day for them. By the way, Chuck Frazier on the *Mariner III* radioed in with a message for you." Lowe shuffled through some notes on the desk and came up with a memo. "Wants you to meet him at six-thirty tonight at Shells' Place. Says he's got proof somebody sabotaged his boat."

Four

I can't believe that guy. He should have talked to me before he went out." Adam stuffed the note in his pocket. "When did he radio in?"

"As he came over the bar." The petty officer looked uncomfortable. "You think he might be in danger, sir?"

"It's entirely possible. You should have let me know immediately."

"I . . . I'm sorry . . ."

Adam picked up the radio and tried unsuccessfully to raise his friend. He then made a call to the Coast Guard patrol boat, asking them to locate him.

Several minutes later a garbled voice reported they had the *Mariner III* in their sights and everything looked fine. Chuck was on deck waving at them.

Adam heaved an audible sigh of relief. "Keep an eye on him and let me know the minute he comes in."

"I'm sorry," Lowe said again. "I didn't think. . . ."

"We'll talk about it later. Come by my office when you get off duty."

"Yes, sir." Red-faced and jaw set, she turned back to the telescope.

Adam escorted Helen back outside. He muttered some choice words, then apologized. "Don't say it. I'm overreacting. You needn't worry. I'll just remind her to follow protocol."

"I wasn't exactly worried—at least not about her." Helen ran to keep up with Adam as they descended the hill. "Sounds like you have cause for concern about your friend, though."

"I'm not sure what he's up to. Telling me someone sabotaged his boat is one thing, but broadcasting it on every radio unit within a fifty-mile radius was stupid."

"Maybe he doesn't know who did it and is trying to flush the culprit out."

"You may have something there." Adam slowed his pace. "Chuck probably figured I'd send a patrol out to check on him."

"And you did."

"Right. I'm just glad nothing happened before I got the message."

"Um, Adam, about meeting Mr. Frazier this evening. Would you mind if I tagged along? I'd like to talk with him."

"Sure, no problem." His lips stretched into a wide smile. "You'll want to include Shells' Place on your list of favorite dining establishments in the book. She's a fantastic chef."

Adam seemed more relaxed when they detoured off the main trail and headed toward Dead Man's Cove. The plan was to hike to the Lewis and Clark Interpretive Center, on to Waikiki Beach, then back along the road to the Coast Guard station before lunch. Three miles in all and Helen loved every step of it. The trail wove in and out of the woods, often bringing them to open stretches that offered spectacular views of the coastline. They paused briefly at the Interpretive Center, where Helen picked up some brochures. She'd have to come back later when she could wander through the Lewis and Clark exhibits and the Interpretive Center grounds at a more leisurely pace. Helen took dozens of photos on the way. Adam provided limited information and Helen eventually gave up asking. The man's mind was obviously on Chuck Frazier.

He left her at the guardrail above the huge circular gun wells. Helen snapped a few photos, then followed him around the building to the grassy slope that ended at a chain link fence. The headland on which they now stood was to the north of Cape Disappointment. From here one could see both lighthouses. Adam stared out to sea, his brow knit in a deep frown—his mind apparently as far away as the boats dotting the horizon.

"Still worried about your friend?"

"What. . . ?" Adam turned a blank gaze on her. "Oh, in a way. I was thinking about Shells. If anything happened to Chuck . . ." His voice trailed off.

"Shells' as in the restaurant?"

"Not exactly. The restaurant is named after her. Chuck's idea. Shells is a nickname. Her real name is Michelle."

"Oh yes. Isabelle mentioned that in her notes. Is Shells Chuck's wife?"

"Sister. Chuck's all the family she's got left. Their dad and an older brother were lost at sea when she was about eight. Their mom took off a year or so later. Met a farmer and moved to the Midwest. Shells says her mom wanted to get as far away from the ocean as possible. They hear from her at Christmas—that's about it."

"How sad."

Adam nodded, his gaze sweeping back out to sea. "Yeah. Can't say as I blame the woman for leaving, though. Soon as my stint is up here I'm heading back to Florida. It's just too blasted cold and wet out here."

Helen suspected his feelings for Shells went beyond concern or friendship. Before she could explore the matter, he pushed away from the fence and suggested they get moving.

After their picnic lunch at Dead Man's Cove, Adam went back to work, leaving Helen to fend for herself. She had an exquisite afternoon exploring Fort Canby and the Lewis and Clark Interpretive Center. Helen was especially enthralled by a set of moss-covered concrete stairs she found in the woods. "Stairs to Nowhere," she named them. Unable to resist, she climbed to the top and was rewarded with yet another stunning view of the coastline.

By five that afternoon, Helen had gone through four rolls of film, hiked three more miles, and still hadn't come close to seeing everything the southern tip of the Peninsula had to offer.

Zipping up her Windbreaker, she made the final quarter-mile trek back to the Coast Guard parking lot. Fog had moved in, turning the landscape a dreary gray and dropping the temperature by at least ten degrees.

Though it wasn't exactly raining, the fine mist soaked through her clothing, leaving her soggy and chilled. She was glad she'd put the top up on her car.

Originally she'd planned to go back into town, give Emily a call, and go straight to the restaurant to wait for Adam. Arriving early would have given her time to meet Shells and perhaps make some notes for the book. Climbing into the T-bird, she thought better of the idea and decided to go back to the bed and breakfast to shower and change.

Emily had been none too happy with Helen's decision to eat elsewhere. Sensing that her annoyance came more from feeling left out than being put out, Helen invited her to come along. On the drive south, she was glad she had. Emily, being somewhat of a historian and a gossip, felt certain she knew exactly who had tampered with Chuck Frazier's boat.

"It's that Pisces International fellow, Scott Mandrel. If you ask me, he's not very bright."

"His name was on Isabelle's list. She'd written a note about him buying up property and small fishing businesses. I haven't had a chance to find out much about him, but I intend to."

"I thought that might be the case. While you were gone, I went through some of the old newspapers. Been planning to toss them out—Isabelle liked to keep 'em in case she needed to look stuff up. Mandrel looks like the proverbial Good Samaritan. I found four different articles from the past year about Pisces International buying out local fishermen who were close to bankruptcy. Mandrel paid off the loans and gave the fishermen a couple thousand besides. Even offered them jobs with his company."

"Doesn't sound like a bad deal to me."

"Humph. Depends on how you look at it. Two of the fishermen he bought out lost their boats only weeks before he made the offer. The losses were too high for them to keep going. They didn't have enough insurance to replace the boats." Emily shrugged. "Looks to me like he might be sinking their boats to force them out of business."

"But if they had no insurance, why sink their craft? And why offer to buy them out? Without their boats there would be little in the way of assets. Doesn't sound like a very smart business move."

"That's true enough. Fishing isn't what it used to be. Was a time you couldn't walk on the dock without tripping over a fish cart. Now you're lucky if you see half a dozen. Harbor used to be full of boats. Now more than half the slips are empty year round."

"I'm not sure I see your point. If the fishing industry is suffering, why would Mandrel want to buy the other fishermen out?"

Emily shook her head. "Beats me. If you want, I'll do some more digging—see what I can find out. I know a couple of the folks he bought out."

Helen hesitated. If Isabelle's "digging" had gotten her killed, she certainly didn't want the same thing happening to Emily.

"I know what you're thinking. You don't need to worry about me. I've got a lot of friends around here who'll know the latest gossip. I'll just keep my ears open."

Helen started to respond when she caught sight of flashing lights in her rearview mirror. "Uh-oh." Her foot automatically released the gas pedal and hit the brake as she looked for a place to pull over. Not an easy task along the dark two-lane road.

"There's a parking lot just ahead," Emily said, "at the cranberry plant."

Helen nodded. Since there were no cars coming and the patrol car hadn't bothered to pass, she figured the officer must be after her. "I wasn't speeding, was I?"

Emily shrugged. "Might have been. Speed limit is only forty-five along this stretch. Folks tend to go faster."

Helen pulled off into the dimly lit parking lot and waited. The siren stopped, but the lights continued to flash as a uniformed officer pulled in behind her, got out, and approached the car.

Helen rolled her window down.

"Any idea why I stopped you, ma'am?" The tall, attractive officer bent at the waist and peered into the car. His eyebrows raised when he caught sight of Emily, but he didn't acknowledge her.

"I'm sorry—I have no idea." Helen couldn't make out the name on his badge, but judging by the expression on his face, this was Emily's nephew, Dan Merritt.

"You were going well over fifty miles an hour."

"Oh. I might have been. I didn't realize. . . ."

"Cut her some slack, Danny," Emily piped up. "She's not from around here."

Clearly disgruntled at his aunt's interference, he cast her a keep-out-of-this look. "I saw the Oregon plates." His hazel gaze shifted back to Helen. "I'd like to see your license and vehicle registration."

"Sure." Helen flipped on the dome light and dug through her bag for her license, then rifled through the maps, napkins, and other miscellaneous papers in the glove box until she came up with the proper card.

"Helen Bradley." The sheriff's piercing gaze settled on her face. "I know that name."

"She's the one taking over Isabelle's book. I told you last week she'd be coming."

"Right. You two stay put. I'll be right back."

Helen watched him in her rearview mirror as he ducked into his car—probably to write her a ticket.

A few seconds later he came back and returned the license and registration in through the window. "I won't give you a ticket this time, Mrs. Bradley, but you'll want to stick to the speed limit. We tend to come down hard on offenders."

"I appreciate that."

Dan's business demeanor disappeared behind a friendly smile. He gave her car the once-over and commented about its mint condition and how it was too bad Ford discontinued the old-style T-bird. "It's a '55, isn't it?"

"That's right." Helen patted the dash. "It's always been my

favorite. And when I found it at an antique car show in Portland a few years ago for eighty-five hundred dollars, I snatched it up. It needed some work, but I found a mechanic in Bay Village who loves to restore old cars."

"Yep—you got yourself a beauty." He tapped the hood and peered into the car again. "Where you two headed this evening?"

Helen didn't think it was any of his business but decided it was best not to say so.

"Shells' Place." Emily volunteered. "Helen's meeting that coastie Jorgenson."

"That so." His grin slid away. "I'll see you there, then—I've got business with him myself."

Five

Helen put away her license and registration, checked for traffic, and eased onto the road.

"Wonder what business he has with the coastie," Emily said.

"I have a feeling we're about to find out."

Following Emily's directions, Helen drove into Ilwaco and made a right at the stoplight, then a left, where she followed the road as it curved west. A brightly lit sign pointed the way to Shells' Place—Waterfront Dining on Baker Bay.

"This used to be an old dilapidated warehouse," Emily said. "Shells bought it and tore down what she couldn't use. By donating part of the land, she got the city to build a public fishing pier and parking lot. She sold part of it to Scott Mandrel. He put up a big fish processing plant just east of the restaurant. Big improvement over what used to be here. Shells built the restaurant and plans to add on eventually—maybe get some shops in here. Don't know how it will fly, though. Money's tight and you can't always depend on the tourist trade—especially with fishing being what it is."

"Shells sounds like an enterprising young woman."

"That she is. Had to learn to fend for herself at a pretty young age. Don't know how she does it sometimes."

"Hmm. Adam told me about her parents." Helen parked the car between freshly painted white lines on the smooth, newly finished black asphalt. At Helen's suggestion they walked along the fishing pier. They could see the lights of Warrenton across the river. Off to her left was Pisces International, the processing plant Emily had told her about, and beyond that lay the Port of Ilwaco, where dozens of fishing boats waited for morning when they'd make their fish runs. Emily had been right about one thing. Over half the slips were empty.

The odor from the fish processing plant took a backseat to the heavenly smells spilling out of the restaurant. The promise of food drew them back to the entrance of Shells' Place. The sheriff caught up to them at the door, and the three walked in together.

The restaurant had been decorated in a shell motif. Nets holding glass balls, shells, driftwood, and other gifts from the sea hung across the ceiling.

Adam was seated at a table near the window with a man in his early fifties—maybe younger. The man glanced at them and turned back to Adam. He must have told Adam about their arrival. Neither seemed pleased to see them—or perhaps it was their police escort. The men both recovered quickly, greeting Dan and Emily like long-lost friends.

Adam pulled out the chair next to him. "Helen, I was about to give up on you. This is Chuck Frazier."

"Hi, Chuck." Helen grasped his outstretched hand. His grip was firm, his hand callused. His leathery skin had the look of a man who never bothered with sunscreen and never would. "Nice to meet you."

After Helen introduced Emily to Adam, Dan surprised her by accepting Adam's invitation to eat with them. Somehow she'd expected him to state his business and leave. The group spent the next few minutes arranging themselves at the table originally set for four.

The restaurant had an eclectic menu, from gourmet-sounding dishes with French names to fish and chips, barbecued ribs, and pizza. When Helen commented on the unusual combination of choices, Chuck laughed. "If it was up to Shells, everything would be fancy-shmancy. She went to cooking school in France and then in New York. I told her the only way she'd get me and my friends to eat here was if she served real food. So she compromised."

He leaned forward. "Don't tell her I said so, but she'd be out of business if she hadn't taken my advice." He tipped back a bottle of beer, finishing it off.

"I doubt that, Chuck." Adam folded his menu and set it on the salmon-colored tablecloth. "Shells is a fine chef. Since she got that write-up in *The Oregonian*, people have been coming from all over Oregon and Washington just to sample her cooking. She's even got a publisher interested in a cookbook."

"Adam's right," Dan readily agreed. "No matter what Shells served, she'd be a success."

Helen held back a smile. Shells must be quite a woman to have the admiration of Adam *and* Dan.

"Where is she, by the way?" Dan stretched to look over the partition into the kitchen.

Chuck shrugged. "You just missed her. She came over to say hello to Adam and me. It's her night off. Said something about going to see a movie. Rusty's cooking."

A too-thin waitress with a white shirt and black pants brought them water. Her pin read *Gracie*. "You all ready to order?"

They were. Chuck and Dan wanted pizza—apparently Rusty's specialty. Adam, Helen, and Emily went for the bronzed salmon.

Once they'd placed their orders, Emily excused herself to chat with two women who'd just been seated across the room. Dan asked Adam to step outside to talk business, leaving Helen and Chuck alone.

"Adam told me you were taking over writing Isabelle's book." His eyes narrowed. Chuck looked as if he wanted to say something more but didn't.

"Yes. I'm excited about the project. I'm hoping you and several of the other fishermen will help me with my research."

"That'll be my pleasure. In fact, I'll introduce you around and maybe get you out on one of the boats. If you're going to write about the fishing around here, you'll want to go out on a charter. I'd take you myself, but the insurance company dropped me—too many accidents. Way things have been going lately, I'm not sure I can afford to take the chance."

"I heard about the *Mariner II*. Adam said you'd lost a crew-man."

He nodded. The lines on his face grew deeper. Chuck leaned back in his chair. His gaze moved to the pier where Adam and Dan were standing, then back to Helen. "Mike Trenton might take you out. He had a cancellation, so he was looking."

"Excuse me?"

"On a charter. You did want to go fishing, didn't you?"

"Yes, but—"

"I'll go call him right now."

"There's no rush. . . ."

Chuck ignored her and hurried out to the entryway. She glanced around the room feeling at odds with being left alone. Emily was still deeply engrossed in conversation with the women four tables down. Three men sat in a far corner booth. Fishermen, most likely—at least two of them were. The two with their backs to her were average build. The one facing her, how-ever, was a bear of a man with an unkempt pale coppery beard and mustache that nearly covered his face. A black Greek fishing hat sat on his head, giving him a continental look. His gaze shifted from his companions to the bay outside the window. He had the demeanor of a sea captain—melancholy, contempla-tive. His blue eyes lifted to meet hers. He glanced away, seem-ingly to focus on the contents of his cup.

She thought of going over and introducing herself and ask-ing if she could photograph him. But before she could get her camera out, the men scraped back their chairs simultaneously and walked toward the entry, where one of them stopped at the counter to pay the bill. He wasn't a fisherman, she decided. At least he didn't make a living at it. A businessman, maybe. His skin was smooth—a coffee-and-cream mix, perfectly suited to the off-white Aran sweater, khaki pants, and brown loafers. He handed the waitress a credit card and laughed at something she said.

Helen's gaze drifted to the other two men. They were standing just inside the door, talking to Chuck Frazier, who'd just come in from using the phone. The bear stood at least a foot taller than Chuck and the other man. One thing she could tell for certain, the men shared a common interest and an easy camaraderie.

Helen caught only bits and pieces of their conversation, noting it had to do with the day's catch. Small. Disappointing. The man paying the bill joined the group, and a few moments later the threesome left.

Chuck came back to the table, panting heavily as he approached. "S'all set." He nearly fell into his chair. "Jus' show up down at the docks' charter office at five tomorrow morning. Pick up a fishing license and they'll show you where to find the *Merry Maid*."

"Thank you. I appreciate that." Helen paused for a moment, not certain what to make of his odd behavior. "Are you okay?"

"Kinda fuzzy, but might just be the booze on an empty stomach. Be okay as soon as I get somethin' to eat." He gave his head a quick shake as if to clear it.

"Are you up to some questions?"

"Sure—fire away."

"Who were those men you were talking to just now?"

"You mean the Carlson brothers?" He nodded toward the door. "Hank and Bill run the *Klipspringer*. The scrawny one is Bill. The yuppie in the sweater is probably a weekender. I've seen him around before. He musta gone out with them today." He paused a moment to dab at his forehead. "You'll most likely get to meet Hank and Bill tomorrow. We usually head out about the same time."

"The big guy looks like quite a character," Helen said. "Do you think he'd mind posing for me?"

Chuck chuckled. "You can ask him. Hank's a shy one—keeps pretty much to himself."

"Maybe I'll take pictures first and ask later." Helen took a sip of water and changed the subject. "I understand Isabelle Dupont interviewed you before she died."

"Wouldn't call it an interview exactly. She wanted to know if I'd noticed anything strange going on down at the docks. Why do you ask?"

Helen shrugged. "Curious. Emily tells me Isabelle died under mysterious circumstances."

Chuck hauled in a deep breath. He rubbed a hand through his thinning hair. "And you want to know if I had anything to do with it. What are you, a cop or something?"

"I was at one time. I'm not implying you were responsible. I'd just like to know what she talked to you about."

Chuck's gaze drifted away from her to the bay outside the window. "Besides asking questions, she wanted me to warn Shells about getting involved with a guy she's been seeing."

"Adam?"

"Ha." Chuck turned back to her. "Don't he wish. Nah . . . much as I like Adam, he's not her type. No way would he settle down here. And to my knowledge, my sister don't plan on leaving anytime soon."

"Dan, then?"

"Wrong again. She's been hanging out with Scott Mandrel." His forehead wrinkled in a deep frown, showing his obvious disapproval.

"Did Isabelle think Shells was in danger?"

"Nope. I think she just wanted to see Shells and Dan get together. Isabelle and Emily kinda look after the orphans around here."

"Orphans?" Helen was having trouble staying on track with the man.

"Yeah, well some of us lost a parent or two over the years. I think they still see us as kids."

"Did Isabelle talk about anything else?"

He closed his eyes for a moment. "If you ask me, Isabelle was getting in over her head. She was asking too many questions. I got a hunch she asked the wrong people. I'll let you in on a little secret. . . ." He glanced behind her and mumbled, "Later."

The man had definitely had too much to drink, Helen mused.

Adam and Dan came back to the table the same time the waitress did.

"Here you go." Gracie set a tray laden with drinks on the table. A beer for Chuck, iced tea for Helen and Emily, and soft drinks for the others.

"Am I the only beer drinker in the bunch tonight?" Chuck's hand closed around the dark bottle of German ale.

"Looks that way." Adam folded himself back into the chair. "Learned early on that boats and booze don't mix."

"I'm on duty tonight," Dan said. "Gotta head out as soon as I finish eating."

"You're not here for social reasons, then." Chuck plunked down the half-empty bottle and rested his arms on the table.

Dan hesitated. "Like I was telling Adam, the Feds think there's been some drug trafficking up this way, but I haven't been able to spot anything. Since you pretty much know what's going on with everybody, thought I'd ask you too."

"I don't know nothin' 'bout drugs," Chuck slurred, "but there's something fishy going on around here and it sure ain't perch."

"This have anything to do with the message you left me this morning?" Adam asked.

"What message?" the sheriff asked.

"Chuck said he had proof his boat was sabotaged."

"That so?" Dan pulled the straw out of his drink and set it aside.

"It was. Did some diving after the *Mariner II* went down. Salvaged what I could. Can't say for sure, but . . . I think somebody punctured the fuel line." Chuck rubbed his hand across his eyes. He seemed to be having trouble staying awake. "Engine kept sputtering—like it wasn't getting enough gas. Then it quit altogether. I swear, that engine was perfect that morning. I checked it out myself before I took her out."

"Accidents happen," Dan said.

Adam agreed. "Engine trouble or no, you were fishing too close to the spit."

"No way. I've fished these waters all my life. It shouldn'ta happened."

"But it did." Adam leaned toward his friend. "So are you going to tell us what's going on?"

Chuck glanced over his shoulder, then leaned closer. The scent of beer settled around them as he spoke in a stage whisper. "It wasn't an accident. Someone . . . wants me out of the way, an' I'm going to find out who."

Dan shook his head. "Just as I thought. You've got nothing. The only problem I see is that you're drunk."

"Oh, I got something all right. And tomorrow I'll have proof."

Gracie approached with a tray and set it on the fold-up stand. The conversation took a backseat to the food. The salmon, served with asparagus and wild rice, had a spicy Cajun flavor and tasted as good as it looked. Chuck ordered another beer and lifted a large slice of the house pizza to his plate.

"Maybe you'd better tell us what you're working on, Chuck." Dan pulled the pizza platter toward him and transferred a slice.

"Not yet. Like I said, I think we're onto something bigger'n drugs here."

"Chuck . . ." Adam forked a piece of his salmon. "If you're in some kind of trouble . . ."

"No! No trouble. Forget it." Chuck slapped a heavy hand on the table.

Emily returned to take her place beside Helen. "Sorry to take so long. Joanna and Libby are writer friends of Isabelle's and mine. They want to know if Helen would come to our writer's group next week. We meet on Wednesday night. Maybe talk a little about how you got started writing."

"It's not much of a story, I'm afraid."

"That's okay. They'd like to hear it anyway." She paused to try her salmon. "Mmm. Rusty's coming along. You tell Shells she's doing a good job teaching that boy."

"D—— right." Chuck reached for his beer.

"Looks like you've had enough, Chuck," Dan said. "Hope you don't plan on driving anywhere."

"Haven't had that much. 'Sides, I'm staying on the boat tonight."

Dan set his pizza down to take a call on his cell phone. "Where?" He glowered at Chuck while he talked to his caller. "I'm on my way."

Dan slipped into his jacket and mumbled an apology. "Some kids partying on the beach up at Klipsan—set fire to the dunes."

Adam scrambled to his feet. "Want me to come too? If there's a fire—"

"We'll handle it." On the way out the door he paused and looked back. "Box up some of that pizza for me, Auntie. I'll come by later on tonight."

"What was that all about?" Helen swung her gaze from the departing sheriff back to Adam. "Dan seemed almost hostile about your offer to help."

"He's probably just in a bad mood about having his dinner interrupted." Adam snorted. "And don't forget, I'm still considered an outsider. And . . . um . . . being interested in the same girl probably doesn't help."

"He's a proud man," Emily offered. "Not too inclined to accept help from . . . others. 'Course, you didn't help his mood much, Chuck."

"That's for sure." Adam turned back to Chuck. "If you know something, you really should . . ."

The rest of Adam's sentence hung suspended in the sudden silence as Chuck pitched forward and fell face first in his pizza.

Six

Adam pulled Chuck off the chair and eased him to the floor. Helen knelt beside him and checked for vital signs. "He's still breathing." She placed two fingers along Chuck's jaw and found a pulse. "We'd better call an ambulance."

"I already did. It may be a while." Gracie put a hand on Adam's shoulder. "Emergency vehicles are all up at the north end. Dispatch operator said we should drive him since it's only half a mile to the hospital. Any idea what's wrong?"

"He just fell over," Adam said.

"Passed out is more like it." From her seat at the table, Emily gave Chuck a disapproving look. "Two beers since we came here and who knows how many before that."

"You might be right." Gracie wiped pizza sauce from Chuck's nose and plucked a slice of pepperoni from his beard. "He had one earlier, and I couldn't swear to it, but he might have started before he came in. He was acting kind of strange."

"His pulse is a bit slow. Otherwise he seems stable." Helen lifted his eyelids to check his pupils, then sat back on her heels. They were pinpoint. "Um . . . does Chuck take any medication or drugs? Something that might react with alcohol?"

"Not to my knowledge," Adam said. "If you're thinking about street drugs, I seriously doubt it."

Gracie shook her head. "Definitely not. Doesn't drink all that much. Guess that's why I noticed tonight."

"Well, we'd best stop speculating and get him in." Helen positioned herself at his feet and instructed Adam to get his head and shoulders. "If he did ingest something other than alcohol, the blood tests should tell us."

Between the four of them, they managed to carry Chuck outside and settle him into Adam's car.

"Should I follow you to the hospital?" Helen asked.

"No need." Adam opened the driver's side door. "I'll give you a call later—let you know what they find out. Might be he had too much to drink, but like Gracie said, it isn't like Chuck to have more than a couple beers. If it is just the booze, I'll take him to my place and sober him up. Maybe I can get him to tell me what he's up to."

After watching Adam drive off, Helen and Emily went back inside. They had only intended to clean up their mess and leave, but Emily's friends insisted they move over to their table.

"Come on, Emily," said one, twisting around in her seat. "You can't just leave. What gives?"

Emily explained what had happened, then introduced Helen to Joanna Black—an ample woman with an easy smile and eyes the color of molasses. And Libby Ainsworth, slightly overweight, with blue gray eyes and long gray hair swept up in a chignon. Helen liked them immediately. Both were published writers and both had been Isabelle's friends.

"I'm glad the publisher decided to go ahead with Isabelle's book." Joanna slid her remaining pizza into a Styrofoam container and reached for a napkin.

"Me too." Libby pursed her lips. "I have to tell you, when we found out the publisher had chosen an outsider, we were—let's say more than slightly annoyed."

"We thought they should have chosen one of us. After all, we were her critique partners. But . . ." Joanna shrugged. "As Emily so wisely pointed out, the editor didn't know we existed."

"I'm glad they picked you, though—at least you live on the coast. I've seen several of your articles—loved the one you did in the *Tour and Travel* a while back on swimming with dolphins. Did you really do that?"

"I did." Helen laughed, recounting the experience. She'd invited her granddaughter, Jennie, to Dolphin Island in Florida. The trip had taken a serious turn when the two of them became involved in a two-year-old murder investigation. "It was quite a thrill."

"I've always wanted to travel like that." Libby sighed. "No money, though. About all I can afford these days is an occasional jaunt to the Bay area to visit friends."

"That's one of the perks of writing on assignment. They pay my way." Helen took a sip of her drink. "Of course I did have to write about six articles on my own before they brought me on as a feature writer."

"You don't have to travel to do that, Libby," Emily said. "Look around you. We have a vacation spot in our own backyard."

"She's right, you know," Helen agreed. "In the short while I've been here, I've seen several possibilities. You could do an article on bed and breakfasts, or on the history and appeal of your lighthouses, or on the fascinating trails . . ."

Libby raised her hands in mock surrender. "All right, you've convinced me."

"Well . . ." Joanna used her napkin to sop up some water she'd spilled. "You two can have the tourist stuff. *I'm* working on a mystery novel that's set here—or a place like this. I probably can't use real names. It's based on a murder we had down here about two years ago."

"Murder?" Helen leaned forward.

Libby raised her eyebrows. "It was an accident."

Joanna's dark eyes widened. "I happen to think otherwise— Isabelle did, too. In fact, she and I were talking about it the day before she died."

"Could you tell me about it?" Helen asked.

"Mike Trenton and Harry Bolton were out hunting, and Mike shot Harry."

"Hunting accidents happen all the time." Emily rubbed her forehead. "Mike isn't a killer." She'd apparently been through this before.

"Just because Dan says so? He thinks Isabelle's death was an accident, too, and we know better, don't we?" Joanna lifted her shoulder-length brown hair from her neck and leaned back. "Rumor goes against the physical findings in the case, but I have a bad feeling about it." She grinned. "Call it a hunch, but I see some connections between Harry's and Isabelle's murders."

Libby sniffed. "I don't see how they can be related."

"Well, we know Mike killed Harry. We just don't know why. We also know Isabelle was killed down here on the docks. Mike's slip is only two down from where Chuck supposedly found her body. I think Mike killed her," Joanna contended.

"Oh, come on, Joanna." Libby tossed her an incredulous look. "You can't be serious. Mike was out of town when Isabelle disappeared."

"Humph." Joanna pursed her lips. "So he says. He could have come in during the night and gone right back out—who's to know? No offense, Emily, but I wouldn't be surprised if Dan isn't in on it, the way he brushed both of them off as accidental."

Helen looked from one of her companions to the other, wondering how much of Joanna's account of the incidents was fact and how much was fiction.

"It wasn't brushed off," Emily insisted. "Dan spent weeks investigating Harry's death. He's still working on Isabelle's."

"Pardon my asking," Helen interjected, "but who is Harry Bolton and why would Mike want to kill him?"

"Harry was born and raised on the Peninsula," Emily answered. "He used to own Bolton's on the Bay—a grocery store and restaurant in Nahcotta. He and Mike went to school together, and I can't think of a reason on God's green earth why Mike would want to kill him."

Helen definitely needed to have a talk with Dan about Joanna's theory. How open would the sheriff be to her questions? Helen couldn't remember reading about Harry in Isabelle's notes. But then she may have had those with her. What had Emily said? They hadn't found her notebook—the one she carried with her everywhere. She had listed Mike Trenton as one of the people she wanted to interview.

Now, interestingly enough, Chuck Frazier, whose boat may

have been sabotaged, was on his way to the hospital. Could Mike—or someone else—be trying to kill him as well? Another possibility existed, of course, that she was being swept up into one woman's fantasy. Despite what civilians often thought, the police—at least most of them—took their responsibilities seriously.

When Helen tuned back to the discussion, the group had moved on to other matters. Something to do with politics within their writer's group. She half listened, thinking about Chuck and Isabelle and wondering whether or not she should even get involved. After all, she'd come to the Peninsula to write a guidebook—not solve a crime. Or crimes, as the case may be.

"Oh my, look at the time." Libby glanced at her watch and made a face. "I hate to break this up, gals, but I need to pick Rachael up from choir practice. My daughter," she added for Helen's benefit, then slipped into her maroon parka. "Speaking of which . . . our church is having a concert Sunday afternoon. I'd love you all to come."

They each thanked her for the invitation and said they'd think about it. Joanna followed Libby out while Helen and Emily collected Dan's leftover pizza and paid their bill. Driving back to the bed and breakfast, Emily spent most of the time defending Danny and assuring Helen that despite her disagreement with him over Isabelle's death he was a "good boy" and a fine sheriff. "I don't care what Joanna says," Emily reminded her again, "Mike Trenton is no killer."

Helen listened agreeably and wondered why Emily felt she needed to defend either of them.

✚   ✚   ✚

Once home, Helen headed for her room in hopes of getting some writing done.

Although she did manage to set up her laptop and open the file she'd started, she didn't get a chance to input much more than the date before Emily knocked to say there was a call for her. "It's Adam. You can use the phone in the entry."

The entry phone was an old-fashioned box-type telephone

with a fake crank ringer. Helen picked up the receiver and heard a click, which must have been Emily hanging up an extension.

"Helen?"

"Adam. Hi. How's Chuck?"

"Not great. You were right about the medication. We found a couple Tylenol number threes in his jacket pocket. Couldn't be sure how many he'd taken, so they pumped his stomach."

"Codeine—" That accounted for the pinpoint pupils and slow pulse.

"Yeah—go figure. You'd think a guy like Chuck would know better than to drink while he was taking pain medication."

"He does know better," a woman in the background said. "Who are you talking to?"

His voice faded as he apparently turned from the phone to answer, "Helen—the writer I was telling you about." To Helen he said, "That's Shells. I called her as soon as I got here. Chuck's been having trouble with his shoulder. Guess he injured it in the boating accident. His doctor put him on pain meds and told him to take it easy for a few weeks."

"Like Chuck is supposed to know what that means." Shells' high-pitched voice betrayed her anger and disgust. "I can't believe he'd pull a stunt like this."

"Apparently he did. Says he must have taken the pain pills and forgot. I'll be glad when he's more alert so I can find out what's going on. Right now, I'm heading home. The doctor says they'll discharge him in another hour or two. You can bet I'll be here to pick him up."

Helen thanked him for calling, then went in search of Emily to give her the news. She found her in the kitchen baking scones for breakfast.

"Looks like our mystery for the evening is solved." Helen helped herself to hot water and a bag of chamomile tea as she repeated the information she'd gotten from Adam. The news that Chuck had mixed his prescription narcotic with alcohol didn't, of course, answer the questions Helen had about murder and mayhem on the Long Beach Peninsula, but it did ease her mind a bit. As did the tea and the cozy kitchen. "The scones smell wonderful."

"You can have one if you like." Emily peeked into the oven, then shut it again. "Should be ready in another five minutes."

"I shouldn't. But . . ." She laughed at her hesitancy, knowing full well she'd give in. "I'd love it."

"Good—gives me an excuse to have one as well." Emily tossed her a companionable smile, and for the first time since she'd arrived at Bayshore Bed and Breakfast, Helen felt welcome.

She watched while Emily puttered around her domain, wiping off the counters and rinsing dishes. She'd have offered to help but knew what the response would be. Besides, it felt good to just sit and relax.

Emily, the scent of fresh scones, and the warmth reminded Helen of home. Back in Ireland long before Mum took sick— before Helen had married Ian and moved to the United States. "My mother used to make scones—we'd have them nearly every day with tea."

"With coddled cream and preserves, I'll bet." Emily pulled out the scones and slid them onto a waiting platter.

"Of course."

"I don't do cream anymore. Cholesterol's too high. But I use low fat whipped topping—it's a tad sweeter but mighty good."

The words low fat took away any guilt Helen felt over indulging in their late-night snack. But their sweet reward hit a sour note when Dan arrived. To say he was in a foul mood would have been gross exaggeration. He lightened up after a swig of decaf and a bite of cranberry scone. The dune party and fire ended up being a drug bust as well. A few of the kids had hand guns and used them. "Found a stash of crank—" he hesitated and shifted his gaze to Emily. "That's street talk for methamphetamine."

"I know what crank is, Danny."

"Yeah, well, I've never seen so much of it in one place. Not down here, anyway."

"Sounds as though you may have a meth lab or two hidden away."

Dan leaned back in his chair and looked at Helen as if he'd only just noticed her presence. "Maybe. You keep hoping things like that will stay in the big cities." He sighed and cleared his throat. "I'm sorry about that. Shouldn't be bringing my troubles to you ladies."

"It's all right. I can empathize with you about the meth labs. Seems you close one down and five more pop up to take its place."

"Right. I hear your husband works for the Feds, Mrs. Bradley."

Helen settled her cup in the saucer. "You've been doing your homework. And with record speed, I might add."

He nodded. "Friend of mine is the sheriff in Bay Village. I talked to him after I stopped you."

"I see. Did he tell you I used to be a police officer?"

"That and a few other things."

Helen met his critical gaze head on. "Are we going somewhere with this?"

"Maybe. I also heard you've done some undercover work for the DEA and was wondering if the Feds might have sent you down here to check into the drug-smuggling allegations."

"No. They haven't. I'm here to write a book."

"So you aren't here in an official capacity?"

"No. Why do you ask?"

"The sheriff down in Bay Village says you've helped them out on occasion. You're credited with solving several murder investigations."

"And . . ."

"Well, Mrs. Bradley, the folks down in Bay Village might welcome your input, but I don't. Regardless of what you might have heard to the contrary, I run a tight ship here in Pacific County. I don't need your help. Do I make myself clear?"

"Oh, very clear, Sheriff."

"Daniel Merritt! Sometimes you have the manners of a porcupine."

"It's all right, Emily. Perhaps he's just trying to protect you.

He's afraid I may try to involve myself in his investigations and drag you in with me."

"That's nonsense." Emily sniffed.

"You're very astute, Mrs. Bradley. But it's more than that. I just plain don't want outsiders—especially a woman—coming in and telling me how to run my business."

Helen bristled but held back her anger and lifted the corners of her mouth into a smile. "I don't think you need to worry about that, Sheriff—at least for the time being. However," she punctuated the word to let him know he hadn't intimidated her, "if I am called in, you'll be the first to go. . . . Oh, did I say go?" She stood and smiled down at him. "I meant *know*."

She took mild satisfaction at the look of surprise on his face and turned to Emily. "Thanks for the treat. I'd love to stay and chat, but I really do need to get some work done tonight. Oh, and Emily," Helen added on a sweet note, "you might want to brief Dan on that incident with Mr. Frazier this evening—seeing as he runs such a tight ship and all."

She bid them good night and went upstairs. Closing the door to her room, Helen took several deep breaths and vowed not to let that territorial chauvinist get to her. Taking a more subjective view, Helen suspected he might have ulterior motives for trying to warn her off.

She made it a point to never fully trust a person who used threats or force to maintain control. Dan was obviously a man who liked being in charge. Was he protecting someone? Keeping dark and deadly secrets?

Too upset to work, Helen allowed herself the luxury of a long soak in the claw-foot tub.

It helped—so had thinking of things she could do to get even. Not that she would. Getting even wasted too much energy. Better to think of him as a poor, unenlightened soul and feel sorry for him. Maybe she'd even add him to her prayer list.

In the meantime she'd use the adrenaline rush her anger had provided to her advantage—and make a few notes of the day's happenings on her computer. She needed to enter some of the information Isabelle had already gathered.

Helen stepped out of the cooling water, dried off, and slipped into her cotton nightgown, then blow-dried her short, serviceable hair and ran a brush through it.

Feeling refreshed and wide awake, Helen fluffed up pillows, set her laptop on the bed, and went to the desk to retrieve Isabelle's files. She could have sworn she'd set them in the top drawer when she'd come back earlier in the day, but they weren't there. She checked her backpack. Nothing. After looking through every possible space including the wastebasket, Helen dropped onto the bed to think where she might have put them. Maybe she'd left them in the car.

A more patient woman might have gone to bed and waited until morning, but Helen knew she wouldn't rest until she'd found those notes. She quickly donned a pair of sweats and stuffed her feet into her tennis shoes.

Emily was coming up the stairs as Helen came down. They met on the landing in the middle and Helen explained what had happened.

"I'll help you look."

The folders weren't in the car. Back in the house they conducted a second search, thinking Helen might have laid them down somewhere. Emily seemed as obsessive about finding the files as Helen. They began in Helen's room and worked down.

On the main floor, several minutes later, Helen finished looking through the living room area and went into the kitchen to find Emily. She was kneeling in front of the basement door at the far end of the kitchen. "Now, how do you suppose this got here?"

"What is it?" Helen knelt beside her.

"Sand. I just cleaned the floor this morning and haven't been down to the cellar in days."

"Could Dan have dragged it in? He was on the beach earlier."

"He came in through the entry and took his shoes off. 'Course he could have had sand in his socks, but I'm sure he didn't come over here."

Helen opened the door and Emily flipped on the basement light. The two of them leaned over to examine the stairs.

Clumps of sand lay on the steps below.

"Looks like someone came in from the cellar." Helen peered into the dimly lit room below. "Maybe we'd better call Dan back."

Emily didn't answer. Helen turned around. The back door stood open. She found Emily around the side of the house staring down at the weathered cellar door. Helen followed Emily's flashlight beam to a jagged hole in the whitewashed wood.

"Looks like someone stepped through it."

Helen reached down and wrenched an ax handle out of the hole. The silvery blade glistened when she held it up to the light. "Or busted it up with the hatchet."

Seven

The alarm buzzed her awake at four the following morning. Helen tried not to think about the fact that she'd had only four hours sleep. She groaned and reached over to pet the furry feline who'd taken her part of the bed out of the middle. "I can't believe I'm getting up at this hour to go fishing."

Swinging her legs off the bed, Helen yawned and stretched. The messy desk in front of the bay window gave proof to last night's bizarre break-in.

Within minutes of their phone call, Dan and another deputy had come to investigate. He verified their findings and insisted Emily take a careful inventory of all her belongings, including the antique jewelry she kept in her room. "Makes no sense that someone would bust in the cellar door just to steal Isabelle's notes."

"Unless there is something incriminating in them," Helen noted.

"Now, that's not likely, is it? Didn't you say you'd read through them?"

"Not all of them."

"Let's say you're right and the thief did steal Isabelle's files. Why wait until now to steal them?"

Helen shrugged. "You've got a point."

That point was something Helen had stewed over half the night. The best scenario she could come up with was that Isabelle's killer—if indeed there was such a person—hadn't felt

67

threatened until they'd heard about Helen taking over the book project. Still, it seemed odd to wait so long. Unless . . . maybe the burglar hadn't been after Isabelle's notes at all. Maybe he—or she—had been after Helen's. And there weren't many of those. Or maybe they weren't after incriminating evidence and only wanted to slow her down.

Whatever the reason, she couldn't deal with it now. If she didn't get down to the docks soon, Mike Trenton and his *Merry Maid* would leave without her.

Fifteen minutes later, dressed in denims, a turtleneck, and a baggy sweat shirt she'd borrowed from J.B., Helen pulled on her tennis shoes and hurried downstairs.

Emily, true to form, had prepared a huge breakfast of cantaloupe, omelet, hash browns, and scones—the likes of which made Helen's stomach queasy just looking at it. "I can't possibly eat this much."

"'Course you can. I fixed you a nice lunch too." Emily opened a cupboard and reached for a prescription bottle and a small clear plastic container. She set both on the table in front of Helen. "Take two of the seasickness pills now and save a couple for later. You'll want to use the sea bands too. Just wear them on your wrists while you're out. I also tucked in a little bag of dried ginger. Supposed to work wonders for seasickness."

"I think I'll pass. I rarely get seasick." Helen scooped out a bite of melon.

"Ever gone over the Columbia River bar?"

"No, but I've been ocean fishing and whale watching along the Oregon Coast."

Emily shrugged. "Suit yourself. I'll pack 'em in with your lunch in case you change your mind."

At five minutes after five Helen slipped on her jacket, gathered her pack and Emily's well-stocked cooler, and headed out the door. In the predawn light, Helen drove the thirteen miles to Ilwaco and parked in the lot near the port. While she unloaded and locked up her car, a Jeep Cherokee and a Ford truck pulled in and parked nearby. The drivers and passengers spilled out—five in all.

Helen recognized one of them as the man she'd seen with the Carlson brothers the night before. A greeting slipped out before she remembered she hadn't actually met him.

A toothpaste-ad smile flashed across his face. "Morning. You going out on a charter this morning?"

"Sure am." Helen adjusted her pack and picked up the cooler.

"Wouldn't be the *Merry Maid*, would it?"

"It would."

"In that case, would you tell the skipper not to leave without us? Knowing these guys, it'll take us at least ten minutes to check in and get our stuff down to the boat."

"Hey, Wilson, who you calling slow?" someone on the other side of the truck bellowed.

Wilson ignored the man, his gaze lingering on Helen. "You look familiar. Have we met?"

"Not officially. We ate in the same restaurant last night."

"Oh, right, I remember seeing you."

"I'm Helen Bradley."

"Earl Wilson."

She switched the cooler to her left hand and shook the hand he held out to her. "Nice to meet you. I'd better scoot or the skipper will end up leaving all of us. See you on board."

"Come on, Wilson. Stop flirting with the lady and give us a hand."

Helen ignored that comment and the ensuing catcalls and hurried on, stopping briefly at the charter office to check in and purchase a fishing license.

From the top of the dock she caught sight of the *Merry Maid*. The white fiberglass craft reminded Helen of a slightly larger and more expensive version of the *Hallie B*. Her stomach fluttered with anticipation. Of course it could have been protesting the breakfast Emily had fed her. Maybe she should have taken those pills after all.

On her way to the *Merry Maid*, she passed the *Klipspringer*, Hank and Bill Carlson's boat. The big black-and-white trawler was badly in need of a paint job. Helen had hoped to see the men this morning—especially Hank. She had her camera loaded and ready.

Seeing no sign of the two men on or around the boat, Helen moved on to the *Mariner III* a few slips down. She didn't see anyone about there either, but then she hadn't really expected to. More than once during the night she'd worried about Chuck and his reluctance to disclose what he had found. He didn't seem to mind who knew that he was on to something. It was almost as if he were asking for trouble.

Wave action, probably from boats leaving the port, set the craft and the dock to rocking, dispelling Helen's thoughts.

A short distance away, Mike Trenton stood on the dock in front of the *Merry Maid*, hunched over, hands in his pockets, the stub of a cigarette dangling from his lips. At least she assumed it was Trenton. He pulled it out of his mouth when she approached and tossed it into the water. It sizzled. So did Helen. She set the cooler down, knelt on the dock, fished the butt out of the water, and handed it to him. "You dropped this."

"Humph." He tossed the soggy butt back in—far enough this time that she couldn't reach it without going for a swim. "Don't tell me you're one of those lame-brained environmentalists."

Helen bit back a caustic lecture about endangering wildlife. This wasn't the time. "Let's just say I care, Mr. Trenton. As for the lame-brained part, I'll let you figure that out." Helen sighed. "We seem to have gotten off to a bad start. If you'd rather not take me along, I'll see if I can find someone else."

"No! I . . . um . . . I'm sorry. Guess I'm just in a lousy mood. My deckhand called in sick, and the men who chartered my boat haven't showed up yet."

"Oh, I nearly forgot. I saw them in the parking lot. Should be down any minute."

Laden with more stuff than could possibly fit on one boat, the men had made it as far as the ramp and were slowly advancing toward them.

Trenton swore and mumbled something derogatory about weekend fishermen, then picked up Helen's cooler and helped her on board. "Did you bring any fishing gear?"

"Gear?"

"Fishing pole, tackle box. A lot of people bring their own."

Helen laughed—at herself and at the odd look on Trenton's face. "You must think I'm two slices short of a sandwich. It didn't even dawn on me to bring a fishing pole."

He grinned at her for the first time. "Don't worry about it. I've got everything you need."

Helen settled into the second mate's seat in front of the console and watched the men load their gear and themselves onto the *Merry Maid*. Mike swiftly and efficiently tucked away coolers, tackle boxes, fishing poles, and bait.

She caught sight of Bill Carlson on the bridge of the *Klipspringer* motioning to Hank, who stood on the dock, preparing to cast off. Helen quickly moved to the rail and snapped several photos. Bill started the engines.

"Mrs. Bradley!" Mike shouted. "I need your attention over here. Before we take off I want to go over some safety regulations." He removed the cushions from one of the benches and scooped out several life vests. Some yellow, some orange. Some new, and some that looked as though they'd been around since World War II. While Helen grabbed one and slipped it on, he told them about the lifeboat, the first aid kit, and how to use the radio to call for help in case he, for some reason, couldn't. "There are two life rings on each side of the boat. Now, I don't anticipate any trouble—weather calls for morning clouds with clearing midmorning. We'll head out around Buoy Ten and do some salmon fishing." He reached into one of his many pockets and retrieved some pamphlets. "These are the fishing regulations. I'll let you read 'em—easier than spending half an hour going over them with you.

"Guess that's about it. If you got questions, you know where to find me." Trenton then ascended the ladder to the pilothouse and within seconds had the forty-foot craft up and running. Helen and Earl volunteered to untie lines and shove off. She was the only one wearing a life vest.

The sky took on glorious shades of red and orange as they motored between Sand Island and the Coast Guard station. The sight brought to mind an old saying: *Red sky at night, sailors delight. Red sky in morning, sailors take warning.*

A chilling wind whipped through her hair as the boat picked up speed. Helen shivered and turned up the collar of her jacket, then stuffed her hands into her pockets. She forced her mind away from thoughts of trouble and focused on the fiery sunrise and the tranquil bay. The black water barely rippled as they sliced through it. Several other boats accompanied them on their trek, but Helen recognized the names of only two: the *Klipspringer* and the *Mariner III*.

Helen was surprised to see Chuck Frazier out and about. He had a passenger, she noticed, but they were too far away for her to see who it was. She waved at Chuck and received a toot from his horn.

The *Klipspringer* chugged slightly ahead of the *Merry Maid*. Bill Carlson waved from the pilothouse, probably in response to the horn. Hank was bent over the rigging on the aft deck. Helen took several photos of the sunrise, but looking through the viewfinder unsettled her stomach.

"Ever been ocean fishing before?" Earl shouted over the chugging engines. He was wearing a bulky sweater in shades of ivory, muted greens, and browns, which again suited his brown skin tone and dark features.

"Several times," Helen yelled back.

"What's the biggest fish you've gotten?"

"A hundred-pound striped marlin." Helen smiled at the memory. "In Mexico." She and J.B. had gone out after a successful drug bust off the coast of Central Mexico. The water there had been a brilliant turquoise.

"Really? How long did it take you to land him?"

"Thirty minutes. At least that's what my husband told me. Seemed more like an hour. He put up quite a fight." Helen smiled. "The fish—not the husband."

Earl chuckled. "What are you hoping to catch today?"

Information. A killer. She shrugged and said neither. "Anything will do. I'm not really out here for the fishing." She explained her mission to write a guidebook.

"So you're a writer. I always thought it would be fun to write a book." He lurched forward, catching himself on the railing. "Water's getting rough."

"Uh-huh." Helen swallowed back a wave of nausea and took a deep breath. Sea air mingled with diesel fuel did little to quiet her churning stomach. "Excuse me." Helen bolted for the side of the boat and relinquished her breakfast to the sea. Oh well. She hadn't wanted it anyway.

Trying to ignore the smirks of her fellow passengers, Helen made her way down to the galley, where Mike had stored the coolers. She pulled out a cold pop and pressed it to her forehead. Digging through the cooler again, she found the Dramamine, wrist bands, and the plastic bag of ginger. Helen downed the pills with ginger ale and slipped the bands on her wrists, placing the buttons over her pulse points. The pills would take a while to work, but at least she wouldn't have to worry about losing her breakfast anymore. She pinched off a square of the ginger and put the rest in her pocket.

Unable to handle the confines of the cabin, she climbed back up the narrow stairs and went aft, settling into the corner. The *Klipspringer* continued to chug along off their starboard side with Bill at the helm and Hank still intent on his task. Helen fumbled with her camera but couldn't focus.

Chuck Frazier still brought up the rear. His passenger stood near the bow looking back at the rugged shoreline.

The red sunrise had given way to gunmetal gray clouds. Behind them and off to the right, high atop the headland, stood the Cape Disappointment Lighthouse and the Coast Guard lookout where she and Adam had been the day before. She could see the narrow inlet of Dead Man's Cove. The Interpretive Center adorned another headland, and a short distance from that was the north jetty and the sandy curve of Waikiki Beach.

"You feeling better?" Earl sat down beside her.

"A little." She raised her can. "The soda seems to be helping. Or maybe it's the dried ginger."

"Good. Can I get you anything?"

"Thanks, but—"

Helen's response went dead as an explosion ripped through the gray morning. She covered her mouth to stifle a scream. Her pop can clattered to the deck.

"God help us," she gasped, then stared horrified as the *Mariner III* turned into a gigantic fireball.

Eight

"Mayday! Mayday!" Mike Trenton yelled into his radio as he turned the *Merry Maid* around and closed in on the burning vessel. He raised the Coast Guard and relayed what they had just witnessed.

The bleating sound of the Coast Guard siren pierced the air before he finished speaking. They'd probably seen it from the tower at Cape D. The *Klipspringer* had turned around as well, Hank's gaze fixed on the *Mariner III*. Bill stared at it, too, the radio mike clasped in his hand.

The flames had diminished some, but Helen could still feel the heat and smell the burning diesel. Thick black smoke rolled up and dissipated on the wind. Debris floated on the water, but she saw no sign of the two men who'd been aboard.

Mike cut the engine and tore down the steps to the aft deck, ripping off his boots and jacket on the way. An instant later he jumped overboard. Helen thought briefly of following, but common sense held her back. Though she'd taken lifesaving courses, she'd never been a strong swimmer, and with her injured arm she doubted she'd be much help. Better to stay on board and assist from there. Besides, jumping into these icy waters even for a few minutes was tantamount to suicide.

"What in the world is he doing?" Earl leaned over the aft rail, watching the water where Mike had disappeared seconds before. Trenton surfaced several feet away, sputtered, spun around, and went under again.

"I don't know. Maybe he spotted someone." Helen released one of the round white life preservers hanging over the side of the boat and handed it to Earl, then grabbed another for herself. She scanned the water again for any sign of Chuck Frazier and his passenger but saw nothing resembling a human being. Mike surfaced again, this time holding on to someone. She heaved the life ring out to him.

Mike hooked his arms through it, his face a study in pain. "Pull us in."

They were still struggling to haul the men onto the boat when the larger of the two Coast Guard vessels approached the *Merry Maid* bow. Adam and two other men wearing orange survival suits and carrying a body board and an EMT jump kit boarded Trenton's craft.

"Got Mandrel." Mike shook salt water from his dark curly hair. "Chuck's still out there." He climbed onto the railing again, ready to jump.

"Trenton, don't be a fool." Adam grabbed him and pulled him back. "We'll find him. Last thing we need is a dead hero."

Mike jerked away and dove back into the water.

"Stupid . . . " Adam yelled to his crew to fish Trenton out of the water. A Coast Guard helicopter from the base across the river hovered above them, adding to the confusion and the wind.

Helen shared Adam's frustration. Trenton should know better. Going in once maybe, but twice—not in water this cold. He'd be hypothermic by now.

Helen divided her attention between Scott Mandrel, who was being checked over by the paramedics, and the gray swells carrying their skipper farther and farther away. She and the others breathed a collective sigh of relief when rescuers fished him out of the water and pulled him into the helicopter.

The rescue team working with Mandrel immobilized his neck and back, then settled him on the body board and transported him over to the Coast Guard vessel, where they could better care for him. He had a head wound and still hadn't regained consciousness. Once Mandrel had been taken inside the cabin, Adam boarded the *Merry Maid* again.

"Any sign of Chuck?" Helen asked.

"Not yet. We'll keep looking. The fifty-two will take Trenton and Mandrel in. I'll transfer over to the thirty-seven and stay out until—"

The ship-to-shore radio crackled. "We found Frazier."

Adam scrambled for the handheld. "What's the status?"

There was a pause, then more static. "He's dead, sir."

Adam replaced the mike and covered his eyes with his hand, dragging it down his face. His shoulders rose and fell. Silence stole over them like a heavy fog. Water lapped against the side of the boat. They seemed to be stranded in eternity. Helen closed her eyes. *Oh, God, please don't let this be happening.*

She felt numb and somehow detached. Swells lifted them several feet up, then dropped them again, but none of Helen's earlier signs of seasickness remained. She opened her eyes again feeling helpless, and at the same time wanting to do something.

"I suppose this means we won't be going fishing," one of Earl's companions mumbled. "Paid good money—"

"Put a sock in it, Kendall." Earl shook his head, his apologetic gaze falling to Helen. "Sorry about that."

"I'll have one of my officers pilot you back to the port." Adam paused and looked at Helen. "You okay?"

Helen nodded. "I'm fine."

He looked as if he didn't believe her. "I'll see you back at the docks then—or at the Coast Guard station."

"Do you want me to pilot the boat in?" Helen asked, eager for something to do.

"Not unless you're a licensed operator."

Helen waited for Adam to leave, then settled onto one of the cushioned seats. A young coxswain climbed up to the flybridge and they were soon under way. He steered away from the Coast Guard boats, giving them wide berth as crews dealt with the burning boat and raced back to the station with their victims.

A number of boats still dotted the water around Buoy Ten. Fishing for salmon, no doubt. Helen and J.B. had talked about taking his boat out salmon fishing, but they hadn't gotten around to it. Helen wished J.B. were with her now. She could have used his skill, his encouragement, and his comforting arm around her shoulder. The coxswain opened the throttle and headed back to port. The engine obliterated the voices of her fellow passengers. They'd been speculating about the explosion. How could it have happened? Had someone planted a bomb? Maybe the engines caught fire. Had it been an accident?

That was the big question, wasn't it? Accident or murder?

"Mrs. Bradley?" Earl sat down beside her and handed her a fresh can of ginger ale. "Thought maybe you could use this."

"Thanks." She popped the top and took a long drink, then settled the can between her legs.

"Do you do a lot of boating?"

"Off and on."

"You mentioned earlier you were working on some kind of guidebook."

She briefly told him about her project.

"I always thought it would be interesting to write, but I don't think I could sit still long enough."

"What do you do?"

"Work for the EPA."

"The Environmental Protection Agency? Are you here in an official capacity?"

"Partly. I've been talking to a few of the fishermen and doing some random checks on their catches."

"Is there a problem with pollution out here?"

"No more than usual as far as I can tell. We've been seeing some mutations in fish in some of the rivers in Oregon and Washington, and I'm checking out fish in different areas. We caught up with one firm in Longview last week. They were dumping toxic waste into the Columbia River. Levied a stiff fine." He smiled. "Tough job, but somebody has to do it."

"What about your friends? Are they with the EPA as well?"

"Nope. Just friends. We usually charter a boat twice, maybe three times a year. Steve Kendall, the one who was mouthing off about not being able to fish, works at a lumber mill in Longview. He's not usually such a grouch. His wife, um . . . my sister, is divorcing him. Ron and Ed Pritchett run a foundry in Oregon City. They're the two guys with matching bowling jackets. And the tall skinny guy eating his sandwich is Nate Hirsch. He's an airline pilot for Alaska Airlines."

Helen listened while Earl rambled on. She wasn't especially interested in learning more about the men at the moment, but she was glad for the distraction. Maybe Earl needed some diversion as well.

Helen swallowed back the lump in her throat as she checked her watch. On an ordinary day she'd just be rising. But today was anything but ordinary. In the twinkling of an eye—less time than it took to tie a shoe—the world had changed for all of them.

The craft slowed in compliance with the "no wake" sign as they entered the channel. Off to her left they could see the Coast Guard station. The boat carrying Scott Mandrel had docked, and an ambulance with sirens wailing was already making its way to the Peninsula's only hospital in Ilwaco. She saw no sign of the helicopter. Chances are they'd taken Mike straight to the hospital's landing pad.

Another rescue boat had docked as well, and another ambulance stood waiting to receive Chuck's body. There would be no hurry for this one. She wondered where they'd take him. Did the hospital have a morgue? Was the coroner close by, or would they have to wait for one to come from one of the larger towns like Longview or South Bend? Helen tucked the morbid thoughts away as the *Merry Maid* neared the docks.

Helen helped tie up, then waited while the men gathered their gear and disembarked. The coxswain questioned each of them about the explosion, getting their names, addresses, and phone numbers in case they'd need to be contacted later. Having completed his task, the young man left.

Earl lingered behind. "Can I give you hand—do anything to help?"

"No. I can manage," Helen told him. "I'd like to sit here a few minutes before I go up."

"I'll be on my way, then. We'll be staying at the Edgewater

Inn for a couple more days in case you want to get in touch."

Helen thanked him and said good-bye. Long after he'd gone she sat on the bow staring into the oil-slickened water. "What now?" She sighed. Part of her wanted to stay on the boat—tucked safely in the harbor. Another wanted to race over to the Coast Guard station to—to do what? Stand around and get in the way? Ask questions no one could answer?

If anything, they'd be asking *her* questions. She'd witnessed the explosion. Yet she had no idea what had caused it. It could have been an engine problem, but Helen doubted that. More than likely someone had planted an explosive device. The only reason she could come up with was that someone, possibly the same person who'd killed Isabelle, wanted to silence Chuck.

The *Merry Maid* shifted and rocked when someone boarded. Helen twisted around. A young man in a Coast Guard uniform stood on deck, hat in hand. "Are you Mrs. Bradley?"

"Yes." Helen rose and made her way to the rear of the boat. "Can I help you?"

"I'm Petty Officer Nixon. Lieutenant Jorgenson asked me to make sure you were okay and ask you to come up to the base."

"I suppose he wants to question me."

"Yes, ma'am. I can drive you if you want."

"No, thank you. I'll drive. My car is here."

He nodded. "Um . . . can I carry anything for you?"

Helen started to decline his offer but stopped herself. "Sure." Nixon followed her below deck where she picked up her back-pack and handed him the cooler.

Walking up the ramp, Helen felt dizzy and weak. She stopped and grabbed the railing. Nixon dropped the cooler and caught her before she could hit the ground. "You okay, ma'am?" He lowered her to the ramp.

"Um . . . not exactly. Just let me sit here for a minute."

After several minutes the nausea passed. "I think I'll be okay now. Probably a mixture of an empty stomach and shock."

"That'll do it. Maybe you should let me drive you. Wait here and I'll bring the jeep closer so you won't have to walk all the way out to the parking lot."

When he left, Helen opened the cooler and extracted a bottle of apple juice and a sandwich. She peeled away the plastic wrap and groaned. Tuna fish. Rummaging through the cooler she found a bag of crackers. That she could handle.

With something in her stomach she felt well enough to drive and did.

When she arrived at the base, Adam was in his office talking, or rather, arguing with Sheriff Merritt.

"You can go in, Mrs. Bradley. Lieutenant Jorgenson said he wanted to see you right away."

"I'd better wait. Has the sheriff been in there long?"

"About five minutes."

Helen nodded and took a seat next to the door, where she could hear them all too clearly.

"It wasn't your fault or mine," Dan shouted. "Brooding about what we should have done isn't going to change things."

"No, but we knew Chuck was looking to get the goods on somebody. He was onto something—just like Isabelle."

"Isabelle's death was an accident."

"I don't believe that now. I'm not sure I ever did."

"You're saying Chuck's death and Isabelle's are linked?"

"It's a possibility. They both had evidence—"

"And you think someone wanted to shut them up?" The door opened, and Dan's lean frame nearly filled the doorway.

"From what you just told me about last night, I'd say yes." Adam waved Helen in. "Oh good. You're here."

Helen stepped into the small office, made even smaller by the two men. "How is Mike?"

"He'll live." Adam's wooden chair creaked when he leaned back.

"And Scott?"

"He's still unconscious."

Dan's frown deepened. He closed the door again, eyeing her suspiciously. "What happened to you?"

"I was on the *Merry Maid* this morning and . . . um . . . witnessed the explosion. The *Mariner III* was right behind us."

"I see." Dan gave her a wry look. "The restaurant last night, the burglary at the B and B, and this morning a bombing. Interesting coincidence, don't you think?"

Helen ignored his innuendo.

Dan leveled a hard, penetrating gaze on her. "You ever heard of chloral hydrate, Mrs. Bradley?"

"Oh, come on, Dan." Adam frowned. "You can't possibly believe Helen had anything to do with that."

Helen glanced from one to the other. "Do with what?"

Adam shifted uneasily. "Last night at the restaurant. We thought Chuck had taken his pain-killers and had too much to drink. Turns out it wasn't that at all. His doctor called this morning."

"He had chloral hydrate in his bloodstream," Dan said. "Somebody slipped him a Mickey."

Nine

C hloral hydrate? You're sure?" Helen asked.

"Puts a whole new light on things, doesn't it?" Dan glowered. "Just wish Chuck had told us what he was up to last night. We might have been able to stop it."

"Maybe." Adam rubbed his chin. "I have a hunch he didn't have enough information to even name names. He was blowing smoke and letting someone think he knew more than he did."

"And he underestimated his opponent," Helen added.

Dan gave her a sidelong glance that clearly questioned her authority to comment, then focused back on Adam. "You suppose he told Shells anything?"

"He might have. He mentioned talking to her." With a worried look, Adam returned to the chair behind his desk. "I took him over there last night to sleep it off."

"Which means Shells could be in danger as well." Helen rubbed at a stiff muscle in her neck. "Have you told her about Chuck?"

"Not yet." Adam's rosy cheeks had turned an angry red. "Haven't been able to get away—didn't want to send just anybody."

"I'll tell her," Dan volunteered. "It's on my way."

Clearly, the idea did not appeal to Adam, but he let it pass.

Helen was beginning to feel woozy again, only this time it wasn't lack of food or seasickness. She slipped off her jacket and sweat shirt and draped them over the back of her chair. "I'm either having a hot flash or it is unbearably warm in here."

"It isn't you. Adam's trying to emulate Florida." Dan stepped over to the window, opened it, then leaned back against it, resting his hips on the sill.

"Sorry." Adam reached over and flipped off a space heater. "I get chilled—takes me forever to warm up."

"You and Sam McGee." Helen retrieved a tissue from her pocket and dabbed at the moisture on her forehead and upper lip and joined the sheriff at the window. "You're hogging all the cool air. Didn't your mother ever teach you to share?"

He chuckled. "Sorry about that." He shifted over a few inches. "I'll be out of here in a minute and you can have all the fresh air you want.

"Before I take off," Dan continued, speaking now to Adam, "we better clarify something. The chloral hydrate business is my jurisdiction, but the explosion is yours—how do you want to handle the investigation?"

"We'll have to work with Marine Safety and probably the Feds. Since Chuck was a friend, neither one of us should be involved in the investigation."

"You have a point."

A determined look that passed between the two men indicated they would both be very much involved, if only in an unofficial capacity. "Since no one else is here yet, it wouldn't hurt to start asking questions," Adam said. "We'll have to contact everyone who might have been a witness." He handed a list of names to Dan. "The passengers on the *Merry Maid* are staying at the Edgewater—with the exception of Helen here." He glanced at Helen. "Guess we could start with you. You were the closest vessel, weren't you?"

"Yes. About two hundred feet away. The *Klipspringer* was ahead of us and to the south. I remember seeing them just before the explosion and right after. They'd turned around too. I lost track of them after that."

Adam nodded. "Bill called in about the same time as Mike, but our lookout had already seen the explosion and alerted us. Unlike your bullheaded skipper, Bill and Hank followed orders and stayed out of the way during the rescue efforts. They stuck around and helped pick up debris from the boat, then headed back out to get some fishing in. I'll talk to them this afternoon when they get back."

"Mrs. Bradley, can you remember anything about the explosion itself?" Dan asked.

"Chuck was at the helm and Mandrel . . . as I recall, he was standing on the portside in front of the cabin, hanging on to the rail. I heard the boom and the whole boat went up in flames. Trenton radioed for help, then jumped in and managed to save Mandrel. I know it's sketchy, but it's the best I can do for now. I may remember more later."

"What do you mean, later? You either remember or you don't," Dan huffed.

"The mind is a tricky thing, Sheriff. The details of what we see—especially in something as traumatic as an explosion—don't always fully register. It can take hours or even weeks to re-create the event and assimilate the information. Some people never take the time to draw these memories to the surface—some don't want to."

"But you do." Dan crossed his arms.

"Helen," Adam mused, "you saw Mandrel just before the explosion. Did he look like he was about to jump?"

"Oh, I don't know . . ."

Dan leaned forward. "You're thinking he might have set the charge, detonated it, and jumped clear?"

"It's a possibility. Probably didn't figure on a concussion, but he knew with all the boats around he'd have a good chance of being rescued." Adam leaned back in his chair and propped his feet on the desk. "With Trenton going into the water the way he did, they might have been in on it together."

"I doubt Trenton had anything to do with the explosion. He was Chuck's best friend." Dan shifted his gaze back to Helen. "Don't suppose anyone was taking pictures."

"I should have been, but I wasn't feeling well at the time. . . . Wait, there was someone. The airline pilot . . . um . . ." Helen searched her memory for a name. "Nate Hirsch. He was taking pictures of the men in matching jackets just prior to the explosion."

"Anything else?" Adam asked.

Helen unzipped her backpack and pulled out a pad and pen.

She wrote each name, trying to place their positions prior to the explosion.

She listed Nate, the pilot, then the brothers, Ed and Ron—P something. All three had been standing to her right on the boat, the brothers against the railing posing for Nate.

"Earl Wilson and I were sitting aft—to the left of the engines." Helen hesitated, trying to picture the fifth man. "There was one more passenger—a man named Steve Kendall. The man was downright rude about our having to go back in. Wanted to stay out and fish."

"Without a skipper?"

"Earl said he was going through a divorce. There's something else about him. He was wearing headphones and had a radio or cassette player hooked to his belt." She closed her eyes. "I remember now. When I came up from the cabin, he was sitting on the stool at the console fiddling with the cassette." Helen hesitated as the possibility sank in. "If it was a cassette."

Dan and Adam exchanged glances. "A detonator?" Adam leaned forward, letting his feet drop to the floor.

"If it was," Helen said, "he's probably ditched it by now."

"I'll pick him up." Dan straightened and picked up the hat he'd set on Adam's desk. "What's the status on Mandrel?"

"Haven't heard. He was still unconscious when the EMTs took him off the base. The hospital is supposed to keep me updated. I'll question him as soon as he's awake."

"I'd like to ask him a few questions myself," Dan said. "Like what was he doing on Frazier's boat."

An hour later Helen and Adam pulled into the parking lot of the hospital. The emergency room doctor had called Adam to report that Scott was awake and stable.

Entering the double-glass doors of the single-story building, Helen noted that the hospital was small but had a competent feel to it. Contemporary chairs lined the small waiting room where no one waited. A receptionist with wide brown eyes and over-permed hair beamed at Adam. "You're from the Coast Guard station, aren't you? The doctor said you'd be coming."

"We're here to see Scott Mandrel."

"I know. He's in room four. Just go through these doors and it's the second room on your right." Her smile faded. "Isn't it just awful about the accident? I feel so bad for Shells. Losing her brother and everything."

Adam agreed, thanked her, and ushered Helen down the hall.

"Scott Mandrel?" Adam stepped into the room.

"That's me." Scott held out his hand. "You must be Lieutenant Jorgenson. The nurse said you'd be coming in." His eyes held a questioning look as he turned toward Helen.

Adam introduced Helen, then said, "How are you feeling?"

"Good, thanks to you and Mike. Got a knot on my head the size of a tennis ball and a few bruises, but I'll be out of here this afternoon."

He looked good, too, Helen noted. The bare chest and long dark hair splayed across the pillow reminded her of the roguish gothic heroes who appeared on many of the historical romances that lined bookstore shelves. Not that she was especially attracted to that type, but at the moment she had to admit Scott Mandrel looked much more like a hero than a villain.

A bruise on his forehead actually enhanced the man's unique features—obviously Native American but Caucasian as well, if the hazel eyes had any bearing. She could see why Shells might have chosen him over Adam or Dan. Yet it wasn't the physical appearance alone that made Scott Mandrel appealing. While Dan and Adam seemed perpetually stiff and anxious, in Scott she sensed a certain charisma and ability to put people at ease. Maybe it was just the difference between uniforms and bare chests.

"I'm hoping you can give me some clue as to what happened," Adam said, pulling Helen's attention back to the reason they'd come.

"I'll sure try. Come on in and sit down." He waved toward a couple of chairs. "I can't remember much. We were heading out toward Buoy Ten and bam!"

"Did you notice anything out of the ordinary?" Adam asked. "Engine trouble, anything that might have alerted you or Chuck that there might have been a problem?"

He moved his head back and forth. "All I know is that one minute I'm enjoying the wind in my face and the next I'm in the hospital." He reached for a glass of water and winced.

"Let me get that for you." Helen held the glass, directing the straw into his mouth.

"Thanks." His gaze fastened on Helen's. "Are you with the Coast Guard too?"

"No. I was on the *Merry Maid*." She explained about writing the guidebook and taking over for Isabelle.

"I remember Isabelle. She came and talked to me a while back about the processing plant—though why she wanted that information for her guidebook, I'll never know." He coughed, holding on to his chest as though it hurt. "Too bad about her accident. She was a nice lady." He looked back at Adam. "Any idea what happened out there?"

"I was hoping you could tell me. Do you know of anyone who might have wanted you or Chuck dead?"

A deep frown etched his forehead. "You're saying it wasn't an accident?"

"I'd be surprised if it was."

"Whoa. I can think of a few people that might want me out of the way—Sheriff Merritt for one. You, too, I imagine. Most of Shells' friends weren't too happy about her dating an Indian. I'm not the most popular guy on the Peninsula." He sighed. "There was a time the Chinook were the only inhabitants around here. By establishing a major processing plant, I saw an opportunity to retrieve some of what was lost to us, but there is a lot of prejudice—still.

"I couldn't have been the target, though," Scott went on. "No one knew I was on the boat. I didn't even know I'd be on board until this morning when Shells called me. Wanted me to keep Chuck from going out. He wouldn't listen, so I decided to ride along. With him being so sick and all, I didn't think he should go out alone. I was afraid he might hurt himself but had no idea someone would try to kill him. What makes you so certain he was murdered?"

Adam cleared his throat. "Someone may have tried to kill him last night and failed. Apparently they decided to finish the job this morning."

"I must be missing something here." Scott bunched the sheets in his fist and released them again. "Shells said he took some pain pills and drank too much last night. I didn't hear anything about an attempt on his life."

"He had pain pills in his pocket but hadn't taken them. Someone slipped him some chloral hydrate."

Scott whistled. "Does Shells know?"

"Probably by now. Dan was going to tell her about the explosion."

"Hi, Adam." A petite woman with hair the color of midnight came into the room. "Dan said you might be here." She looked up at Helen, who was at least six inches taller. "You must be the writer Adam was telling me about."

"Yes, I'm Helen Bradley. And you must be Shells." Though Helen considered herself slender, she felt awkward and oversized next to Shells. The woman's waist looked no bigger than one of Helen's thighs. Well, almost. She even had a small voice—the kind you might expect to come out of a cartoon mouse.

Shells had a pixyish face and a shaggy haircut that emphasized her doll-like features. Her cocoa brown eyes held evidence of recent tears. There was a haunting vulnerability about her, and at the same time Helen sensed a certain strength and resilience. Her unflinching gaze met Helen's head on. "This may seem like a stupid question, but why are you here? Adam said you were writing a guidebook."

"Yes. I met your brother last night and was with him when he, um, passed out."

"I asked her to come along," Adam said. "She witnessed the explosion this morning. Shells, I . . ." Adam looked as though he wanted to hold her.

She glanced away. "Whatever you do, don't tell me you're sorry. If anyone's to blame, it's me."

"You couldn't have stopped him, Shells," Scott said. "No one could."

Shells approached the opposite side of the bed from where Helen and Adam stood and greeted Scott with a lingering kiss. "But you shouldn't have gone out either. I don't know what I'd have done if I'd lost you both."

Scott took hold of her hand. "Don't think about that."

Adam cleared his throat again. "I . . . uh . . . I need to ask you both some questions. But if you want we can do it later."

Shells looked blank for a moment, then, without relinquishing her hold on Scott's hand, pulled a chair next to the bed. "What do you want to know?"

"Did Chuck tell you anything that might help us find his killer?" Adam directed his question to Shells.

She shook her head. "Dan asked me that too. I didn't even see Chuck this morning. He was gone when I woke up. Left a note saying he was going fishing. I called Scott to see if the boat was still in. He said it was. I asked him to try to stop him."

"Chuck told me he was on to something big," Adam said. "He seemed to be closing in on some illegal activity. He didn't think it was drugs but wouldn't tell me much more than that. Did he give either of you any indication of what he was up to?"

"No, nothing." Shells paused, tears close to the surface.

"Can't you wait with the questions?" Scott asked. "She's just lost her brother. . . ."

"It's okay, Scott." She squeezed his hand and looked up at Adam. "Chuck and I hadn't been talking much for the past couple weeks. He didn't think I should . . ." She hesitated, weighing her words. "Let's just say we disagreed about something." Shells paused to dig a tissue out of her jacket pocket and blow her nose. "It had nothing to do with what happened out there today. It was personal."

Helen suspected it had something to do with Scott Mandrel. Isabelle had warned Chuck about him. Isabelle had also written the word *curious* beside her entry on Scott. It was indeed curious.

Adam asked several other questions, but neither Scott nor Shells could shed any more light on why anyone would want to murder Chuck. He had no enemies that they knew of.

But he did have at least one, Helen thought. Like Isabelle, Chuck had come too close to discovering a secret. A secret that person meant to protect at any cost.

Ten

H elen declined Adam's invitation to dinner. She needed time
alone. Needed to assimilate the bits and pieces of information she'd been soaking up all day. She was bone tired and badly
in need of a nap.

When she pulled into the long, narrow drive at Bayshore Bed
and Breakfast at four P.M., Emily clucked over her like a mother
hen. "You look like something the cat dragged in."

"Gee thanks." Helen thought about objecting until she
caught a glimpse of herself in the mirror. Dirt and charcoal
smudged her face. Though she'd tried to clean up earlier, the
paper towels she'd used had only managed to move the dirt
around. Her hair looked as though a bird had tried to build a
nest in it. And she had a nasty bruise forming on her cheekbone
where a piece of debris from the *Mariner III* had hit her. Emily
was being kind.

"I know you'll be wanting to clean up, but go on into the
parlor and relax for a spell. I was about to have some tea. That
should perk you up."

"Tea would be nice." Helen hung her jacket on one of the
hooks by the door and followed Emily inside. "Did you hear
about the explosion?"

"It's all they were talking about at the post office this morning. Must have been awful seeing something like that."

"Hmm." Helen rubbed her forehead, wishing she hadn't
brought it up. But it wasn't fair to keep Emily in the dark either.

"Too bad about Chuck. Guess Shells is taking it pretty hard—but then she would." Emily sighed. "Don't feel like talking about it, huh? Well, I can wait. You just sit and rest. I'll get the tea."

Helen settled into an oak-framed gliding rocker with comfy dark green cushions, then stretched her aching legs out on the matching ottoman and set it into motion. Tipping her head back, she closed her eyes. When images of the explosion burst into her mind, Helen thrust them aside, willing her mind to think on more pleasant things. She wasn't ready to relive the tragedy yet. Maybe tomorrow. Maybe not.

J.B. hadn't called, she realized. But then she hadn't called him either. After her making such a fuss about needing time alone, he probably didn't dare interrupt. The corners of her lips lifted in a smile. She missed him and made a mental note to call after tea.

"You had a couple phone calls today," Emily announced as she set the tray on the coffee table. "One was from someone named Kate."

Helen accepted the china cup and saucer. "My daughter. Did she say what she wanted?"

"Nope. Checking up on you, I suspect."

"Yes, daughters have a way of doing that." Helen brought the cup to her lips, breathing in the comforting and distinct aroma of her favorite tea. "You said there were two."

"Other one was your husband. Said he'd either be at the office or the condo, and for you to call him as soon as possible."

"When did he call?"

"This morning. I told him you'd gone fishing. He didn't sound too happy."

Helen nodded and took a sip of tea. She would make her calls soon. At the moment, however, she had no intention of moving.

"I boarded up the cellar door today," Emily reported. "Still no word on who tried to break in. No fingerprints. Dan said they must have been wearing gloves or weren't in the house. He couldn't get a decent footprint either. We'll probably never know who did it. He says it was probably vandals—some kids messing around."

"Kids wouldn't have taken Isabelle's files."

"Yes, but you don't want to know what he said about that."

Helen raised her eyebrows and gave Emily a wry smile. "Let me guess. Dan thinks I'm senile and probably misplaced them." She chuckled. "He knows better than to come right out and say something like that to me. Especially since I have a better memory than he does. He was thinking it, though. Said unless we came up with something more pressing than a bunch of papers, I should fix the cellar door and forget it."

"I take it nothing else was missing, then."

"Not that I can see."

"Odd. As far as I could tell Isabelle hadn't written anything incriminating, but then I didn't read everything."

"It's a puzzle. Just hope we can solve it before they come after us."

Helen sat up straighter. "That brings up an interesting point. Why didn't the killer come after you? How would he have known Isabelle hadn't told you what she'd found?"

"Don't know unless he overheard her talking to me on the phone that night. She did say she'd fill me in later, so if someone was listening they might have figured they were safe."

"Yes. That's probably the case. And who knows? Maybe Dan is right. The break-in may have been an act of vandalism. In all honesty, I have been known to misplace things on occasion." Helen eased out of the chair. "Guess I'd better make my phone calls. Then I'm taking a shower and going to bed."

"What about dinner? I took the liberty of making reservations at 42nd Street Cafe in Seaview at six-thirty. Wonderful spot. You really do need to try it."

"Oh." Going out was the last thing Helen wanted to do.

" 'Course if you're too tired I could postpone it. Joanna and Libby will be disappointed, but . . ."

"I'm sorry—"

"Don't give it another thought. They called me today to see what I knew about the explosion. Libby's all set to write an article for the paper. Thought it might be easiest all the way around if we met at the restaurant. Kill two birds with one stone that way. You did say you wanted to check out the best restaurants for your guidebook."

"I wish you'd asked me first. I'm not sure I'm up to an interview. Maybe she could talk to Dan or Adam."

"You know she's not going to get much out of them."

"Um . . . I'll tell you what. Let me get cleaned up—I'll take a nap and see how I feel later on."

"Fair enough. In the meantime, I'd best get myself ready. Think I'll go even if you don't."

Helen waited until Emily was upstairs, then called J.B. from the phone in the entry. He wasn't in the office or at home. She left a message on both machines and called Kate.

"Oh, hi, Gram," Lisa, Kate's oldest, chirped. "How's the book coming?"

"I haven't made much progress yet." Helen pictured her sixteen-year-old granddaughter and smiled. Lisa was just about the most adorable redhead Helen had ever seen. "Your mother called—any idea what she wanted?"

"I'm not sure. She and Dad went out to dinner with Aunt Susan and Uncle Jason. Jennie's here with me and we're watching the boys. Hang on a second." After a muffled, "You can talk to her in a minute, Jennie," Lisa came back on. "Sorry about that. Anyway—I think Mom wanted to ask you to stay with Kurt and me when they go on a cruise in November. I hope you'll say yes. They are both getting way too cranky."

"I'd love to . . . um . . . I'd better ask J.B., though. He may have plans."

"Actually, Mom asked him earlier today and he said it was up to you."

"He was there?"

"Not exactly. He called around noon to talk to Mom about something, and then they went out to lunch."

"Oh?" Helen turned around and leaned against the wall. Though she loved the way her family had so readily accepted J.B., she felt a pang of jealousy at being left out. Of course, J.B.

and Kate had tried to call. Her annoyance turned to concern. "Is there something going on that I should know about?"

"They didn't tell us anything. . . ."

Helen could hear Jennie's voice in the background. "Come on, Lisa. Let me talk to her."

"Oh, okay. Gram, tell Jennie to cool it. She's way too hyper."

"Hmm. I'll see what I can do. Be sure to tell your mom I called."

"I will. Love you."

"I love you too, honey."

Jennie skipped the preliminary greetings and jumped in. "You're at the beach where that boat exploded, aren't you?"

"How did you—"

"It was on the news. The authorities think somebody bombed the guy's boat. Did you see it? Are you on the case? Do you have any leads? I wish I could be there with you."

"Whew. Lisa's right, you *are* hyper." Helen could imagine Jennie pacing the floor as she spoke. The girl had an even stronger propensity for fighting crime than her father or her grandmother. Unfortunately that crime-solving bent had gotten her into hot water on more than one occasion. "To answer your questions, yes, I saw it. The *case* is being handled by the Coast Guard and the local sheriff. And no, I have no leads."

"You're looking into it though, right? Who do you think did it?"

"Jennie, dear, I'm here to write a book, not solve a crime."

"That's what Dad said. He won't let me come see you. J.B. told him you didn't even want *him* around 'cause you need to concentrate on writing." She sighed heavily. "Is that really true? You don't want any of us around?"

Helen hesitated. "It's only for two weeks. This is a longer project than what I usually write. It isn't that I don't love you. . . ."

"I know that . . . but I don't think J.B. does. He seemed sad when he talked about you."

Helen rubbed her eyes. "He'll adjust. Um . . . Jennie, when did you see J.B.?"

"This afternoon. He stopped by for a minute to say good-bye."

"Good-bye? Did he say where he was going?"

"No, just that he had to go away for a while."

Away. Just what did away mean? Helen didn't ask, of course. J.B. had apparently not confided in the girls. She'd have to wait until he contacted her to find out what he was up to.

They spoke a few minutes more and after telling Jennie to give the boys a hug from her, she rang off. Guilt over J.B.'s sadness sank its tentacles deep in her heart. Was she being selfish? Should she be spending more time with J.B.? Maybe she should have been more sensitive to his needs. On the other hand, he'd known she was a writer before they married. It wasn't as though he hadn't had any idea what to expect. And what about him? Knowing J.B., he probably decided to come out of retirement and was on some plane to the Middle East again.

Helen tossed off her frustration and headed upstairs. She ran bath water and soaked in the tub until the water cooled and the bubbles disappeared, then slipped into her cotton pajamas and crawled into bed.

She slept without dreaming and awoke to the distant sound of a jangling telephone. A three-quarter moon shone over the water, creating a silver path to her bed. Helen stretched lazily, then winced. She'd pulled some muscles in her shoulders and lower back helping to bring Mandrel and Trenton on board that morning.

The phone was still ringing—five, maybe six times now. Why hadn't Emily gotten it? Helen swung her legs over the side of the bed. The neon green numbers on the clock read eight o'clock. The phone stopped ringing, but she didn't hear Emily's familiar voice. Then Helen remembered the dinner engagement. Emily must have gone on without her.

Fully awake now and stomach grumbling from lack of attention, Helen put on her robe and made her way down the stairs. Except for the light in the entry and the moonlight coming through the large bay windows, the house was dark. A movement on the back wall startled her. She yelped and jumped back, then clasped her robe more tightly around her.

"Silly goose," she muttered when she realized it was only the shadow caused by tree limbs waving in the wind. Not normally given to fears and fantasies, Helen chided herself for being so jumpy. She ran a hand through her hair and rubbed the back of her neck. Determined not to scare herself with wild imaginings, Helen crossed through the dining room to the kitchen. She fumbled for the light switch, encountering only a bare wall. Wishing she'd paid more attention earlier, she stepped farther into the darkness toward the kitchen door. Surely she'd find a switch there. A faint thump sent her heart into overdrive. Something crashed to the floor.

Eleven

W ho's there?" Helen clutched the lapels of her robe.
"Meow." Ginger tore past her.

Relieved to know it was just the cat, Helen hurried to the back door. This time she found the switch—two of them—and flipped them on. Light flooded the kitchen. Helen moaned. Ginger had knocked over a glass canister. Flour and glass shards covered half the floor.

"You stinker," Helen called after the errant cat. "Look at this mess."

From the utility closet Helen retrieved a broom and dustpan and methodically worked her way around the perimeters of the spill—sweeping inward and trying to keep from stepping in the broken glass. When she'd finished she filled the teakettle and set it on the stove.

Emily would undoubtedly want tea, and Helen needed food.

Someone pulled into the driveway—not Emily and not a car. The vehicle sounded more like a motorcycle. Perhaps Emily had a guest. Helen wandered back to the entry and reached for the knob at the same time the doorbell rang. Helen peered through the curtains. Not knowing whether to be happy or annoyed, she swung open the door. J.B. gave her an odd grin. "Evening, luv. Aren't you going to invite me in?"

Helen backed up and made room for him to enter, then closed the door. "I . . . I didn't expect to see you until the weekend." He looked different—more handsome if that were possible, but distant as well. Part of that might have been the clothes. He was wearing a black leather jacket and jeans, and a black biker T-shirt with a colorful Harley. Definitely not his usual style. And part may have been the smell—his clothes reeked of stale cigarette smoke and liquor.

"Yes. I'm truly sorry to bother you. I know how much you were wanting to be away to write. I tried to call. Emily said you'd gone fishing."

A swatch of apprehension sliced through her as wide and deep as the chasm that kept her from hauling him into her arms and kissing him. "I meant to call back around four, but—"

"You wouldn't have caught me. When I heard about the explosion and I didn't hear from you, I imagined the worst."

In all their years together as friends, and in their past few months as husband and wife, Helen had never felt so far away from him. It disarmed her. Was he moving on? His clothing seemed to indicate he was up to something. "But that's not the only reason you came."

"No, I've come to a decision. Since it involves both of us, I thought it best to talk it over with you."

"I see." She lowered herself onto the arm of a sofa and watched him settle into a big chair. "Could this have anything to do with your meeting with Jason and Kate?"

"So you know about that? Good. As I told them, I know how much you wanted this to work out," J.B. continued. "But the truth is, Helen, I was never cut out for this sort of life."

Helen hadn't known quite what to expect, but it wasn't this. Jennie had said he seemed sad. She was beginning to understand why. He was leaving her. Helen's heart sank into whatever murky depths hearts sink into when they've been broken. "And you want out." It was all she could do to maintain a steady voice. But she was not given to outbursts and fits of crying and had no intention of starting now.

"I know you're disappointed, but I suppose I do. I never should have made the commitment in the first place."

Helen swallowed back the baseball-sized lump in her throat.

"I suppose part of that is my fault. I expected more than you were willing to give."

"I knew you'd understand, luv." His blue eyes connected with hers. "It won't be so bad. I'll no longer be underfoot. We'll go back to the way things used to be."

Oh, J.B., I want you underfoot. I never meant that you should leave for good. She thought the words but couldn't say them. "I'm not sure we can go back. So much has happened."

His lovely smile faded. "I'm afraid I don't follow."

Helen didn't know what to say. The look in his eyes and the words they'd just spoken didn't seem to match. "I'm not sure I do either. But if you divorce me I don't think—"

"Divorce. . . ?" The blank look on his face might have made her laugh if the subject hadn't been so serious. "What on earth are you talking about?"

"J.B., you said you wanted out. That you shouldn't have married me. . . ." Helen got up and walked over to the window.

"I said nothing of the sort." J.B. came up behind her, his large hands cupping her shoulders. "You thought I was talking about us?"

"Weren't you?"

"No! I was trying to tell you that I'll not be retiring after all. I've been working on some prospects of things to do to keep busy, but so far nothing seems to be clicking for me. I came down here in hopes of persuading you to go along with me on it."

Helen turned and looked up at him. "That's it? All this stuff about not making a commitment to me just to say you don't want to quit working?"

"Of course. Do you really think I could leave you?"

"Oh, J.B., I thought—you seemed so different. Your clothes and that guilty look on your face make you look like a man on the run."

"Ah." A broad smile spread across his face and into his eyes. "Yes, well—this is part of what I've been trying to tell you. I hope you won't be too upset about the change in plans. Adam Jorgenson called while I was in the office. Wants us to take over the case. Says the lines are blurred as to who has jurisdiction, and since we've been concerned about the drug issue, and now with the bombing . . ."

"And you're going to work on the investigation?"

"Undercover. Only people who'll know are Adam and you—and perhaps the local sheriff. It's the best way to find out what's going on. I hit a few local pubs and made some initial contacts to feel out the territory."

Helen nodded, not quite knowing what to make of this man of hers—not knowing what to make of the conflicting feelings jumbling about inside her. Along with the rush of relief in knowing their marriage was intact, the old concerns for his safety crept in.

"I hope you're not too angry with me, luv." He stroked her cheek, his tender blue gaze searching her face for approval.

Helen closed her eyes, melting under his touch. She still didn't like the idea of J.B. taking risky assignments but understood full well his need to go on working at what he did best.

"I do love you." She brushed her lips against his. "I want you to do what's right for you."

J.B. hauled her to him and kissed her soundly.

Several minutes later gravel crunched in the driveway. J.B. dragged in a ragged breath. "Someone's coming. I'd best go."

"You're not staying the night?" Helen asked, somewhat winded herself.

J.B. groaned. "Don't tempt me, luv. I'd best not. The fewer people who know about us, the better."

"What will I tell Emily?"

"That I lost my way and came in to ask for directions."

Helen chuckled. "At least I won't be lying."

He cast her a look of pure longing. "I'll be going back to Portland in the morning to pick up the *Hallie B*. Thought I'd dock her down here and live on board. It'll be a good cover for me."

"Since when do bikers ride around in fancy boats?"

He glanced down at his leathers. "Since businessmen and yuppies decided it was *cool*. I won't be in this getup for long. Decided it might be best to hang around the docks for a few days. See what's coming in and going out."

The front door opened. "Oh my!" Emily stared at J.B., looking him up and down as though he might have been last night's burglar.

"Emily, I'm glad you're here. This gentleman needs to know how to get into Long Beach. I'm afraid my directions aren't up to speed yet."

Emily shrugged out of her jacket, still eyeing him suspiciously. "Just go out to the main road and make a left. Look for Cranberry Road—turn right. When you get to Highway 103, go left and you'll soon be in Long Beach."

"Thank you." He turned back to Helen. "And thank *you*. I'm terribly sorry to bother you two this late."

"No problem, Mr.—?" Helen followed J.B. to the door.

"Logan." He paused in the doorway and glanced back at Emily. "Very nice place you have here. Don't happen to have a room available, do you?"

Helen suppressed a grin.

"I might," Emily said. "There's a room upstairs—queen-sized bed with only one other person in it—if you don't count the cat. 'Spect that's where you'll want to stay."

Helen gasped. "Emily!"

"I may be old, dear heart, but I'm not stupid." She turned to J.B. "I take it you're the husband?"

J.B. opened his mouth, then closed it again.

"It's all right, you don't need to explain. People get their kicks doing all kinds of crazy things these days."

Helen looped her arm through J.B.'s when he started to object. "The jig is up, darling. You may as well stay."

"How did you know?" J.B. stepped back in and closed the door.

"Are you kidding? With you two mooning over each other like love-starved teenagers, I'd have to be blind not to know something was going on. Besides, I recognized your accent."

"It's all right, darling. I'm certain we can trust Emily to be discreet."

"I can," Emily said. "If need be."

The teakettle whistled. Helen offered to fix a tea tray while J.B. explained to Emily his presence on the Peninsula, as well as his disguise. Several minutes later, tray in hand, Helen entered the parlor.

"I understand your cousin may have been killed by the same person who murdered Frazier," J.B. said.

"That's my suspicion. Chuck and Isabelle might have been on the same trail."

J.B. frowned. "That's one of the reasons I volunteered actually. I suspected my dear wife would feel compelled to lend a hand."

Helen bristled. "Jason Bradley. You came down here to keep an eye on me, didn't you?"

"Not exactly, luv." J.B. hesitated, leaned back in his chair, and accepted the cup Helen handed him. "I'm here for the very reason I said. But Adam did mention you'd been asking questions about Isabelle. I told him I wasn't the least bit surprised."

Helen served Emily and, after taking her own cup, perched on the arm of the sofa. "Let me guess. You're both going to gang up on me and tell me to stay out of it."

"No. Not at all. Adam asked about having you drop your writing project for a time and concentrate on helping with the investigation. He thought since you were already here and interested you'd be ideal. But I took the liberty of telling him no."

"You what. . . ?"

J.B. raised his hand in mock surrender. "Before you lose that temper of yours, let me finish."

"It better be good." Helen couldn't believe he'd do something so underhanded. In all the years they'd worked together, he'd never made decisions for her. Now that they were married perhaps he felt justified. She set her teacup down on the tray and glanced at Emily, who seemed quite enthralled by it all.

"I tried to call you," J.B. went on. "When you didn't call back . . . well, knowin' how much you wanted to work on the book, I volunteered to take on the job myself." His blue gaze settled on her face. "I know you, luv. You're not the type to let something like this rest. I only wanted to set your mind at ease so you wouldn't feel compelled to take up your gun instead of your pen."

"I didn't bring my gun."

"But you did bring your pen."

Helen tilted her head and examined his face. Was he handing her a line? Maybe. She supposed she should give him the benefit of the doubt. He did seem sincere. And J.B. had been one of the few men she'd worked with who treated her with the same respect with which he treated male agents. Still, old resentments bubbled to the surface from years past, when she'd worked as a police officer.

"Helen, me luv," J.B. crooned in that irresistible Irish accent of his—well, part Irish. He was actually part Scot and part English—a mixed breed. "I'm not moving in on your territory. In fact, if you'd rather, I'll go back to Portland and put you on as a special agent and you can work the case with Adam. Ye'll answer to me, as we've always done."

Helen shook her head, a smile breaking across her face. "No. As much as I hate to admit it, you're right. I do want to write the book. And I have been wanting to get involved in the investigation. Having you here is perfect."

And it would be even more perfect, Helen decided, once she got J.B. up to her room, out of those silly clothes, and into her bed. J.B.'s tender smile suggested he was thinking along similar lines.

"I hope you'll excuse us, Emily, but it's time we turned in." Helen set her cup aside.

"You'll do no such thing. You haven't had dinner." Emily turned to J.B. "Have you eaten?"

J.B. nodded.

"You needn't go to any trouble," Helen said. "I can fix myself something quick."

"No trouble. Already got a meal ready—just have to heat up the rice and panfry the oysters. Besides," Emily said, walking toward the kitchen, "I got some news you're both going to want to hear."

Helen and J.B. followed her and settled onto the wooden chairs at the table.

"All right, you've got us." Helen slipped her hand in J.B.'s. "What did you want to tell us?"

"Well, it looks like you two have been arguing over nothing. If you'd have let me get a word in edgewise, I could have told you that."

"What do you mean?" Helen and J.B. asked together.

"Ran into Dan at the restaurant tonight. He made one arrest in the bombing case and is ready to make another.

Helen gasped. "Really? Who?"

"One of the men on the *Merry Maid* this morning confessed. Fellow named Steve Kendall. Says Scott Mandrel hired him to blow up Chuck's boat."

Twelve

I 'll be leaving now, luv." Leaning over the bed, J.B. nuzzled the back of Helen's neck. She'd asked him to wake her before he left. Even with the pending arrest, there would still be an investigation. Apparently Kendall's confession included naming Scott Mandrel as a drug kingpin.

"So soon?" She turned onto her back and draped her arms around his neck.

"I'll call you the moment I dock in Ilwaco." He kissed her again and drew away, taking her clasped hands from his neck and brushing his lips against them.

"Be careful." She watched him go, then snuggled back under the covers. Feeling warm and soft and feminine, Helen stretched lazily and closed her eyes. Oh, how she loved that husband of hers. She wondered how she'd managed alone all those years after Ian's death.

Helen showered, dressed, indulged in tea and her morning devotions, then went to work. She typed her notes into the computer and began outlining the guidebook. It was sketchy at best, but that would be remedied over the next few days. She set up a schedule that allowed her to write in the mornings and leave afternoons free to sight-see, gather information, and conduct interviews. Today, however, would be mostly devoted to discovery.

When Emily called her for breakfast at eight-thirty, Helen was more than ready for food and a break. She set her work aside and hurried downstairs.

"I still don't understand why J.B. is going ahead with all this undercover stuff." Emily set a plate of English muffins on the table. "The Kendall fellow confessed—what more do they need?"

"Even with a confession he has a lot of work to do," Helen explained. J.B. had talked with Adam the night before and would be meeting with him and the sheriff before heading back to Portland. "They need to make certain they have sufficient evidence to take to trial." With drugs involved, they'd also want to infiltrate the operation to get names of suppliers and buyers and find out how far-reaching it was. She didn't tell Emily about that part. Nor did she reveal what she'd told J.B. about Chuck's insistence that drugs were not an issue.

Fortified with juice, baked oatmeal, half a grapefruit, and a muffin, Helen headed out at nine-thirty with her notebook, camera, and a picnic lunch. Not even the partly overcast day and the threat of rain hampered her spirits. Helen couldn't help smiling as she drove south on Sandridge Road. She planned to drive as far as the Astoria-Megler Bridge, then backtrack, hitting points of interest. With luck, she'd make it back to the docks and Shells' Place about the time the boats came in. Helen wanted photos of people bringing in their catch. Maybe she'd do a nostalgic piece about fishing in the past when salmon were in abundance and one could always be assured the thrill of catching at least one.

The sound of a siren interrupted her reverie. She glanced in the rearview mirror. "Oh no, not again." She took note of her speedometer, slowed down, and drove on until she could find a safe place to pull over. Once stopped, she got out of the car and leaned against the door. Dan Merritt crunched to a stop behind her.

"Good morning, Sheriff," she called as he approached. "What's the problem? I know I wasn't speeding this time."

"Nope. Just wanted to see how you were getting along. You had a pretty busy day yesterday." He seemed friendlier this morning—more in charge.

"How nice of you to ask. Except for a few sore muscles, I'm doing fine."

"Did Emily tell you about Scott Mandrel?"

"Yes, yes she did. I must say, I'm rather surprised."

"You and a few others. He denies having anything to do with it. Claims he was set up." Dan shook his head. "If I had a dime for every time I've heard that one. But I'm not worried. We got an FBI agent on the case—between us we should be able to get the evidence we need to put him away."

Helen nodded, attributing Dan's good mood to the fact they'd been able to find their killer so quickly. If indeed they had the right man. "Doesn't it seem odd that Scott would have blown up Chuck Frazier's boat? From what Shells told me, she and Scott planned to marry soon."

His lips curled in a churlish smile. "Chuck didn't want Shells to have anything to do with Mandrel. Now I see why. My guess is Chuck suspected Mandrel was into drugs and planned to get proof. Makes perfect sense. Mandrel buys up small businesses— sometimes at a loss—eases out the competition. Only he's not buying them out for the fish—that never jived. He's eliminating potential witnesses."

"I see." Helen had a hunch Dan's dislike of Mandrel stemmed from the fact that Shells loved him. He'd made up his mind about Scott and would work to find the proof. That in itself wasn't necessarily a bad thing. Unfortunately, predeter-mining a guilty party could result in overlooking important ev-idence that pointed to another suspect. It also opened the door to a witch hunt of sorts. "Sounds like you're certain Scott is guilty."

"You'd better believe it." The sheriff adjusted his hat and hitched up his belt.

Not able to resist, Helen asked, "Didn't Chuck say it *wasn't* drugs?"

"Chuck was wrong!"

"Hmm. Well, I'd best be going. I have a lot of ground to cover today." Helen opened her car door.

"Oh—what are you up to?"

Helen told him about her plans. "With any luck I'll be able to finish out my day with a hike to McKenzie Head. Might time it so I can catch the sunset."

"I'm not sure that's a good idea, Mrs. Bradley. You'd be coming back down the trail in the dark—not that the park is dangerous, but we have had some trouble on occasion. Best to go in daylight."

"Your point is well taken, Sheriff. I appreciate your concern."

Good-byes said, Dan returned to his car, reported in on his radio, then headed back in the direction he'd come. Helen found herself wondering if he'd run into her on routine patrol, or if he'd purposely sought her out. She suspected the latter. But there would be no point—unless he meant to keep an eye on her.

Had J.B. told Dan about her being his wife? Helen doubted that. For security reasons he'd want as few people as possible to make the connection. Unless Emily had told him. But why would she? And when it came down to it, why had Dan stopped her? There had been nothing urgent in his message. Maybe he just wanted to gloat over his success in apprehending his criminal.

An uneasy feeling floated through her, and for a moment she wished she hadn't told him where she was going. "Helen Bradley, you're being absolutely ridiculous. Next thing you know you'll be suspecting Adam."

Helen arranged her long frame into the narrow space behind the wheel and within a few minutes was back on the road. Her good mood had drifted behind clouds of apprehension. She plugged one of her favorite tapes into the player, cranked up the volume, and belted out Handel's "Hallelujah Chorus" with the Philadelphia Orchestra and the Mormon Tabernacle Choir.

Helen drove about half a mile past the bridge and turned around at a rest area. There she picked up half a dozen brochures, used the facilities, then headed west. The area nearest the bridge, Megler, had served as a ferry station until the Astoria-Megler bridge was completed in 1966. There had once been an Indian village called Chinookville, but it was abandoned before the turn of the century when most of the Native Americans died from diseases the early settlers brought in. Helen paused briefly at the Robert Gray historical marker, then went on to St. Mary's Catholic Church at McGowan. There she wandered around the still-used, weather-beaten building that settlers had built in 1904. Helen loved to visit old churches. Though she couldn't get inside, she lingered at the entry for a few minutes, soaking up the saintly feel of it.

Helen loved the feel of the day as well—no pressures—almost. No danger—she hoped. It was a day for enjoying life and hanging out with God, nature, and history. It would be a day of mourning too. Though Helen hadn't known Chuck Frazier well, she couldn't help being saddened by his death and sharing the grief of the friends and family he'd left behind. "Poor Shells," Helen murmured. "Somehow it doesn't seem fair that one person should suffer so much." Before leaving the church, Helen paused to say a prayer for Shells and the others affected by yesterday's tragedy. She prayed also for J.B., Adam, and Dan, and for the quick resolution of the case—with no more lives lost.

Over the next three hours she explored the Lewis and Clark campsite, had lunch at the awesome Fort Columbia, then meandered through the town of Chinook and the small community of Baker Bay.

It was two-thirty when she pulled into the parking lot at Shells' Place, and Helen was more than ready for a break. She settled into a seat near the window, where she could watch the boats come in. Gracie finished up with the only other customer and brought Helen a menu.

"I don't need that. I'll have an Irish Cream latte, single, tall, and iced."

"Sure." Gracie hesitated. The grief etched on her face had aged her ten years. "You were out there, weren't you? You saw it happen?"

"Yes. Such a terrible thing. I'm so sorry. You loved him, didn't you?"

Gracie nodded. "It wasn't mutual—not really. We dated some, but . . ." Gracie dabbed at her eyes with a napkin. "I suppose I shouldn't have come in today. Shells told me I could stay home. But she had to make the funeral arrangements and everything. It's Thursday, if you want to come." She sighed heavily. "Oh, listen to me babbling on."

Shells came through the swinging door of the kitchen carrying two glass pedestal mugs. "Here's your latte, Mrs. Bradley." At their questioning looks she added, "I heard you order it." She placed the cups on the table and touched Gracie's forearm. "Why don't you take off early, Gracie? I can get one of the other servers to cover for you."

"No, I'm okay. You're the one who should be home."

"I suppose, but . . ." Shells shook her head. "I can't stand being there alone having nothing to do. At least here I can keep busy so I don't have to think about . . ." She faltered.

"Yeah, I feel the same way. Nothing to do at home but cry. Guess we're both better off here." Gracie offered Shells a half smile. "Thanks for getting the latte."

"No problem. I wanted to talk to Mrs. Bradley anyway."

The waitress nodded. "I'll leave you alone, then. Call if you need me."

"Do you mind if I sit down?" Shells slid into the chair opposite Helen and pulled the second cup of what looked like black coffee toward her.

"Not at all. What did you want to talk to me about?"

"I know it must seem strange, but when I met you at the hospital yesterday, I said to myself, now there is a person I can trust. Maybe it was a premonition or something, but I had this feeling we'd be friends. I didn't know then that I'd need your help, but . . ." She pinched her lips together.

"Go on. What can I help you with?"

"I suppose you heard about Scott." Her doe brown eyes held a mixture of grief and anger.

"Yes, Sheriff Merritt made a point of telling me this morning."

Shells grasped her steaming cup in both hands. "Did he also tell you I disagree? Not that it does much good. Adam and Dan both seem pretty anxious to blame Scott."

"Not without just cause. There is the matter of Steve Kendall's confession."

"He's wrong. I know Scott." Shells' eyes filled with tears, but she didn't wipe them away. "I know he didn't kill Chuck. I just wish there were something I could do."

Helen wasn't certain how to deal with Shells. In some ways she, too, was having a hard time seeing Scott as a killer. "Hopefully the truth will come out in the investigation. For now I can only suggest that you pray that happens."

"I haven't stopped praying since the explosion—well before, really. I've been worried about Chuck for the last few weeks—ever since the *Mariner II* went down." Shells fastened her gaze on the water and took a drink. "Frankly, I'm not sure how much good it's doing. I probably shouldn't say this, but I'm pretty upset with God right now."

"Hmm. I can certainly understand that." Helen turned to watch a sea gull walk along the deck, wondering whether or not she should comment. The last thing Shells needed was to hear religious platitudes about having faith or reassurances that everything would work out fine. "I was angry with God for a long time when my first husband died," she finally said. "For a while I blamed God for taking him from me."

"How did your husband die?"

"In a bombing."

Shells jerked her gaze back to Helen. "How? What happened?"

"Ian was working as a government agent. He'd been sent over to Beirut—I never did learn why. Not that it mattered. A terrorist group bombed the embassy. Ian was there. He may have been the target—Ian's superiors alluded to the possibility—but I never knew for certain."

"Wow! Were the terrorists ever caught?"

"I don't know. For a while I pushed for details, but after four years, I gave it up. Decided it didn't really matter anymore and I'd be better off leaving the revenge to God." They sat in silence for a time—Helen's thoughts drifting back over the years. Though she still experienced twinges of pain and rage, God and time had healed her. It had taken many years to work through her grief—it would for Shells as well.

"Thanks." Shells' gaze drifted back to Helen.

"For what?" Helen pulled herself back to the present.

"For not telling me something good will come of Chuck's death. Like if I have enough faith everything is supposed to work out. I thought that when I was a little kid, but nothing happened the way I prayed it would. I just wish I knew why God lets stuff like this happen."

"You sound terribly bitter."

"I guess I am sometimes. Wouldn't you be?"

Helen's resolve to shut up and listen flew off in the face of a need to dispel what she saw as myth. "I learned long ago that having faith doesn't always keep tragedies from happening, but it does make us strong enough to overcome them." She hesitated, then plunged in with perhaps a bit more vigor than necessary. "I don't believe for a moment that the bombing was God's will—not in Ian's case or in Chuck's. Murder is never sanctioned by God. God's desire is that people love one another. Unfortunately, too many people ignore God's will and make choices based on greed and anger—and revenge. Their choices destroy lives, and God is left to clean up the mess." Feeling she'd said too much, Helen concentrated on her latte.

Shells stared out at the water again, looking vulnerable and teary eyed. Her childlike features made Helen want to hold and comfort her.

"I'm sorry," Helen began. "I told myself I wasn't going to get preachy."

"You didn't." The corners of Shells' mouth curved into a wry smile. "What you said makes sense. God didn't kill Chuck. Someone with a sick, twisted mind did. I need to stop thinking about it and do something. I'm going to find my brother's killer. It's obvious to me that whoever did it is framing Scott. I don't know why Steve would lie like that."

"Steve? You know Steve Kendall?"

"Sort of. He and some of his buddies have been in here before. He seemed like an okay guy—kind of quiet. Don't know what he'd have against Scott, though. I don't think Scott even knew him."

"You didn't know Steve well, then."

"No. Just didn't figure him for a liar. Makes me mad. Dan and Adam aren't going to bother looking anywhere else, so it's up to me."

"Shells, I don't think—"

"Would you help me, Mrs. Bradley? Adam told me you used to be a homicide detective. And you agree with me, right? About Scott not being a killer."

Helen couldn't very well tell Shells about J.B. or FBI involvement in the case, but she had to do something to prevent Shells from getting involved and maybe getting hurt. "I'll look into it," Helen heard herself say. "But you must promise not to do any investigating on your own. We're obviously dealing with dangerous people here, Shells. They've already killed Chuck, and I have a hunch they may have killed Isabelle too. If they find out we're looking for information, we could be the next to go."

Shells nodded. "I'll be discreet. What can I do?"

"Eavesdrop. Listen to your customers. You'd be surprised what interesting tidbits you can pick up. Let me know if you hear anything that might be of interest. And think back to the days before Chuck was killed. See if you can remember who he talked to and what they talked about."

The bell ringer on the door dinged and two women walked in. When Gracie didn't come out, Shells excused herself to wait on them.

Helen heaved a deep sigh, gathered her belongings, and picked up her check.

While ringing up the tab, Shells asked, "What are you planning to do now?"

The bell jingled behind Helen, announcing the arrival of two new customers. Hank and Bill Carlson.

Helen dug into her bag for her wallet and extracted a five. "If there's time I'd like to hike up to McKenzie Head, then meet Emily at Bubba's for pizza."

"Oh, you'll love Bubba's. Maybe I can get someone to take

over for me here and I'll join you." She closed the register and handed Helen her change. "I hope people won't think it's weird for me to be going out. It's just . . ."

"You don't have to explain. People grieve in many different ways." Helen glanced at her watch. "I think I'll go down to the dock—take some pictures before my hike. Hopefully I can get a shot of some lucky fishermen—or women."

Helen stuck the change in her wallet. "That reminds me, what's the politically correct term for a woman who fishes? Fisherperson sounds ridiculous, and I can't very well call them all fishermen. Someone might feel slighted."

"How about fishwives?" Bill Carlson chuckled at his own joke, then sauntered up and leaned against the counter, introducing himself and Hank.

Helen grinned despite her resolve not to. "Somehow I think 'fishwives' might alienate my readers even more."

He winked at her. "All that fussing for the right word. Isabelle—um—a friend of mine used to do the same thing." A hint of sadness flickered in his gray-blue eyes.

"Did you know Isabelle?" she asked.

"Everybody knew Isabelle," Hank said. "And Emily."

Bill's gaze moved from Helen to Shells. "So you two are eating at Bubba's tonight, huh? Mind if Hank and me tag along?"

"Nothing like inviting yourself." Hank Carlson shook his head. "Maybe the ladies have other plans."

"As a matter of fact, we do have some business to discuss," Shells said.

"Oh? Like what?" Hank asked. His bulk made Shells look more like a little girl than a mature woman.

"It's none of your business." Shells gave him a good-natured tap on the shoulder. "If you must know, Helen is going to help me prove Scott's innocence."

Helen chewed on her lower lip. So much for discretion.

Hank's wide forehead creased in a frown. He stroked his thick fuzzy beard. "Why would you need to do that? Somethin' happening we should know about?"

Shells pulled two menus off the counter. "Steve Kendall told

Dan and Adam that Scott hired him to blow up the boat."

"That's crazy," Bill said. "Scott was on the boat, wasn't he?"

Shells explained the theory and added, "Anyway, I've got to find evidence to the contrary. Helen's an ex-cop and has agreed to help me."

"Oh yeah?" The corner of Bill's eyes crinkled in a smile. "Don't that beat all. And here I thought you was just another writer like Isabelle."

"I'm a writer too, of course. That's primarily why I'm here. I've been asked to finish the guidebook she started."

Hank's thick arm went around Shells' shoulder. "We'll help you too, honey. If you say Scott's innocent, I believe you." He turned to Helen. "You just let us know what we can do to help."

"There might be something," Helen said as she followed them to a table. "Do you mind if I ask you a few questions?"

Bill shrugged. "Ask ahead." He sat next to the window and pulled out the chair beside him for Helen. Hank nearly took up both spaces on the other side.

"Bring me the usual, Shells." Hank handed her back the menu without looking at it. "Can't wait to start in on that chowder of yours."

Bill glanced at the menu. "Bring me a burger and fries."

"Did you want anything to eat, Mrs. Bradley? Another latte?" Shells asked.

"Thanks. Water will be fine." She turned to Bill when Shells left. "You two seem to know Shells quite well."

"She's like a kid sister," Bill said, sadness apparent in his eyes. "We went to school with Chuck—best friends since I can remember. After her mom left, we all kinda felt responsible for her."

"Is what she said true?" Hank reached for his cloth napkin. "You going to help her prove her boyfriend didn't do it?"

"Shells is prematurely optimistic, I'm afraid. I'm not sure I can do that. The case is already being investigated by the authorities, but I'll do what I can."

"Well, I wish you luck," Hank said. "Poor kid. She's had a rough life with her old man dyin' and her mom taking off like she did. Now with Chuck gone, she needs somebody to look after her. Doesn't look like Mandrel's going to be much help."

"I just hope Scott ain't involved." Bill folded his sinewy brown arms and leaned on the table. "Shells don't need any more heartache."

Shells came back with coffee and a large bowl of soup for Hank. "Here you go. Yours will be right up, Bill."

When she'd gone again, Bill leaned back and twisted slightly in his chair. "You said you wanted to ask us something?"

"Yes. I'm wondering what you can tell me about one of the men who was on Mike Trenton's boat yesterday morning . . . Earl Wilson. He had dinner with you here the night before. His brother-in-law is the man who admitted to detonating the bomb."

"Yeah, we know Earl." Hank shoveled a spoonful of clam chowder into his mouth. A small amount dribbled onto his beard, and he paused to wipe at it with the back of his hand. "Earl went out with us to check our catch. He's EPA. Why do you ask?"

"Just curious," Helen said.

Bill's eyes narrowed into thin slits. "You don't think Earl had anything to do with Chuck's death? Cause if he did—"

"I just find the connection rather interesting—that's all."

Bill settled back in his chair. "I like the way you think, Mrs. Bradley. It does seem kind of strange that Earl and his buddies charter out and one of them just happens to be a bomber. I guess just 'cause he's with the EPA don't necessarily mean he's innocent, huh?"

"That's true enough," Helen agreed.

"Maybe we could check him out."

"That might be better left to the sheriff. You can best help by keeping your eyes open and reporting any suspicious activity to the authorities." Helen stood. "In the meantime, I'd better be going. I'd like to talk to the two of you later, if you don't mind."

"No problem." Bill stood and ducked slightly in what could have passed for a bow. "Might see you at Bubba's later."

Thirteen

Helen was on her way out for the second time when Shells whizzed past her and landed in the arms of the man coming through the door.

"Scott!" Her voice was muffled as she buried her face in his shoulder. "Thank God. Dan said he was going to arrest you. What happened?"

Scott held her against him, kissing her before he spoke. "My lawyer said they didn't have enough to hold me." He glanced toward Helen, then back to Shells. "I didn't do it, babe. I didn't kill Chuck."

"I know." Shells took hold of his hand and pulled him forward. "You remember Mrs. Bradley."

"Of course. You were with Lieutenant Jorgenson." He gave Shells a what's-going-on look.

"Helen said she'd help us prove you didn't have anything to do with Chuck's death."

"I thought you were working with Adam," Scott said. "He sure isn't interested in saving my skin."

Helen shook her head. "I'm not officially working with anyone. Shells, you make me sound like a miracle worker. I only said I'd look into it."

Shells' lower lip quivered. "I know. But with your help I'm sure we'll be able to find out who really hired Steve—or at least prove Scott is innocent."

Helen wished she shared Shells' confidence. Though she

may not have been as quick to accuse Scott as Adam and Dan had been, Helen wasn't by any means ready to eliminate him as a suspect. Once again she bid Shells and the others adieu and set off for the docks.

Helen's timing proved perfect as she arrived on the boat dock just in time to watch Mike Trenton pull into his slip. She took several photographs, then helped him tie up.

"How was the fishing today?" she asked when Mike jumped onto the dock and set up portable steps for his passengers.

"Not bad. Everybody caught something—mostly salmon."

One of the women joined Helen on the dock. "It was wonderful. I got a sturgeon just under six feet."

Mike lifted the lid on the fish box and hauled out a giant fish that looked like a throwback to prehistoric times.

"Would you mind posing with it?" Helen asked. "I'd like to get some photos."

"I'd love it. Will you send me a copy?"

"Be happy to." Helen spent the next half hour acting as the trip photographer, getting release forms signed and writing down names and addresses of Mike's eight delightful fishermen—and women, as the case may be.

When the group finally left, Mike Trenton joined her on the dock. Helen found herself thinking he'd be an attractive man if he smiled more. His troubled countenance remained in place while he thanked her for giving his customers the added bonus of pictures.

"Can I buy you a cup of coffee?" He rubbed the back of his head, then adjusted his Trenton Charters baseball cap.

The man obviously had something on his mind, and though Helen had other things on her agenda, she agreed. They walked up to the small deli near the dock entrance, ordered, and took their drinks outside. The clouds had lifted, and Mike led the way to a table on the sun porch.

"Turning out to be a nice day," Helen said.

"Not bad." He put the Styrofoam cup to his mouth, sipped, and grimaced. "You ready to try your hand at fishing again? I got an opening on Friday."

"That's kind of you," Helen murmured. "I appreciate the offer, but—"

"Seeing as how you didn't get to do any fishing yesterday and . . . well, I figure I owe you."

Did she really want to go out again? Helen sucked in a deep breath and took a sip of coffee, then shuddered. No wonder Mike had made a face. The stuff was strong enough to stand a spoon in. "Maybe I will go," she said.

"Good. That EPA guy wants to go out again too. Guess he's bringing his buddies—except for the one that admitted to detonating the bomb on Chuck's boat."

"Doesn't it worry you to take them out?"

"What for? Earl told me he felt real bad about the whole thing. Didn't know his brother-in-law was having such a hard time. Said he knew the guy was upset, but . . ." Mike reached up and pulled the bill of his cap down. "Guy must have been pretty desperate to let Mandrel talk him into killing somebody."

"Sounds like you think Scott was behind it."

He nodded. "Who else would it be? From what Dan said, the guy's got motive, means, and opportunity. 'Course it was pretty stupid to be on board when it blew. Sure not something I'd do."

"How well do you know Scott?"

"Not well enough by the looks of things. Glad we found out now, though. It'll be tough for Shells, but not so much now as if she'd married him. Just wish we'd known sooner." He paused to clear his throat and look down toward the docks. "Chuck might still be alive."

"I take it you and Chuck were good friends."

"The best. We went to school together—Chuck, me, Dan, Hank, and Bill. Did everything together."

Grief seemed to take its toll on the big fisherman. He hunched over the table and didn't appear to notice when she stood.

"I'd best be going." Helen sensed his desire to be alone. "I want to climb McKenzie Head before dark."

"Better hurry." He looked to the west where the colors of sunset were already painting the late afternoon sky. "You only got about an hour and a half of daylight left."

⁂ ⁂ ⁂

It was nearly five when she parked her car in the small lot near the trail head. She'd almost talked herself out of going, but the promise of a spectacular sunset lured her on. Besides, she wouldn't be meeting Emily at Bubba's until seven, and the caffeine from the coffee she'd downed was not about to let her sit around doing nothing. Helen ignored the niggling voice in her head urging her not to go. It was the voice of fear, she decided. She glanced around, assuring herself she had nothing to be afraid of. *You're the only person around*, Helen reminded herself. *You've hiked dozens of trails alone.*

It would take her only fifteen minutes to hike up the half-mile trail and probably ten to jog back down. That left her more than half an hour to explore. She tossed a fresh water bottle into her pack along with two new rolls of film. The flashlight, first aid kit, and camera were already in.

Upset with herself for vacillating, Helen slipped the straps of her backpack onto her shoulders, locked the door, pocketed the keys, and set off.

Moments later she was glad she'd made the decision to come. The path was easy and clear—and beautiful as it wound through the trees and occasionally afforded a view of the ocean. She hurried along the path, dwelling not on murders and murderers, but on how she'd describe the hike in the guidebook.

When Helen reached the concrete bunkers Adam had described, she bypassed the long dark tunnel which led to living quarters that had been home to dozens of soldiers over the years. She planned to walk through the bunker on her way back. Helen scrambled up the short, narrow trail and emerged at the summit. The clearing offered a panoramic view of the coastline north and south. Below her stretched Benson Beach. She took several photos, then concentrated on the circular concrete hole where artillery guns had once protected the shoreline. The gun placement, similar in size to those near the Interpretive Center, was about six feet deep and eight feet across. To her right was another concrete building—a square lookout with narrow openings across the top. Helen climbed inside, fancying herself a soldier keeping watch in a fort completely hidden from enemy eyes. Thrilled with her find, Helen took the steep, eroded, slippery path to the top of the lookout. The view was even more spectacular from there. Helen sat cross-legged near the edge, looking down at the steep incline to the beach far below.

If someone wanted to get rid of her, this would be the place to do it. One push and gravity would do the rest. She shuddered. "Helen Bradley, what an imagination you have."

She glanced around, reassuring herself she was still very much alone. After taking more photos and watching the sun turn the sky into a vivid canvas of color, Helen rose, stretched her arms to the sky, and started back. She still had time to walk through the tunnel and make it back to her car before it turned completely dark.

Pausing at the entrance to the first bunker, Helen pulled out her flashlight, then stepped inside. The temperature dropped immediately. It smelled musty and dank. She trained the flashlight beam on the floor and over the walls. Just a short distance in was a small room, then another. As she walked through the maze of tunnels stopping to examine each room, Helen tried to imagine what it might have been like new. Soldiers talking to one another, lonely, showing each other pictures of girlfriends, wives, children, and parents.

She stopped at a hallway leading to a room that must have served as a lockup of sorts. A metal door stood at an angle slightly ajar. That one she'd skip. She moved faster now—stepping carefully over puddles of coffee-colored water toward the opening at the other end of the tunnel.

This was not a safe place—even in daylight—and she chided herself for coming alone. Unfortunately, even at her age, curiosity sometimes won out over common sense.

Helen heard a scraping noise behind her. She whirled and aimed the flashlight's beam toward the direction of the sound. A small gray mouse skittered across the floor. She covered her mouth—but a yelp escaped just the same. Her cry bounced off the walls and echoed back at her. She took deep breaths to settle her racing pulse.

Fear pounded in her ears and raced through her veins. The sound she'd heard had not come from a mouse. Something or someone was in the tunnel with her.

"Who's there?" She took a step forward, jerking the flashlight back and forth.

Something hit her from behind. Helen pitched forward. The light at the end of the tunnel disappeared.

Fourteen

W here . . ." Helen moaned. Her head hurt, and not just from the baseball-sized lump on the back of her skull. She felt fuzzy and disoriented—as if she were waking up from surgery. She opened her eyes hoping the hard, damp floor, the drip-drip-dripping on her forehead, and the total darkness were only the lingering effects of a dream gone bad.

Opening her eyes made matters even worse and seemed to heighten her awareness of the cold floor and the smell—musty mold, decaying leaves. Helen rose to her knees and tried to orient herself. Lights exploded behind her eyes as a wave of pain tore through her head. She wove her hands through her hair, wincing as she touched the lump.

"Oh, dear God, what's happened?" Her whimper echoed in the darkness. "Where am I?"

When the pain and accompanying nausea subsided, she crawled forward, feeling for a wall—something stable she could lean against when she tried to stand. The last thing she remembered was watching the sky turn rose from the top of a hill—she couldn't recall the name. She'd started back and—flashlight . . . she'd had a flashlight and her backpack . . . and matches and drinking water. They were all gone.

Her memory came back in snatches. She'd been exploring a bunker—part of the old army barracks. Had she fallen? She remembered pitching forward, but the hit had come from behind. Had something—a piece of concrete—dropped from the ceiling? "Too much force for that," she murmured. Someone had hit her. But why? Had she come upon a vagrant?

Or had Chuck and Isabelle's killer struck again?

Her hand connected with an object and sent it skittering across the concrete floor. Her heart careened into overdrive. "It's okay," she gasped. "Probably a discarded aluminum can." She needed to calm down—be rational. She'd been in worse situations—like the prison in Mexico where she'd gone undercover for the DEA. There she'd shared her quarters with rats. Here at least there was a way out. An open doorway at both ends. She just had to find one of them . . . and hope her attacker wasn't still there.

Helen moved ahead, crawling on all fours again. Her hand grazed a ledge and plunged elbow deep into a water-filled hole. "Ugh." She touched something slimy and jerked her hand back. She dried it on the front of her jacket. Panic surged through her like an electric shock. She sat back on her legs. "It's just water," she reminded herself.

She stopped and took several deep breaths. Complete darkness had always frightened her. She wasn't sure why. Perhaps something had happened to her as a child. As she often did when fear assailed her, Helen began to recite the Twenty-third Psalm. "The Lord is my shepherd. . . ." When she finished she repeated her favorite line for emphasis. "Though I walk through the valley of the shadow of death, I will fear no evil: for thou art with me." Believing that had brought her through more trials than she cared to remember. God had been with her through them all—no reason He'd quit now.

Inch by inch, Helen continued to move ahead and nearly cheered when she butted her head against a wall. She cautiously eased herself into an upright position. Dizziness and pain made it next to impossible to concentrate on her task. After a few minutes she regained her equilibrium. Using the wall for support, she crept alongside it. When she reached a corner, she whispered a short thank-you and turned to exit the cubicle she'd been dumped in. Helen stepped forward and moaned in despair. Her hands closed around the rusting iron bars, and she knew exactly where she was. Whoever had attacked her had dragged her into the brig. She was trapped.

When the terror subsided again, Helen struggled against the tide of emotions to bring herself back to rational thought. She'd only gotten a brief look at the iron bars, but it seemed unlikely that they'd still have a working lock after all this time. The barred door had been standing open when she looked at it earlier. Perhaps it still was and all she had to do was maneuver around it. She reached for the bars again. They swung away, screeching on rusty hinges.

Free of her imagined prison, Helen felt her way along another wall until she reached what she hoped was the main walkway through the tunnel. A gust of wind whistled through, rustling up dry leaves and chilling her to the bone. Helen found the wall again and followed it. When it didn't give way to another room, she knew she was on the west wall—the solid one that would lead her to freedom.

Helen emerged from the tunnel and sank to her knees thankful and exhausted. She hoped the moon would provide enough light to guide her back down the trail.

Voices splintered the cold, clear night. Someone was calling her name.

"Helen!" It was Emily.

Another voice joined in—maybe Dan or Adam. "Helen! Are you up here?"

"I'm here!" She waved as if they could see her. "Up by the bunkers."

Several beams of light flickered through the trees. Voices stilled and footsteps thundered.

Suddenly they were standing around her, lanterns and flashlights creating a bright circle of light. Emily, Hank, Bill, Adam, and Dan.

"My goodness gracious, child," Emily said. "What happened to you?"

"I was exploring the tunnel and someone knocked me out. My pack and flashlight are missing—might still be in there. And my camera." She patted her pocket and groaned. "He got my keys."

"Your keys are in your car." Dan looked as though he wanted to lecture her on that point but apparently thought better of it. "Could be the other stuff's there, too, but we'll have a look here first." He directed his flashlight around the group and added, "Hank, why don't you and Bill help Mrs. Bradley down to the road. I'll radio ahead for an ambulance. Adam and I'll have a look around and catch up."

Helen would have liked to search the bunkers, too, but her head hurt and she could barely stand. She'd have to question Adam and Dan later. Hank and Bill made a makeshift chair by clasping their hands together and carried Helen between them. Emily walked just ahead lighting the way.

As promised, an ambulance was parked at the trail head. Two EMTs stood beside a stretcher, which they pushed toward the rescue party when they emerged from the woods.

"I don't really need an ambulance," Helen protested. At her insistence Hank and Bill put her down.

"Thanks for all your help," she began.

"Are you sure you can drive?"

"I'm fine." *As soon as I sit down*, she added to herself. She took one step and the nausea returned. Another step and the lights started spinning. On her next step, someone caught her as she went down.

❖   ❖   ❖

When Helen next awoke, her headache was nearly gone. The mattress was almost as hard as the concrete she'd been lying on earlier. It was still dark outside. Helen lifted her arm to look at her watch. The small numbers blurred.

"It's twelve-thirty." Her daughter's face moved into Helen's line of vision.

Helen smiled—or tried to. "Hi."

"Hi yourself." Kate's questioning gaze fastened on Helen's face.

"Did they take me all the way back to Portland?"

"Not yet. Adam called Jason and he called me. I thought one of us better come get you."

"Get me?" Helen scooted back against the pillows and reached for her water. Kate fetched the glass for her and held the straw to Helen's lips.

"I'm taking you home for a couple weeks so we can keep an eye on you." Kate turned on the light behind the bed.

Helen squeezed her eyes shut. "Nonsense. There's no need for you to do that." Her headache was coming back.

"Mother, you've been mugged. The doctor says you have a concussion and that you'll need to rest."

"Mugged?" Helen gripped the guardrail on the bed and rose up on her elbows. "Is that what Adam told you?"

"He and the sheriff are pretty certain that's what happened. From the looks of things, some vagrant hit you on the head and took off with your pack. He left the keys in your car and your pack in the trunk after dumping it out. There were papers scattered everywhere. Your wallet's missing. The sheriff was going to check for prints but didn't leave much hope for catching him. Might be a camper, so they're checking that out."

"Wonder why they didn't steal my car. It's worth almost as much as my house—certainly more than what was in my backpack or wallet."

"He probably realized a classic car would be too easy to track."

"I suppose." That made sense. But a vagrant? She wasn't so sure.

"You shouldn't have been out hiking alone. It's not safe anywhere these days." Kate twisted her hands around the bed railing. "I think I've mentioned that before."

"Where is the call light? I'd like the bed raised." Helen ran a hand through her hair—it felt matted. "I need a shower. Look at my hands." She held her hands up and inspected them. "I look like I've been crawling in the dirt." She smiled. "Maybe because I have."

"Mother, please don't make jokes. This isn't funny."

"Relax, darling. I'm fine."

"You're not fine." Tears gathered in Kate's cobalt blue eyes. "You're going to fight me on this, aren't you?"

"On what?"

"Taking you back to Portland with me. Jason said you probably wouldn't come."

"Jason's right. There's no need for that." Helen clasped Kate's slender fingers. She was so like Helen in appearance but so different in personality. "I don't mean to sound ungrateful, darling. I know you're doing what you think is best, but I have work to do here."

Kate sighed. "Okay. I'm not going to argue."

"You're not?"

"If Mohammed won't go to the mountain, I'll bring the mountain to Mohammed."

At Helen's puzzled gaze, Kate added, "I talked to Emily Merritt. She said I could stay in one of the rooms until I'm satisfied you're all right."

Kate could be as bullheaded as her mother, but of course that was a trait that seemed to run through her entire family. Helen mulled over Kate's decision. Kate probably wouldn't take no for an answer, and it would be nice to spend a few days with her. Helen just hoped she'd be able to write. She squeezed Kate's hand. "I think that's a wonderful solution."

A nurse came in, checked Helen's vital signs and pupils, and raised the head of the bed. "How's the head, Mrs. Bradley?"

"Better."

"Good. Would you like an ice pack? It'll help the pain and keep the swelling down."

Helen nodded, then turned to Kate. "You look tired."

Kate yawned. "I am—but I'm not going anywhere, so don't try to talk me into it."

Helen closed her eyes. She felt incredibly sleepy. "I suppose I should get word to J.B."

"Jason and Adam are trying to do that. Any idea where he might be?"

"On the boat . . . he . . ." Helen frowned, trying to cut through the fog that still lingered in her brain. When her mind cleared, fear sliced into her heart. J.B. should have been there by now.

Fifteen

Helen spent the next few hours telling herself that J.B. had gotten caught in the usual governmental red tape. Refusing to dwell on the fact that no one had been able to reach him, or that he hadn't checked in with his superiors, she filled her thoughts with reasonable explanations.

He was on his way downriver and had probably pulled into one of the ports along the way to get some sleep. Perhaps he'd had a change of plans. He may have found new evidence and detoured briefly. He'd be there. She just needed to be patient. *No news is good news*, she told herself again and again.

Still, the moment Kate left to get herself some breakfast, Helen called her friend and J.B.'s immediate superior at the FBI office in Portland. Tom Chambers hadn't heard from J.B. either.

"I don't know whether to be mad or worried," Tom said gruffly. "I wish we hadn't agreed to bring him back on. He called just before he left, said everything was fine." Helen could imagine Tom leaning back in his chair, legs propped on the desk, an unlit cigar in his mouth.

"Helen," Tom went on, "did J.B. have any health problems that you know of?"

"No—he's as fit as always. Might have gained a few pounds since he's been off work, but . . ." Panic clawed at Helen's insides. "Why are you asking?"

"I got a call today from the doctor who does company physicals. Seems he found some irregularities in J.B.'s cardio tests."

Cardio? "Something's wrong with his heart?"

"The doctor said it might not be anything, but he wanted to run some more extensive tests."

Helen let out an uneven breath. "I wasn't even aware he'd gone in."

"Had to before we could take him back. J.B. went in on Monday. The doc put him through the paces and, since he's known J.B. for years, signed him off. It wasn't until this morning he noticed there might be a problem."

"Exactly what is the problem?"

"I'm not sure. Doc wouldn't say."

"We need to find J.B. You know him, Tom. He would have found a way to contact us if he could."

"You're right about that. It's too soon to panic. J.B.'s a good agent, Helen. He can take care of himself."

"Yes, I suppose you're right. But you will keep trying."

"You can bet on it."

Adam arrived just as Helen hung up. "Still no word about J.B.?" she asked, hoping his verbal answer would be different from the one written on his face. And hoping the Coast Guard would have had better luck than the FBI.

"I'm sorry. All we know for certain is that he got home okay yesterday," Adam assured her. "Jason said J.B. met with him around noon at the Newport Bay Restaurant. He told him he was working on a case and would be out of town for a few days."

"What about the boat—did he take it out?"

Adam nodded. "It's gone. Close as we can figure he had lunch with Jason, and left the marina around two."

Helen rubbed her forehead again, as if she could ease away the headache. "Could he have stopped along the way? Had engine trouble?"

"Jason's got people checking all the ports now—both sides of the river. If he's in any of them, we'll find him."

"What about helicopters? Suppose something happened and he drifted into some remote area. There are some rugged places. . . ."

"Got that covered too." Adam squeezed her hand. "He'll show up."

Helen wished she could be more positive. She hated gut feelings like this. As desperately as she wanted to believe J.B. was safe, part of her knew something had gone dreadfully wrong.

A short time later the doctor came in and saw no reason not to discharge her. Leaving her in Kate's care seemed the reasonable thing to do. Kate drove them back to the bed and breakfast, where she and Emily joined forces to make certain Helen had every possible need met.

Helen spent the rest of the day in a drug-induced daze, vaguely aware that Emily had gone to Chuck's funeral. The doctor had given her pain medication for her headaches, which had been incessant all day.

Eventually, she stopped asking about J.B., figuring Emily and Kate would tell her the minute they learned anything. At one point she tried writing, then reading, but soon gave up when she couldn't make her eyes focus on anything. About the only thing she managed to do was sleep and eat, which Kate kept saying was the best thing for her.

Helen disagreed. The best thing would be to find J.B. Awake now, she turned to look out at the bay. Soft pink cotton candy clouds gave evidence of another lovely sunset. Tears gathered in her eyes and ran down her temple and into her hair. "J.B.," she whispered. "Where are you? Please, God, let him be safe."

She'd run out of prayers, run out of energy. Now she wished her mind would run out of things to stew about. When she wasn't thinking about J.B. she was thinking about the mugging—if that's what it was. Helen didn't believe much in coincidences and strongly suspected the attack on her, the break-in at the bed and breakfast, and Isabelle's and Chuck's deaths were all linked. The one common thread was information. Now J.B., who'd gone undercover, was missing. Could there be a connection there as well?

But who'd known about J.B.'s part in all this? Adam, Dan, Emily. J.B. had already made some contacts in Long Beach. He'd been to at least one of the taverns. Could one of those people have suspected he was an agent and followed him?

Helen closed her eyes. Too many questions.

The door opened a crack. Kate stepped in. "Mother?" she whispered. "Are you awake?"

Helen brushed away her tears and sat up, glad for the distraction. "Come in, darling."

"Emily and I were about to have tea—would you like to join us? We can bring it up here if you'd rather."

"No, I'll come down." Helen pushed the covers aside and sat up. Swinging her legs off the bed, she waited for the woozy feeling to pass, then stood.

"Are you sure you want to go downstairs?" Kate held Helen's white terry bathrobe.

"I need to move around." She took a deep breath and slipped into the robe. "Have you heard anything about J.B.?"

"Jason called about an hour ago. Still no news, I'm afraid."

Helen nodded, not trusting herself to speak. Kate waited while her mother brushed her hair and used the facilities. Walking down the stairs was an arthritic experience. Every joint in her body ached, partly from all the hiking she'd done the last few days, but mostly from last night's injuries. Yet sitting in front of the fire with Emily and Kate was worth the effort.

"Tell me about the children," Helen said once she'd settled into the gliding rocker. "I want to hear every detail."

"Lisa has been shopping nearly every day, and Jennie can hardly sit still. They're excited about school starting."

"Jennie and Lisa are my sixteen-year-old granddaughters," Helen said for Emily's benefit. "Lisa is Kate's oldest and Jennie belongs to my son, Jason."

"They both wanted to come with me today."

"I'm surprised they didn't."

"Kevin's out of town. I told them I needed them to baby-sit. Besides, school starts next week. And I thought I'd be bringing you back."

"I miss them—almost wish I could go back with you."

"You can. Maybe you should. Seems to me it would be better with J.B. . . . well . . . missing."

"I need to get this book written. Stay busy. I still have a lot of research to do." Helen sipped at her tea and rocked. "How are the boys?" Again for Emily's benefit she identified Kate's ten-year-old son, Kurt, and Jason's five-year-old son, Nick.

"Nick misses J.B.," Kate said. "They must have really bonded while he and Jennie stayed at the coast with you. He's all excited about school too." Kate smiled. "Thinks he's hot stuff now that he's in kindergarten."

Helen chuckled. "A little knowledge . . ."

Kate launched into how well the boys were doing with their reading. Well above average. When she moved into the problem of choosing the right school, Helen's thoughts drifted back to J.B. The man of her dreams. She chided herself now for thinking he'd been in her way. She'd much rather have him underfoot than not have him at all. Try as she might not to give into the fearful, negative thoughts, she couldn't change the hard, cold facts. J.B. would never neglect to call her or his superiors unless he'd been injured, captured, or . . . no, she wouldn't let herself think the worst. Maybe he'd had a change of plans. Still, wouldn't he have called?

Her mind drifted back to the trail her thoughts had taken earlier. Perhaps J.B.'s disappearance was somehow connected to the other incidents. She waited until Kate had finished praising the private school the children attended, then asked, "Emily, did you say anything to anyone about J.B. working undercover?"

"You asked me not to." She looked hurt—annoyed.

"I know. I was just trying to make some sense of J.B.'s disappearance. The only logical thing I can come up with other than an illness or injury is that someone discovered who he really was—" Helen felt like she'd been hit in the stomach with a baseball bat. Everyone was looking for an FBI agent named Jason Bradley. But he'd gone undercover. He was using another name. One she couldn't even remember. And he probably had a fake ID as well. If something had happened to him or if he'd been in an accident . . .

"Mother? What's wrong?"

"J.B. was working undercover. Emily, did J.B. mention the

name he was using? I can't remember if he even said."

"I don't recall. Why is that important?"

"Because that's who he is right now. It's one of the dangers of working undercover. With a false ID, if something happens and you can't communicate who you really are, it could take days or weeks to straighten things out."

Kate leaned forward. "So if J.B. was in an accident or had health problems, we wouldn't even be called."

"Not unless he had a name or number on his person." Helen set her cup aside, moved the ottoman, and stood. "I need to call Tom." If anyone would know, he would.

"I have no idea which name he used," Tom said when she reached him. "He told me he'd let me know when he checked in."

"He was dressed as a biker," Helen said. "But he might have been planning something else as he was bringing the boat down."

"He's got a handful of IDs besides the ones we set up for him—some we got registered, some we don't. I'll see if he told anybody here and print out a list of the ones we have on file. I'll get on it right away and call as soon as I have anything."

Helen hung up, willing herself not to worry. This was one time when ignorance would have been bliss. She wished she hadn't called Tom, or learned about J.B.'s possible heart problem, or realized how difficult he might be to trace.

Tom was right. J.B. did have a drawer full of fake IDs and phony registrations he'd picked up in Belize and Colombia. How he'd gotten them and from whom was not something he shared with anyone—not even her. As necessary and good as law enforcement agencies were, Helen was also keenly aware of their shortcomings. They tended to be careless at times. Their record keeping—mostly because they hated paper work—left something to be desired. She didn't trust them to find J.B. Which meant she'd have to.

She called Adam and hit another dead end. J.B. hadn't told him or Dan his alias.

"He must have told someone his name," she said aloud

much later as she paced back and forth across the braided rug in her room. He'd been nosing around the local pubs and the docks. Maybe someone there remembered him. Tomorrow she'd start looking for that person. She needed a name to go with that handsome Irish face. And if she didn't find one, she'd personally search every hospital in the area and every . . . When the word *morgue* crept into her thoughts, Helen trashed it. *Don't even consider such a thing,* she told herself.

Before climbing into bed, she glanced at her computer and the notes for the guidebook. "Sorry, Isabelle," she murmured. "J.B. comes first."

Sleep came easier knowing she'd be doing her part to find J.B. She closed her eyes and envisioned him alive and well and prayed herself asleep.

⁓   ⁓   ⁓

The next morning she awoke well before dawn. Creeping around like an errant child running away from home, Helen dressed in jeans and a turtleneck, then added a bulky, oversized cable knit sweater. She'd borrowed it from J.B. a few months earlier to keep him close to her heart when he'd gone off on another of his secret missions. He'd had to marry her to get it back. Wearing the sweater always gave her a strong sense of his presence and reminded her of his strength and capabilities. He'd rescued her on several occasions. And now, if need be, she would rescue him.

Of course the possibility still existed that J.B. was fine, but experience and common sense cut the logic of her fantasy to shreds.

Kate and Emily, Helen wrote in a note she planned to leave on the kitchen table. *I've gone fishing. Don't worry—I'm fine—no headache. I'll call you later.*

Helen grabbed up a few snacks and, after making tea, filled a thermos and headed out. The temperature had dropped during the night. She tugged on rag wool mittens and her jacket and unlocked the car. Her warm breath fogged up the windows. She set the defroster on high, then slowly made her way out the long driveway. By the time she hit Sandridge the front window was mostly clear.

Helen had given her plan a lot of thought. She'd get to the docks early enough to catch Mike Trenton. He'd invited her to go on the charter with him, and that gave her an opportunity to talk to Earl and his friends again. A reunion of sorts. Discovering J.B.'s name was not her only mission. But it was the most important one. Once she learned that, she would let the authorities know immediately so they could begin a search. If he were lying in a hospital somewhere, they'd find him.

The possibility occurred to her that J.B. had been betrayed. Dan or even Adam could be involved in the drug-smuggling operation—if that was indeed the problem. For that reason she hadn't said anything to them about investigating on her own.

Though her heart wasn't in it, she would move ahead with the guidebook—at least that's what she would lead everyone to believe. To those who knew about her relationship to J.B., she'd be working to alleviate her worries and fears. To others she'd just be a writer with a retired husband staying in Portland.

"I see you decided to join us." Mike reached for her backpack with one hand and helped her board with the other. "Wasn't sure, what with your getting mugged the other night."

"I wasn't either. Amazing what a day of rest can do."

"Hmm. You need any Dramamine? I noticed you got sick last time."

"Took some this morning." Helen looked up toward the parking lot, where several vehicles were pulling in. "Are Earl and his friends still coming?"

"Better be. They didn't cancel. Still a little early. I'll give them another half hour."

Catching sight of Bill and Hank Carlson down near their boat, Helen grabbed her camera. "In that case, I'll see if I can get a few photos." She scrambled out onto the dock and aimed the lens at Mike. "Look busy."

He laughed and stooped to pick up her cooler. "What do you mean, 'look'?"

She caught him in a rare smile, and when he disappeared

into the galley, Helen walked down to where the *Klipspringer* was docked.

"Ahoy!" she called. "I was hoping to catch you. To thank you again. Do you suppose I could get some photos of my two rescuers? I appreciate your bringing me back down the trail."

"Glad we could help. A little dark yet for picture takin', isn't it?" Bill asked.

"Not really." She focused her lens. Bill yelled for Hank to join them.

The big fisherman emerged from the hold wearing a plaid shirt over a black turtleneck, and to Helen's delight he had on his Greek hat. He carefully lowered the wooden cover over the hold.

Obviously not used to being photographed, the men grew restless after the first shot. "I hope this ain't gonna take long," Bill said. "We gotta head out."

"Just a couple more." When finished, Helen covered the camera lens. "Say, guys, maybe you can help me. A couple of days ago I saw a guy on a motorcycle. About this tall"—she held her hand six inches above her head—"clean-shaven. I wanted to get some photos of him but didn't have my camera. He was in town Tuesday night."

Bill frowned. "I might know the guy you mean. Said he was thinking about mooring his boat down here."

"Yes," Helen worked at keeping her tone level. "He told me that too. Unfortunately, I didn't catch his name."

"Can't help you there. Not much good at names. How 'bout you, Hank?"

Hank wagged his head back and forth. "Nope. Don't know what you'd want with the likes of him, though. He was hanging out with some druggies. Told Dan to keep an eye on him. Wouldn't surprise me if the guy was into dealing."

"Quit the jawing, Hank—we gotta go. Sorry, Mrs. Bradley—maybe we can talk some more when we get back."

Helen waved them off, then hurried back to the *Merry Maid*, where Earl and Mike seemed to be arguing about something.

"Look, I'm sorry to bail out on you," she heard Earl say.

"Don't expect a refund. It's too late now for me to get anyone." Mike glowered.

"That's fine." Earl shifted his gaze to Helen as she approached. "Hi, Mrs. Bradley."

"Hi. I couldn't help but overhear—you're not going out?"

"No. I have to head home—to Longview." Earl wore the mask of tragedy.

"Not bad news, I hope."

"I'm afraid it is. You remember Steve Kendall?"

"Your brother-in-law—the one who confessed to detonating the bomb?"

"Yeah. Cops found him in his cell. Died of a drug overdose."

Sixteen

Hate to take just one person out, Mrs. Bradley." Mike jumped onto the dock, setting it to swaying. "I'll run up to the office and see if anybody's waiting for a cancellation."

Helen grabbed onto a piling to steady herself. "You don't need to go out on my account, Mike. In fact, if it's all the same to you, I'd just as soon wait. I'd like to talk to Earl."

"Sure, no problem. I could use a day off. Got some business to take care of anyway."

Mike boarded the boat, handed Helen her bag and cooler, and went back to the helm. As she and Earl walked away, Mike started the engines and headed out. He seemed almost relieved to be rid of her, and she wondered where he was going.

Reluctantly, she turned her attention back to Earl. "I'm sorry about Steve," Helen said as they walked.

"Yeah—it's heavy stuff. I could understand why my sister divorced him, but we'd gotten close over the years. He was pretty messed up. I just didn't realize how bad. What gets me is how he could have overdosed in jail."

"Drugs are available everywhere for a price, even in prison— maybe I should say especially in prison."

"I suppose that's true," Earl said. "Still, I can't help but feel responsible. He'd been despondent for several weeks. I thought he was handling it. S'pose I shouldn't be surprised. After all, he did agree to detonate that bomb for Mandrel."

"You're sure it was suicide?"

"That's what the authorities told me." Earl shivered and put his hands in his pockets. The temperature had dipped into the forties and he was wearing a T-shirt under a thin cotton jacket. "Hard to believe. When I went to see him yesterday he seemed up. Said the DA was willing to cut him a deal—lighter sentence if he'd testify against Mandrel."

"You mustn't blame yourself—though it's a natural tendency." Heaven knew she'd been suffering enormous guilt over letting J.B. go. Not that there was much she could have done.

"Wish I'd known what he was up to . . . maybe. . . ." His gaze met hers. "Can I buy you a cup of coffee, Mrs. Bradley? You're an easy person to talk to, and my goose bumps are getting goose bumps."

"Of course." Helen had wanted to talk to Earl and this was as good a time as any. The Charter House Cafe was open—had been since three in the morning.

"Good morning, Mrs. Bradley, Earl. You can sit anywhere— just pick a spot." Gracie, the waitress from Shells' Place, picked up two menus and followed them to the table.

"I'm surprised to see you here," Helen said. "Thought you worked for Shells."

She half smiled. "I do. Fill in here most mornings. Shells doesn't open until eleven. By then the day shift is here."

"Long hours for you." Helen removed her mittens and slipped out of her jacket.

"Yeah, well, keeps me busy. I need it right now. Coffee?" Earl pushed his cup toward her and she filled it.

"I'd rather have herbal tea if you have it."

"Sure do. We usually carry a good supply of teas. I'll bring you a basket and you can choose." She glanced from Earl to Helen and frowned. "This may seem like a stupid question, but what are you two doing down here so early—not that it's any of my business . . . I mean . . . ."

"If you're wondering if we've got something going, the answer is no." Earl winked at Helen. "At least not yet."

Helen rolled her eyes. "In case you hadn't noticed I'm old enough to be his mother. Besides, I'm happily married." *At least*

I was. No, she wouldn't let herself think of J.B. or her marriage in the past tense. She bit her lower lip and swallowed hard to still the wave of grief crashing in her stomach. "We were going fishing, but Earl and his friends needed to cancel."

"Death in the family." Earl went on to explain about his brother-in-law.

Gracie shook her head. "Nothing but bad news these days. Which reminds me . . ." Gracie headed toward the kitchen. "I saw an article in *The Oregonian* this morning about an FBI agent named Bradley being missing. I wondered at the time if you might be related, but I guess not, huh?"

Helen's heart lurched. "May I see the article?" Tom must have been extremely worried. For the FBI to go public so soon was practically unheard of. Yet with the possibility of J.B. having a heart problem. . . . Her wall of stoicism was beginning to crumble.

"Sure. There's a copy on the counter."

"I'll get it." Earl got up before Helen could and looked over the article on his way back to the table, then handed it to her.

J.B.'s photo had been placed beneath a headline that read, "FBI AGENT MISSING." Tears blurred the rest. She dabbed at her eyes with a napkin, but it wasn't doing much good.

"You do know him." Gracie placed a hand on Helen's shoulder. "Your husband?"

Helen nodded.

"Didn't you know he was missing?" Earl asked.

Avoiding his question, Helen asked, "Could you read it for me please?"

Earl turned the paper around and began reading.

" 'FBI Agent Jason Bradley of Portland, Oregon, disappeared Wednesday during a routine investigation. Officials became concerned when Bradley failed to show up at a scheduled rendezvous point on the Washington Coast, where he was working with local law enforcement officials. Bradley is 6'2", 185 pounds, has silver gray hair, and speaks with an Irish accent. If you have any information regarding Agent Bradley's whereabouts, contact the Portland Federal Bureau of Investigation immediately.' "

"Doesn't tell you much. They listed a couple numbers at the end. Want to keep the article?"

Helen reached for it, tore out the article, and set the paper aside.

"Do you know what kind of case he was working on? Bet it was drugs." Earl answered his own question. "It's always drugs." Earl leaned back, somber faced, thinking no doubt about his brother-in-law.

Helen closed her eyes. They hadn't mentioned J.B.'s alias, or the fact that he'd been working undercover, or that he might have a heart condition. He may have even lost his accent for his role. He'd done it before. The photo of J.B. bore little resemblance to the man he was pretending to be. God forbid they would want to jeopardize his mission with the truth. She wondered how many days would pass before they let the public know he'd been on the Peninsula. That he had been wearing leathers and riding a motorcycle. And that he'd colored his hair black and now looked a lot like James Bond. She'd often linked J.B. to James Bond of movie fame—and with good reason. J.B. had worked for British Intelligence and done similar work. He even had the same initials.

She wasn't being fair. Knowing the way J.B. worked, it was entirely possible they hadn't seen him in disguise. As Tom had said, J.B. could have used any one of over a dozen aliases.

Gracie brought her tea. "I'm so sorry, Mrs. Bradley. What an awful way to find out. I can't believe they didn't contact you."

"I alerted them—when J.B. didn't call me. It's just such a shock to see it in writing."

"Yeah, I know—like when I read the obits and saw Chuck's name. It was so final." She crossed her thin arms and blinked back the tears. "Um . . . that reminds me, I heard what happened to you the other day."

"News does travel fast."

"Being a waitress I hear a lot."

"What happened?" Earl asked.

Helen filled him in on the details of her fiasco at McKenzie Head.

"I can't believe I'm hearing this conversation," Earl responded. "This is crazy. Frazier killed in an explosion, you getting hit over the head, your husband missing, and Steve committing suicide. What's going on around here?"

"You forgot about Isabelle's death," Gracie added. "One thing for sure, it's more than a run of bad luck."

Fading out of the conversation, Helen chose a raspberry tea and concentrated on dunking the bag in the hot water until it turned a deep shade of red. She brought it up to her lips and inhaled the fruity aroma. All she really wanted to do was go back to the bed and breakfast, curl up under the comforter, and cry. But she couldn't afford herself that luxury. J.B. had been missing for nearly thirty-six hours.

Gracie left to wait on a couple who'd walked in. Earl's gaze left the waitress and focused on Helen. "You want to ask me something. I can tell."

"You're very astute. I do have a question. There was a man in town on Tuesday"—Helen chose her words carefully—"and I wondered if you might have seen him. Dark hair, tall, blue eyes, wearing jeans and a worn leather jacket. He had a motorcycle with Oregon plates and was frequenting some of the pubs."

Earl's eyes turned to narrow slits when he frowned. "I might have seen somebody like that at the Lightship. Couple of the guys and I had dinner there. I remember thinking he seemed out of place. Tough-looking character. Why are you asking?"

"Adam and Dan seemed to think he might have something to do with the drug-smuggling operation they've been investigating. I'm wondering if he's somehow connected to my husband's disappearance. The biker seems to have vanished as well."

Earl looked thoughtful. "I can see why they might think he was dealing. Wish I could help you, but I didn't actually talk to him. He was having dinner with Scott Mandrel."

Seventeen

"M orning," Adam grunted, looking about as cheerful as Helen felt.

She had gone up to the Coast Guard station directly from the restaurant. Catching Adam on his daily walk up to the lighthouse, Helen fell into step beside him.

"I need to talk to Scott Mandrel," she explained. "I tried to call Shells, but she wasn't home. I need a phone number or an address for him."

"I could give you the information, but it won't do much good."

"Why?" Helen stopped him. "Don't tell me he's skipped town." She felt out of breath, but it wasn't from walking up the steep hill.

Adam shook his head. "I don't know. Dan and I went to talk to him last night. No sign of him or his car. The relief chef at the restaurant—Rusty—told us Scott and Shells had gone to Portland on business after the funeral. He thought they'd be back last night. They never showed up. Dan and I think maybe he might have run and forced Shells to go with him."

"I see." She hated being wrong—almost as much as she hated wrongdoing. Had she been wrong about Scott? At the moment, Mandrel had too many strikes against him to be considered an innocent bystander. Now it seems he may have had something to do with J.B.'s disappearance. "I thought he was your prime suspect. How could you—"

Adam glanced away. "Don't say it. We should have had a tail on him." He started walking again. "What do you need to see Mandrel about?"

Helen told him about her conversation with Earl. Adam denied knowing anything about Scott's meeting with J.B.

"Are you sure J.B. didn't mention talking to Scott?" Helen asked.

"All J.B. told Dan and me was that he'd baited some hooks and may have gotten a couple bites. He was in a rush to get back to Portland to pick up his boat and said he'd fill us in on the details when he got back."

"So it's possible J.B. may have gotten too close." Helen closed her eyes. "I'm worried, Adam. I'm really worried. What if Scott saw through J.B.'s cover? I need to talk to him. I need to find out why he was with my husband. He may know where J.B. is. If anything's happened to . . ." She stopped the negative thought before it came out and concentrated on putting one foot in front of the other. And on the puffs of steam released by her mouth as each breath hit the cool morning air.

"We're trying to track Mandrel down—got the state police searching both sides of the river. It isn't looking good. Mandrel could be anywhere by now—he could even be in South America."

"Let's hope not."

Helen walked the rest of the way up the hill, then lingered awhile after Adam had gone back to his office. She tried a relaxation technique in order to come up with J.B.'s phony name. Sometimes clearing her mind and taking deep, steady breaths worked. Today it didn't. Anxiety formed a thick fog in her brain—thicker than the heavy fogbank that kept her from seeing anything on the horizon but gray. Still, she stood at the chain link fence, staring out into the distance, praying, aching to hear God's still small voice tell her everything would be okay.

But all she could hear was the plaintive cry of sea gulls, the mournful bellow of a foghorn, and her own weeping.

After twenty more minutes of ruminating, Helen returned to her car. She'd stopped briefly at Adam's office, but he'd had no further news of J.B. or Scott Mandrel. While there, Helen called Emily to let her know the fishing trip had been canceled, then filled her in on the other details she'd learned that morning.

"You might have told me you were going—I'd have made you a nice breakfast and packed you a lunch."

"I didn't want to bother you," Helen said. "Besides, I was afraid Kate would have a fit. She hovers over me like a mother hen. I'm beginning to feel smothered. She's a wonderful daughter and I love her dearly, but she seems bound and determined to get me into a rocking chair."

"Don't know much about getting around this younger generation, do you? Maybe I can give you a few pointers. Been fighting Danny since I turned fifty. He used to be underfoot all the time trying to take care of his old auntie. Now his old auntie's taking care of him." Emily chuckled. "In fact, he's coming over for breakfast this morning. Which reminds me, I'd better see if your daughter is up."

Helen glanced at her watch, surprised to find it was only seven-thirty. Unlike Helen, Kate was not a morning person. "I don't suppose anyone's called there about J.B."

"Nope. I'll ask Dan. 'Spect we'd hear right away if they found him." Emily paused. "You planning on coming back soon? Want me to set an extra plate for breakfast?"

"N-no." Helen hesitated. "Since I'm here at the south end, I'll do some exploring. I'd like to see the North Head Lighthouse and make a few notes."

"Lunch, then?"

"Maybe. Don't look for me, though. I'm not good company just now. I may catch a bite at Shells' Place. Need to talk to somebody over there anyway. I'm hoping Rusty can shed some light on Scott and Shells' disappearing act."

"Come again?"

"Shells and Scott left town. The way news travels I was sure you'd have heard by now. Ask Dan to give you the details over breakfast."

"I will. What if I hear anything about J.B.?"

"Call me." Helen gave Emily her cell phone number. "I'll keep it with me."

"Okay." Emily hesitated. "What shall I tell Kate?"

"That I'm working." Helen bit her lip. "On second thought, have her meet me at Shells' Place at twelve-thirty. Since she's here, I may as well put her to work."

After promising to be back in time for dinner, Helen rang off.

Out of sheer desperation to keep from going to pieces over J.B., Helen focused on the guidebook. She left the Coast Guard station, parked at the trail head, and hiked the three miles to the North Head Lighthouse. There she took a tour, climbing the stairs to the top of the lighthouse. The fog was finally lifting and the day promised sunshine.

Going back, she stopped to see the lightkeeper's house—now newly remodeled and open to tourists. Enthralled with the look and feel of the house—and maybe to give herself hope—Helen made reservations for herself and J.B. for the weekend after next. She'd be done with the book by then—or at least ready to put together all of the material she'd gathered. It would be a perfect way to end their stay on the Peninsula.

Helen stared out at the spectacular view of the lighthouse and the ocean beyond it, lingering for a few moments after the guide descended the stairs. She felt an odd camaraderie with the wives of men lost at sea. Unbidden tears filled her eyes, blurring the landscape. "Lord, please bring J.B. back to me," she whispered.

The tour complete, Helen hiked back to the state park, then drove toward the jetty. She parked in a paved lot overlooking Waikiki Beach and worked on her laptop until the battery signaled its recharge warning. Saving her files, Helen put the computer away.

She'd be meeting Kate soon. Dear Kate, who felt it was her God-given duty to care for her aging parent. Helen smiled at the irony of it. She didn't need taking care of yet. Maybe the day would come, maybe it wouldn't. One thing for certain, she had no intention of being a burden to her children if she had anything to say about it.

Helen stepped out of the car and stretched, then picked her way over the rocks to the sandy beach. While she walked the length of the short beach, she rehearsed the conversation she'd planned to have with her daughter. Helen dreaded the thought of facing Kate after her hasty departure earlier that morning. Kate would be . . . troubled. Helen sighed. Her overprotective daughter would give her that mother-you-need-a-keeper look. But, Helen reminded herself, it was far better to have children who cared a bit too much than to have them completely ignore her. And she did have a wonderful family.

In fact, it was time for another gathering at her home in Bay Village. She hadn't had a get-together for a long time—not since she'd married J.B. It was that promise of a weekend together with which she placated Kate when she arrived at Shells' Place a few minutes later.

Kate hugged her. "That sounds lovely, Mother, but I'll need to coordinate all of our schedules."

"Good. You let me know and we'll plan to be home." They walked arm in arm into the restaurant.

"Thanks for inviting me to lunch," Kate said. "When Emily told me you'd gone, I was pretty upset."

"I'm sorry about that. It was a spur-of-the-moment decision, and to be honest, Kate, I guess I was running away."

"From me?" Kate's eyes widened in surprise.

Helen smiled. "Sounds silly now." She paused to greet Gracie, who led them to a table at the window. A boat sat at the end of the dock—a container of fish—rock cod, Helen guessed, being delivered to the processing plant. A plant owned by Scott Mandrel.

When they'd been seated and had ordered drinks, Kate picked up the conversation. "Mother, I . . . I guess I owe you an apology. I don't mean to come off sounding like an army sergeant."

"Oh, Kate, you don't."

"Emily thinks I do. And she's right. I have no business trying to run your life. I worry about you. Maybe I always have." She tossed her mother a wry smile. "I come by it honestly. With Daddy off doing his secret agent thing and you solving murders, somebody had to worry. I sure couldn't leave it to Jason. He thought having parents in law enforcement was cool."

"I appreciate your concern, darling. It's normal to be worried about people you love and want to protect them. Take J.B., for example. I'm so afraid I might lose him. He was supposed to be retiring. I thought that was what I wanted. But I know now that's not the answer for him—or me. At least not right now. He needs to be working and productive." Helen glanced out at the calm bay and squinted as the bright reflection of sun on the water shone into her eyes.

"Emily told me I should be grateful you're as active as you are . . . and I am." Kate sipped at her water. "But I can't help worrying."

"You always were the sensitive one." While her twins had shared similar physical features—both tall and slender with dark hair and navy blue eyes, they were opposites in many ways. Jason had gone on to study law, then joined the DEA. Kate had taken up art and design and become an interior decorator.

"I guess I was. Remember how I used to get tummy aches when Daddy was out of town? And when you worked nights I'd go to sleep in your room so I'd wake up when you got home. Then, when Jason disappeared I . . . well, I nearly went crazy. When I think of all you three have put me through, it's a wonder I'm not a basket case."

"Poor Kate," Helen cooed. "Were we really that hard on you?"

"Terrible." A smile crept across her face, softening her delicate features. "Growing up with you and Dad and Jason was—" Kate stopped. "It was scary and exciting. I was so happy when you retired from being a police officer. I thought, Thank God it's over. But it wasn't by a long shot. For a while it was wonderful, then you started taking those secret trips. And you playing detective and getting shot at last month didn't help. You should be settling down—enjoying your golden years."

"I'm not there yet. And you, my darling daughter, need to

stop pushing me over the hill. Goodness, I'm not even silver—at least not completely." Helen reached up and brushed her fingers through her short graying hair.

"You're right. I wanted to apologize, and here I end up grousing about my miserable childhood." Kate's gaze met Helen's. "And it wasn't all that bad. Anyway—you must have done something right. Look at how well I turned out."

"At least you recognize that." Helen squeezed her daughter's hand. "I'm glad you came down. It's good having you here—especially with J.B. missing. You and Emily have been a great comfort."

"Emily told me you might have a lead."

Helen shared what Earl had said about Scott's dinner with J.B. "I hate to admit it, but Steve Kendall's confession may have been accurate."

"At breakfast Dan was worried that Shells might have been taken as a hostage."

"Yes. I hope not. She's been through so much already."

"You two ready to order?" Gracie refilled their cups.

"How fresh is your fish?" Helen asked.

Gracie tossed them a you've-got-to-be-kidding look. "See that boat out there? We get fish and seafood—shrimp, oysters, crab—delivered fresh every day. Chuck used to supply all the fish, but now that he's gone we'll get it from the Carlson brothers mostly."

Kate and Helen both ordered the sturgeon with a hazelnut coating, polenta, and a salad with raspberry vinaigrette dressing on the side.

Gracie hesitated, chewing her lower lip, then said, "I couldn't help overhearing what you said about Shells. Um . . . I saw Shells leave with Scott yesterday. Like I told Dan, she asked Scott to go into town with her to pick up supplies. I don't know where Dan got the idea that Scott forced her."

"But she was planning on coming back?" Helen asked.

"As far as I know. It's not like her to leave and not call." Gracie shrugged. "Maybe Adam and Dan know something we don't. Anyway, don't pay me any mind. No one else seems to."

Helen watched the waitress walk away. For the first time, she began to consider Shells as a possible suspect. If Scott was smuggling drugs, could he do so without Shells knowing? Was she an accomplice—had she helped him escape?

"Mother? Are you okay?"

"Wha—? Oh. I was just thinking about what Gracie said. It occurs to me that I've been making assumptions about the innocence of certain people around here. It's possible that Shells and Scott are a team. The restaurant is a good cover—and with the wharf so close. What's to stop them from bringing in something besides seafood?"

"Like cocaine or marijuana?"

"Hmm. Shells could be making her kitchen available for storage. She has delivery trucks coming and going at all hours. Most of them would be bringing supplies, but some could be picking up the drugs and distributing them any number of places."

"Do you think J.B. suspected them?"

"Maybe. All I know is that J.B. being missing at the same time Scott and Shells are is too much of a coincidence." Helen stared out at the boat that was now chugging away, riding high in the water, its hold as empty as her heart.

After lunch, curiosity about the fish processing plant drew Helen and Kate to the end of the pier. The entire setup smelled fishy—literally as well as figuratively. In Helen's mind, the plant would work perfectly for drug smuggling. A small coastal town—easy access where many people whose livelihood once depended on the fishing industry but were now forced to find other ways of earning a living. Like smuggling drugs. Helen thought about the fishermen Scott Mandrel had bought out. Perhaps his generosity had a catch.

Eighteen

Helen and Kate approached the processing plant wishing they'd brought nose plugs. The strong smell of fish and some kind of cleaning solution permeated the air around the plant. As they approached a security gate, a worker dumped a large container of blood, fish heads, and entrails into the water where hungry squawking sea gulls waited.

"Gee, Mom. You see what a rough life I lead? When other mothers take their daughters on outings they go to flower gardens. We end up in a fish morgue."

Helen chuckled. "Hush. We'll do flowers next time."

"Right."

The locked gate barred their way. A large metal sign read, *Pisces International. No admittance.* Another said *Enter at Your Own Risk.* Still another instructed them to ring the buzzer for assistance. Helen rang the buzzer. A young-sounding female voice came out of a speaker attached to a piling above them.

"Welcome to Pisces International. How may we help you?"

"Is it possible to tour the facilities this afternoon?"

"We hold tours on Saturday and Sunday between one and four."

"Oh." Helen took another tactic. "Mr. Mandrel said I could come by anytime. I was hoping—"

"What's your name?"

"Helen Bradley. I'm writing a guidebook—"

"One moment please," the voice interrupted. Seconds later she was back. "Dad—I mean, Mr. Black will be right with you."

Mr. Black, a congenial man in his mid-forties, greeted them with a smile that didn't reach his eyes. "Mrs. Bradley, yes. Scott mentioned you might come by this week." He was wearing a blue dress shirt and jeans. His neon Ziggy tie was the type kids might give a dad on Father's Day.

Helen introduced Kate, then added, "Is this a bad time for you? We can come back later."

"No, no. Not at all. It's been a busy morning. S'pose you heard the news about Scott being wanted on murder charges. Fool cops. Only reason they're going after Scott is he's not a local boy. Humph. Ancestors were here decades before any of the rest of us. You'd think that would count for something."

"We heard. You have to admit it doesn't look good with him leaving town."

"No, don't suppose it does." He adjusted his hard hat. "I hear you're writing a guidebook about the Peninsula."

"Yes. I thought it might be an interesting perspective to do a piece on a seafood processing plant, since seafood is so much a part of this area."

"Right—that and cranberries. Be glad to answer any questions you might have. Can't let you in through this gate, though—too dangerous with all the heavy equipment. You'll have to drive around to the main entrance—just go back out to the road and turn right at the next driveway. I'll meet you in the office."

Mr. Black—Pete, as he insisted on being called—reached the office door before Kate and Helen and escorted them inside. The office consisted of a large waiting room with a reception area. A hallway on the right led to several offices. The room smelled of cedar, which had been used to finish the interior walls. Colorful banners hung from the high open-beam ceiling. With its glass-cased exhibits and display of books and pamphlets, it looked much like a fisheries resource center.

"Nice," Kate murmured as she wandered over to look at a metal sculpture of a fly-fisherman and his fighting trout. "Definitely a Northwest flavor."

"Hi, Helen." A familiar-looking woman came out of one of

the offices and set a file folder on the receptionist's desk. "How's the guidebook coming?"

"Good." Helen recognized her as one of Emily's writer friends. "You're Joanna, right?"

"Right. I can't believe you remembered." She turned to Pete. "Honey, why don't you let me show them around. Goodness knows you have enough to do today without a tour. Besides, it'll give me a chance to talk writing."

"Thanks, Jo. I owe you one." Pete hung an arm over her ample shoulders. "My wife is the office manager and bookkeeper for the plant." He nodded toward the receptionist. "That's our daughter, Becky. She fills in for our regular secretary."

Becky looked up at them and smiled, revealing a full set of braces. "Mom told me about the book you're writing. Sounds neat. If you decide to write about the cranberries, let me know. My grandfather raises them. He's got bogs right off Cranberry Road."

"Thanks, Becky. I'll keep that in mind."

"I'd best be getting back to work," Pete said. "If you have any questions just give me a jingle."

Pete went into the first office and closed the door.

The tour, though interesting and informative, provided no answers to Helen's concerns about the plant being a cover for a covert drug operation. Toward the end of the tour, Kate excused herself to find a rest room. Helen lingered in the plant viewing room, which looked out over the warehouse where fish were brought in and processed, and used the opportunity to question Joanna.

"Drugs? Here? Oh dear, no." Joanna looked genuinely shocked. "We'd never work for a company that was into anything illegal. And we certainly wouldn't bring our daughter into an environment like that."

Below them a dozen or so workers, mostly Hispanic, pulled fish onto tables in front of them, cleaning and cutting them to specification. They worked so quickly with their knives, Helen could hardly keep track of what they were doing. Within minutes of delivery, the fish was refrigerated and ready to ship out to waiting customers. "Could the workers be involved in a drug operation that you and Pete don't know about?"

"I seriously doubt it. Pete's been the operations manager here since it opened six months ago. How could you even suggest such a thing?" She paused, her mouth dropping open in shock. "Surely you don't suspect *us*."

So complete was the indignation, Helen doubted the Blacks, at least Joanna, had any inkling. "Innocent people have been used before, Joanna," Helen said. "It's obvious something is going on. Isabelle and Chuck are both dead—probably because they got too close to uncovering the truth. Emily's home was broken into. I was hit on the head. My—" Helen stopped just short of telling Joanna about J.B. "The man who accused Scott and was willing to testify against him is dead."

"He committed suicide. Mr. Mandrel was terribly upset over that. Says he can't imagine why the man would lie. He and Shells even drove to the jail in South Bend on the way to Portland."

"Wait a minute. Scott went to see Steve Kendall? When?"

"Yesterday."

"Joanna, he died yesterday."

"You don't think—" Joanna shook her head. "No, I won't hear of it. Scott Mandrel is one of the nicest men I know. Why, he paid us well over what our charter business was worth when he bought us out. He even offered us jobs at the plant."

"I see." Desperate times called for desperate measures. "Scott bought out several fishermen, didn't he?"

"Yes. And it was a good thing. We were close to declaring bankruptcy."

"Did he offer jobs to the others as well?"

"He did. But only three of the men took him up on it. The two who didn't are still grousing about how unfair life is while they drink away their unemployment checks."

They walked back to the reception area where Kate was examining the colorful banners suspended from the ceiling.

"Joanna," Helen paused, making one last effort. "If Scott is as innocent as you say, where is he now?"

"Wish I knew. Maybe the pressure got to be too much. Maybe he knew the law down here would crucify him and he felt he had no choice but to run." Joanna crossed her arms. "The one thing I do know is that Scott Mandrel is not a killer."

They chatted awhile longer and finally left on good terms with Helen promising to see Joanna at their Wednesday night writer's meeting.

"Well," Kate prodded on the way back to their cars, "do you still think the plant is a front for a drug-smuggling operation?"

"I certainly didn't see any signs of it. If something is going on, I don't think the Blacks are involved—not Joanna at any rate. I doubt she'd have her daughter working there if she so much as suspected drug involvement on the part of Pisces International."

Helen paused at Kate's maroon Taurus. "Are you up for a drive and a walk on the beach?"

"I guess." Kate grinned. "Beats looking at dead fish."

"Good. I'd like to walk the boardwalk in Long Beach. Low tide is at four, so we should have plenty of time to drive up to the north end of the Peninsula. We can come in at the Ocean Park approach. Emily said I should stop at Colleen's Creations at the beach approach for desserts or lattes. She mentioned a gift shop as well—Sweet William's."

Leaving Kate's car in Long Beach, mother and daughter spent the afternoon walking, exploring, and getting acquainted with the Peninsula and reacquainted with each other.

"I'm glad we decided to do this." Kate spooned out the last of her burnt cream from Colleen's and set the dish on the small round marble table. "It's been great."

Helen had opted for a piece of marionberry pie and tea. Though Colleen had jokingly assured her she'd removed all the calories, Helen felt stuffed. "We were long overdue, I think." Helen looked at the brown stain on her shoes and frowned. "The only downside of our little excursion was that awful stuff on the beach."

"I wonder what it is. Even the waves looked brown. Must be an oil spill or something."

"I'll have to ask Earl. He's with the EPA. If anyone would know about a pollution problem, he would."

"Sorry to barge in on your conversation," a woman two tables down said. "Couldn't help overhearing. That brown gook out there is a natural-occurring algae—clam food, actually. Not very pretty, but there it is. Been around for as long as I can remember—some days it's worse than others."

"Really?" Helen frowned. "I don't recall seeing it on the Oregon beaches."

"Might have something to do with the river being so close. If you want to know for sure, you can check over at the shellfish laboratories in Nahcotta."

Helen pulled out her map and asked the woman to show her where to find it, then wrote down the name. She'd either drive out there or call tomorrow. When they finished their drinks, they popped into Sweet William's to browse, then headed back to Long Beach, where Kate picked up her car. All in all a fruitful day for the guidebook. All she'd managed to do on the investigation was to raise more questions. It would take days, maybe even weeks, to follow and tie up all the threads. Maybe it was time to put Emily and Kate to work.

❖ ❖ ❖

"Logan." She said the name aloud when it came to her the next morning as she drifted into wakefulness. The night before she'd prayed that if J.B. had told her his name, she'd be able to recall it. Helen tossed the covers aside and slipped into her robe. "Logan," she repeated again. She didn't know if it was a first name or the last, but it was a name.

Helen hurried downstairs, told Kate and Emily the news, then called Tom at the FBI in Portland. Tom promised to check the files to see if J.B.'s alias was on file from a previous usage and call her back. She called Adam, who promised to alert other local law officials. Soon, she thought. Soon they'd find him. She tried not to think where or in what condition he'd be. She only held on to the image of the two of them staying in the lovely turn-of-the-century house where keepers of the light had helped scores of ships navigate safely along the treacherous coastline.

Nineteen

I understand you've been asking questions around town." Dan Merritt bent at the waist and peered into Helen's car. He'd passed her on Sandridge Road going south. She'd been heading north toward the bed and breakfast. The moment they passed, he had flipped on his lights and siren, done a U-turn in the middle of the road, and come after her.

She hadn't been speeding.

"The last I heard, there was no crime against that." Helen was tired of Dan's games. Her head and her stomach hurt. She felt jittery, as if she'd been on an espresso binge. At breakfast she'd given Kate and Emily the job of tracking down the people Scott Mandrel had bought out. She wanted the stats on all of them— what they were doing, who they were working for. Then, after making some notes to herself and writing for two hours, she'd set out for Seaview and worked her way north to Long Beach, taking photos, finding places of interest, and interviewing people on a variety of subjects. With nearly all of them, she'd managed to swing the conversation around to the biker named Logan. She'd gone into nearly every eating and drinking establishment listed in the phone book.

As far as she could tell, Dan didn't know about her relationship to J.B.—maybe this was the time to tell him. On the other hand, what if Dan was responsible for J.B.'s disappearance?

Dan's challenging gaze fastened on hers. "Got an interesting phone call today. From the FBI office in Portland. Said if I ran

161

into you I should give you a message."

"From Tom?" Helen's discomfort created a tight band around her chest. She bit her lip. "I mean Agent Chambers?"

"Yeah." His nostrils flared when he drew in a deep breath.

"He called you?"

"Apparently they tried Emily, but she says your cell phone isn't working. Emily gave them my number thinking I could track you down. Might want to check your cell phone. They do need recharging now and then."

Helen glanced at the phone lying on the seat, where it had been since the day before. Berating herself for being so forgetful, she said, "What did Agent Chambers say?" Her heart beat out a hard and heavy pattern of growing fear. "Have they—"

"Found your husband?" Dan rubbed his jaw. "No. Look, Mrs. Bradley. I think we'd better have a talk. How about I follow you to my aunt's place?"

Helen swallowed hard and nodded. She didn't like the accusing tone of Dan's voice. Though he'd said they hadn't found J.B., she couldn't help but think he might be holding something back. That's what people often did when they had bad news. Did he want to get her off the road before he told her?

Reminding herself over and over not to think the worst, Helen led the way to the Bayshore Bed and Breakfast. The empty driveway gave her a start. Where was Kate? And Emily? Dan pulled in at an angle behind her, blocking her in. He climbed out of his vehicle and opened her door. "Emily and Kate have gone into town, so we'll have the place to ourselves."

Two possible scenarios scrambled through Helen's head as she walked onto the porch and waited for Dan to open the door. Either the news was very bad, or he had some malevolent plan to put an end to her and her questions.

Making himself at home, he went straight to the kitchen and poured two cups of coffee. If Emily had left the machine plugged in, she must have been expecting him. He handed a mug to Helen. She accepted it without comment, though she would have preferred tea. Bad news always went better with tea.

"Why did Tom call?" Taking a small pitcher of cream from

the refrigerator, she slid into a chair and set her cup on a place mat.

"I'll get to that." Dan hooked a chair leg with his foot, pulled it out, and sat down. "In a minute. First I want to know why you lied to me."

"I didn't lie. I came here to write a guidebook. That's what I'm doing." Her hand shook as she poured too much cream into the already full cup. She grabbed for napkins from the center of the table to mop up.

"Maybe not, but you omitted some important details. Okay, so I know you used to be a cop. And I knew you were married to an FBI agent. But today when I tried to talk to Agent Chambers about you, he clammed up. Now I figure you are either in a witness protection program or you're one of them."

"Not necessarily."

"I think you owe me an explanation. Especially since you're so bent on moving in on my territory. Were you sent in to investigate me or something?"

"No." She sipped at the warm brown brew. "I'm not here in an official capacity. What was the message you had for me?" Helen steeled herself to hear it.

"Chambers said, and I quote, 'Tell Mrs. Bradley her husband's name isn't on file.' Now I may be a backwoods sheriff, but I'm not stupid. And every once in a while I even read the papers. Why didn't you tell me the missing agent was your husband?"

"You know how the Feds are. J.B. didn't want anyone to know about our relationship. Adam knew, of course, and Emily. I didn't know how much J.B. had told you, and I didn't want to compromise his investigation."

"In case I was dirty? In case I had something to do with his disappearance?"

Helen's fears about Dan faded. She read no real malice in his eyes—only annoyance at being left out of the loop. "It did cross my mind. After all, besides myself and Emily, you and Adam were the only ones who knew J.B. was with the FBI."

"Don't be too sure. Could be someone he'd talked to the

night before got it into their head to follow him. They might have seen him when he met with Adam and me."

And they'd have seen him come to the bed and breakfast. Helen focused on Dan's badge.

Dan leaned forward, pushing his half-empty cup to the center of the table. "Look, Mrs. Bradley, I'm sorry about your husband. We're doing all we can at this end to find him. But for your own safety, I gotta ask you to quit poking into this case. I'm working on about four different angles here. If you stir things up, you could jeopardize the investigation."

"Do you have any idea what happened to J.B.?"

"Yeah—but you don't want to hear them."

"Have you been able to locate Scott and Shells?"

"Not yet. Found Mandrel's car in a long-term parking lot at the Portland airport. Nothing on the passenger lists, though. Looks like he used phony IDs or maybe took a private plane. On the other hand, he may have parked there to throw us off the trail."

"Which means they could be anywhere." Helen told him about her visit to Pisces International and her suspicions that some of the people Scott had bought out might be involved in drug trafficking.

"As a matter of fact, I've asked Black to keep an eye out. He's a volunteer deputy. If they were pulling in contraband, they've put a moratorium on it. At least for the time being."

"And you feel you can trust Mr. Black?"

"More than I trust your friend Adam."

"Adam? You're not serious."

"Don't tell me you've ruled him out. As you said yourself, you, Emily, Adam, and I are the only ones who knew about J.B. being FBI. Now, I know I didn't do it. I doubt seriously my aunt is into the drug scene. And you—probably not, but I wouldn't rule out the possibility. Adam? I'm not hedging my bets there either."

"Touché."

Dan was just leaving when Emily and Kate arrived with a large take-out pizza and seafood salad from Bubba's. Kate set the boxes on the table and opened them while Helen set out plates and utensils. Emily poured tall glasses of iced tea, then led them in a table prayer.

Dan's comment about Emily being involved in drug trafficking niggled at her. Was it possible? Only two weeks ago, a seventy-year-old great-grandmother whose only other crime had been crocheting afghans for her children every Christmas had been arrested for cooking methamphetamine for two of her drug-dealing sons.

Helen pushed away the ridiculous image of Emily as a doper and tried to concentrate on the wonderful blend of shrimp, artichoke hearts, dried tomatoes, and cheeses that made up what Bubba called the "Yachtsman." It was excellent, but she wasn't in the mood for pizza, or anything else for that matter.

After raving about the pizza, Emily shifted the conversation to the information she'd gathered that day. "Three of the five fishermen Scott bought out are working for him at the plant," she reported. "I asked a friend of mine who works at the police department in Long Beach to check their records. The three working for Scott were clean—not so much as a parking ticket. Now, the two who aren't working for Scott . . ." Emily paused. "That's a different story. They've both had recent arrests for drunk driving. One was busted for possession last year. Unsavory characters, the both of them. Divorced, deadbeat dads, in and out of treatment centers. If anybody was suspect in drug smuggling, I'd pick them."

"You're certain Scott bought them out?" Helen sipped at her tea in hopes it would settle her churning stomach.

"Oh yes. I got as far as finding out where they lived. Tomorrow I'll pay them a visit."

"That may not be such a good idea. Perhaps we should give Dan the information and let him take care of it."

Kate and Emily both stopped eating and glared at her.

"Mother, don't tell me you're giving up now."

"Not giving up. But for you two to confront known drug users could be dangerous."

"You think maybe that's what happened to Isabelle?"

"Maybe."

"Mother's right, Emily. There's a point when you have to leave investigating to the authorities." Kate arched an eyebrow, leaving no doubt that the comment had been meant for her mother as well.

"Did you contact the shellfish laboratory?" Helen asked, changing the subject.

"I did," Kate said. "The woman at Colleen's Creations was right. It is a type of algae—food for the clams and other shellfish. It has plant and animal characteristics. Basically one-celled animals hooked together in long chains. They have four hairs and tiny rectangular shells or houses around themselves. The houses break and look like silt in the water, and that mixes with silica . . ." Kate smiled. "That's probably more than you need to know. Right?"

"It's interesting, but you're right. I just wanted to know if it was a pollutant."

"Nope. I was sure glad to hear it. I had this horrid feeling it was from a big oil spill. There's so much pollution these days."

"True." Helen dabbed at her mouth with a napkin. "Earl was telling me he found some mutated fish in some of the rivers around here."

Kate screwed up her face. "Maybe I'll give up fish."

"It is a scary prospect." They talked on through dinner about the widespread contamination of the earth's water supply. Not the most pleasant conversation, but like so many other things, it helped Helen through the day. Though she'd been busy, thoughts of J.B. were never far away.

It hit her now, as she sat in Emily's living room, like a fist in the stomach. Where was he, and why hadn't they found anything? Helen wished she had more confidence in the law enforcement agencies. It was J.B. himself who'd found her in that Mexican prison. He hadn't even been on the case and got into trouble for stepping in the middle of it. He hadn't trusted anyone else to do the job. *"Half the time these guys can't find a piano in a one-room house,"* he'd told her later. She was beginning to think he was right.

If she didn't hear anything tonight, she'd take up her personal search again in the morning.

Emily picked up her knitting. Kate sat in an overstuffed chair reading. Helen watched the fire and prayed. Her stomach felt queasy, probably from stress. Maybe she should have tried to eat more, but she just hadn't been hungry.

The buzz of the doorbell jarred her out of her reverie. She bounced to her feet. "I'll get it." Adam stood on the porch, his face drawn, his eyes full of pity.

"They found him?" Helen's heart must have stopped beating. Everything seemed to slip into slow motion as Adam stepped inside and closed the door.

Twenty

Helen felt light-headed. Her knees went spongey. Adam's voice sounded hollow, as if it were coming from a well. What was it he'd said?

"Maybe you'd better sit down." Adam cupped her elbow and guided her to the living room.

"What's going on?" Kate was on her feet. The two of them settled Helen into the chair and none too soon.

"I started to tell her we found J.B.'s boat."

"I'll get her some water," Emily said.

"Don't try to get up, Mother. Just sit there a minute."

"I'm . . ." Helen forced herself to take several deep breaths, then accepted the water Emily brought. "I'm sorry," she said when her head finally cleared. "I don't know what came over me. Where's J.B.?"

Adam shook his head. "I—we don't know."

"But I thought you said you found the boat."

"We did. J.B. wasn't on it."

Helen dragged a hand through her hair. "Maybe you'd better start over. Exactly what did you find?"

"The *Hallie B* ran ashore about thirty miles west of Longview on the Washington side. The area is uninhabited. River patrols said it had drifted into some brush along the bank."

"It doesn't make sense." Helen leaned back and sipped at the cool water. "J.B. wouldn't leave his craft. If there'd been trouble he'd have radioed for help."

"Um . . . he may have, Helen. River patrol said they got a Mayday call at sixteen hundred hours on Wednesday. The call came in garbled and when they asked the caller to repeat the message, they got nothing. The mike on the boat was hanging like he'd dropped it."

Had he been the victim of pirates? Had Scott, or whoever the murderer was, followed him and waited until he was in a secluded spot, then . . .

Helen set the glass down and took a deep breath. She needed to remain rational, calm. One thing for certain, someone had taken J.B. off that boat. They'd either taken him hostage or left him in the river to drown. *Stop it!* Helen thought the words with such vehemence she nearly said them aloud. She couldn't let herself even think that J.B. might be dead.

"I'm sorry," Adam was saying. "We're checking different angles. At this point it doesn't look good."

She recoiled at Adam's suggestion, her mind racing with possibilities. "Maybe his disappearance has nothing to do with the investigation. He may have gotten sick." Heart attack came to mind, or a stroke. Or he could have fallen and hit his head. It could be serious but not fatal. Surely not fatal. "I need to check the hospitals. Maybe someone picked him up."

"Helen . . ."

"No, don't . . ." Helen gripped the arms of the chair. She didn't want to be reminded of the odds. "Just promise me you'll keep looking."

Adam nodded. "I talked to Jason. He was able to find half a dozen Logans and some John Does in the hospitals upriver, but none of the leads have panned out. It's hard to say where J.B. left the craft. We have no idea how far downstream it drifted. It was set on automatic pilot. I'm guessing around Cathlamet. That means if someone did take him in, it would have been to Longview—maybe Astoria. Jason's taking a couple days off to check it out personally."

"We could go too, Mother. With the three of us . . . Mother?"

Helen fought against the tide of nausea rising in her stomach. A cold sweat sent chills through her. Darkness threatened to engulf her. She struggled to escape. Her breaths came in ragged gasps. Somehow she needed to pull out of it. She had to find J.B. The headache she'd had earlier came back with head-splitting force.

"Mother, talk to me. What's wrong?" Kate gripped Helen's shoulder, rising panic in her voice. Helen tried to reassure her but couldn't find the words.

"Maybe we'd better call an ambulance." Adam moved away.

"No . . ." Helen grabbed at her stomach and pitched forward, succumbing to the pervasive darkness.

⚜   ⚜   ⚜

For the second time since she'd been on the Peninsula, Helen woke up in the hospital. She'd drifted in and out of consciousness during the night. Each time she awoke, Kate had been at her side. "Just rest, Mom," she'd said the first time. "The doctor says you probably have a bad case of the flu."

"Then why am I in the hospital?"

"For a while we thought it might have been because of the head injury. If you're feeling better he'll let you go home today."

In a way Helen felt better. She was more alert. More aware of her discomfort. More aware of her weakened state. Kate wasn't there now, Helen noticed. Maybe she'd gone out to eat.

Helen's stomach threatened to rebel at the thought of food. The flu. Unbelievable. "Lord," she grumbled, "your sense of timing couldn't be worse." She needed to be out looking for J.B., not stuck in a hospital bed in what even the locals called the *lost corner* of the world.

"I'm so sorry, J.B.," she murmured. "I'd like more than anything to help." Her gaze drifted from the IV tubing taped to her left arm to the bag dripping above her. "But I'm sort of tied up at the moment." She sighed in resignation.

"Hi." Kate walked in carrying a colorful gift bag covered with roses. A muted pink tissue hid whatever she carried inside. "How are you feeling—and don't say with your hands."

Helen smiled despite her rotten mood. "Better. I'm at the

point where I think I'm going to live, but I'm not sure I want to."

"The doctor says he wants you to try clear liquids this morning. If you're able to keep those down you can go home." She set the bag on the bedside stand. "I brought you some things to cheer you up."

"That's sweet, but the only thing that will cheer me is to have J.B. back and find whoever is responsible for . . . whatever happened to him—and Isabelle and Chuck."

"You're in no condition to do any such thing. Jason and Adam and a lot of other people are doing their best to find J.B. You, my dear mother, need to take your own advice and let go. God can handle this—better than we can. He knows what He's doing."

"Yes, I suppose He does." How often Kate's words had been her own. She'd always believed that when you came to the end of your own abilities, when you simply could not facilitate a change or find an answer, the only solution was to let go and let God. She'd even asked Kate, who did calligraphy among her other talents, to create a watercolor, weaving in the words "Maturity is the art of living in peace with that which we cannot change." So easy to say—so hard to do. Talking faith and living it were often two entirely different things, and she was still in the process of learning the art.

"You know how you say things happen for a reason. Some good will come of this. You wait and see."

Helen gave her daughter a halfhearted smile. "I hate it when you're right."

"Open your present." The light in Kate's eyes held a mischievous gleam.

Helen reached into the bag and retrieved a novel she'd been wanting to read, Earlene Fowler's latest quilt mystery. "Thank you. I suppose if I'm to be laid up, I may as well try to enjoy myself."

"There's more."

Helen dug through and found a cranberry-scented packet.

"The clerk said a lot of people use those for bookmarks. I thought that might be nice."

She put the packet to her nose and drew in a deep breath, savoring the scent of cranberries. Amazing how little things could lift one's spirits. There was a tape called *Celtic Moments*, a get-well card, and a box of her favorite chocolates. And a cloth angel wearing a country dress and straw curls for hair.

"This is all wonderful, darling. Thank you." Helen sank back on her pillow, her fingers grazing the silken angel wings.

"You're welcome. Now try to get some rest. You need to concentrate on getting well."

Helen mumbled an apology for being too tired to stay awake, then drifted off to sleep. Over the next few hours she dozed on and off and took sips of water, tea, and apple juice. Everything stayed down, and by lunch, she'd graduated to that famous cure-all, chicken noodle soup.

Emily, Dan, and Adam had come by at different times. No word yet on J.B. The Feds had assigned another agent to take the case. She took little solace in how quickly the world moved ahead to fill in the empty space a person left behind. She realized, too, that the agencies would only spend another day or so actively looking for J.B. Even federal agents like J.B. who'd given their entire lives to serve their country were expendable. Helen scolded herself once more for letting her thoughts drift into such negative waters. She needed to think positive.

The doctor stopped on his rounds and gave Helen the option of staying one more night or going home. Helen chose the latter. Not that it did much good. She'd need help leaving the hospital and was stuck there until someone came to pick her up. Kate had disappeared around lunchtime and still hadn't shown up at two. Helen was beginning to worry.

Kate finally arrived at two-thirty, face flushed and looking as excited as a new parent. "Mother, you are never going to believe this. I went to lunch at Shells' Place, and a couple of the nurses from here came in. They recognized me and I asked them to join me. Anyway, we got to talking, and they mentioned a patient who had come in a couple of days ago. They'd been trying to locate a family."

Helen's heart lurched. She clutched Kate's hand. "J.B.?"

Kate nodded.

"Is he. . . ?"

"He's okay. I just talked to the doctor." Kate looked away. "Mother . . . he . . . he had a heart attack—a mild one. He must have fallen from the flybridge and hit his head. His jaw's broken too. He's been out of it since he came in. A fisherman picked him up Thursday afternoon when he saw the *Hallie B* drifting not far from where he was fishing.

"Anyway, this fisherman found him lying on the deck and managed to get him transferred to his boat. Figured the quickest route to get help for J.B. was to head downriver to the port of Chinook and have an ambulance meet him there and take him into Ilwaco. Mom, he's been here the whole time. One of the nurses said the man's decision probably saved J.B.'s life."

"Are you sure it's J.B.?"

"I'm sure. I just came from his room. He was admitted under the name of J. Woods."

Tears stung Helen's eyes. She tossed her covers aside. "I've got to go see him."

Kate helped her into a robe. Since Helen was still weak and unsteady, the nurse brought in a wheelchair.

Helen thought she'd break into a million pieces if anyone so much as touched her. She couldn't remember feeling so torn up inside since the authorities had come to tell her about Ian.

J.B. had had a heart attack. It was unthinkable. But he was here. She uttered a dozen thank-yous to God on her way down the hall to the Intensive Care Unit. Kate opened the door to the room, then stopped. "I'd better see if it's okay for us to visit him."

Nothing could have prepared Helen for the sight of J.B. lying there. She'd always thought of her husband as invincible. Even over the last few days of not knowing, she hadn't allowed herself to imagine anything like this. Kate came back with a nurse, who stepped in front of Helen, blocking her view. "Oh, Mrs. Bradley. I'm so glad you're here."

"May I go in?"

"Of course, but I'd like to speak with you first."

The nurse closed the door and wheeled her a few feet down the hall. "I'm so sorry you had to find out like this. We tried to contact relatives, but we didn't have a phone number. There was no contact person in Mr. Woods' wallet—I mean Mr. Bradley. He's been agitated and in a great deal of pain. We've been sedating him. Today he's depressed. Won't talk to us. Won't even try to write us a note. We had no idea he was the missing FBI agent." She shrugged. "I'm so glad your daughter happened to be at the restaurant."

She could understand why they hadn't recognized him from the photo in the newspaper. The man in the hospital bed bore little resemblance to her J.B. "He had a heart attack?" Helen still couldn't believe it. J.B. had always been so healthy.

"Yes. A mild one, which fortunately occurred on the front of the heart and resolved itself. His EKG alerted the doctors to a possible problem and they ran cardiac enzymes. The enzymes were slightly elevated when he came in, but they're back to normal now. Still, he's a very lucky man. If that mysterious fisherman hadn't come along—"

"What do you mean, mysterious?" Helen interrupted.

"He popped back into his boat and disappeared right after he turned Mr. Bradley over to the EMTs. We have no idea who he is or where he came from." The nurse smiled. "Personally, I think he was an angel."

"An angel." Helen took a deep breath. She really didn't care whether the fisherman was an angel or a mere mortal at the moment. Nothing mattered except the fact that God had answered her prayers. "May I go in now?" Helen bit her lip. "On second thought—maybe I shouldn't. I've had the flu."

"We'll get you a mask. I have a feeling seeing you will do far more for him than anything we could do."

If she could rely on the monitor above his bed, J.B.'s heart shifted to a higher rhythm when he saw her, but it soon settled into a steady, normal pace. "Mmm." He lifted his head and tried to speak, then sank back in frustration.

"He underwent surgery Friday afternoon. His jaw's been wired shut," the nurse explained. "He's still in a great deal of pain and has some swelling. This is the most alert he's been since surgery yesterday. We should have a pen and note pad in his bedside stand. Also, you'll find wire cutters by his bed. Those will go home with him when he's discharged. If he should happen to choke, the wires can be cut."

His blue Irish eyes no longer smiled. As always, though, they spoke volumes. Gazing into them, Helen read relief and love and frustration and fear. Helen brushed the dark hair from his forehead, wishing more than anything she could take the mask from her face and kiss him senseless.

The nurse opened the bedside stand and pulled out pen and paper. "I'm not sure he'll use it, but we can try."

Helen placed the pen in J.B.'s hand and held the pad at an angle.

Love you, he wrote, then dropped the pen and shifted his gaze to her.

"I love you too." She squeezed his hand and brought it to her lips. "It's going to be all right, darling. I know that now. God led me to you. Though why He felt I had to get sick to do it, I'll never know."

At J.B.'s questioning gaze, she added, "I got the flu. But if I hadn't we might not have found you for days."

His eyes held compassion for her.

"I'm fine," she assured him. "Enough about me. We need to concentrate on getting you well and out of here."

He smiled—or tried to—then closed his eyes. Helen held tight to his hand and rested her head on the bed beside him. Now that she had found him, she had no intention of letting him out of her sight.

At Helen's request, Kate went back to the bed and breakfast to collect her essentials—the laptop and her notes, a few clothes, and her T-bird. Once she'd settled in, Helen suggested Kate go home to Portland. "It's time," she said. "I think they need you more than I do right now." Surprisingly Kate hadn't argued.

Over the next two days, Helen stayed in the hospital with J.B. She had him moved to a private room and had a recliner brought in for her. When she wasn't seeing to J.B.'s needs or talking with him, she worked on the guidebook and got out for some walks to gain back her strength. Though she hadn't forgotten about the investigation, she'd set it in the far corners of her mind. J.B. needed her, and at the moment nothing else mattered. Sometimes, though, when she least expected it—on a walk to the marina or just before sleep—she'd think about the murders and wonder who the killer was and if he—or she—would strike again.

Twenty-one

*Y*ou two don't have to fuss over me, J.B. wrote on his pad. *I'm not an invalid.*

Helen chuckled. "You're getting feisty. Must be feeling better."

I'd feel much better if I could get these wires out of my mouth.

"Be patient, darling." She kissed him on the forehead and sat on the arm of the chair where she could see the rest of his message more clearly. His words sent a flutter of warmth skittering through her.

"Me too. But the doctor says you need to wait awhile." Helen got up, walked over to the window, and stretched, ignoring the longing look in J.B.'s eyes and the desire in her own heart.

She watched a crane extend its long neck looking for food in the tidelands of Willapa Bay. It felt good to be out of the hospital and back at the Bayshore with Emily. She'd become like family in their short time together. She'd insisted on Helen and J.B. returning to the bed and breakfast, where they could both take care of him. The weekend had come and gone as had the six guests, so they had the place to themselves again.

"You need to finish the book," Emily had said. "And you'll need help with J.B." The scent of fresh savory stew and baking bread wafted out of the kitchen.

Helen turned back to J.B. "I'm going up to Oysterville tomorrow—and to Leadbetter Point State Park. Are you up to an outing?"

He shook his head and wrote, *Need to get hold of Tom. Want to see how investigation is going.*

Helen bit her lip. J.B. was off the case. Having had a heart attack, he was also out of a job—permanently. No way would the Feds take him back now. He knew that as well as she did. "Why? You've already typed up your final report." Which hadn't amounted to much. His talk with Scott Mandrel had been set up to feel Scott out. J.B. didn't think Scott was involved in any criminal activity. Dan and Adam disagreed, holding firm to the idea that if Mandrel was innocent, he wouldn't have run. Helen could understand why J.B. felt betrayed. The powers that be no longer wanted him or his opinions.

J.B. slapped the pad down on the floor.

"Being angry isn't going to help." Helen picked up the pad and set it on the coffee table.

Folding his arms, J.B. sank back into the chair. The agency had let him know before he even left the hospital that he'd been retired. Mandatory.

"Come with me tomorrow. We'll have a picnic on the beach, and if you're up to it we can walk."

J.B. closed his eyes. He'd lost weight, she noticed. Still handsome as ever but depressed. She wished there was something she could do to cheer him up.

"The guidebook is nearly done." She told him about the reservations they had at the lightkeeper's house at North Head. "We'll have a wonderful time there."

J.B. gave her a skeptical look.

"Dan's coming for dinner," Emily announced from the kitchen doorway. "We'd best set the dining-room table."

"I'll do that." Thankful for the interruption, Helen left J.B. pouting and took the china and silver from the rosewood hutch. Even though J.B. would be drinking his meal, Helen set a place for him.

A few minutes later they sat down to a dinner of stew, salad, and fresh bread. Dan told them that the autopsy of Chuck Frazier's body and examination of the boat indicated an explosive device had indeed been used and that it had probably been placed near the fuel tank. Chuck had been killed almost instantly from the severe heat and force of the bomb. "It pretty well fits with what Steve Kendall told us."

"Did you determine whether Steve actually killed himself?" Helen tore a thick slice of bread in half and reached for the butter.

Dan nodded and slurped in a spoonful of the hot broth. "He was despondent. Probably figured he didn't have much to live for."

The subject turned to less gruesome matters when Emily brought up the matter of the fishermen who hadn't gone to work for Scott after he bought them out. "They seemed like a couple of ne'er-do-wells."

"Who're you talking about, Auntie?"

"Jake Summers and Eddie Randolph."

Dan snorted. "You're too kind. Those two dopeheads need directions to tie their shoelaces. If you think they're involved in any of this, you're way off base." Dan went on to tell them he'd run up against a brick wall trying to find out where the kids who started the dunes fire got their drugs for their party they'd had. No one was talking.

Halfway through dinner Dan got a call. "No kidding." He hesitated. "You're sure they're headed this way?" He glanced at his watch. "They should be here in about two hours. What do you say we surprise them with a little coming-home party?"

"You seem pretty pleased with yourself," Emily said when he hung up.

"That was an agent in Portland." His gaze slid to J.B., then back to his stew. "We got Mandrel. He landed at the Portland airport about an hour ago. I asked the Feds to keep an eye on him. Wanted to see where he'd go."

"And Shells?" Helen asked.

"She's with him."

"I'm certainly relieved to hear that," Helen said. "Tell me something, Dan. If Scott is a killer, as you seem to think—and if he ran to avoid prosecution—why is he coming back?"

He shrugged. "Maybe Shells talked him into turning himself in."

"Do you know where they've been all this time?"

"Not yet." He pushed his chair back. "But I aim to find out. Hate to eat and run, Auntie, but I gotta go."

✤　✤　✤

News spread fast, and by midmorning the following day, most of the Peninsula knew about Scott Mandrel's arrest. The mystery over his and Shells' disappearance had been solved as well. They had eloped to Las Vegas to be married. At J.B.'s insistence, he and Helen drove to Ilwaco to find out firsthand what had happened.

Not certain where to find Shells, they went to the restaurant.

"Yeah. She's here. Only Shells could work with her fiancé— excuse me—her *husband* just getting arrested. She's one tough lady." Gracie seated them at the only available window seat and poured coffee. "I'm sure she'd like to talk to you, but it may be a while before she can come out. Rusty's off today."

"He'll need a straw." Helen pointed at J.B.'s coffee. "He broke his jaw in a fall."

Gracie smiled. "Sure, no problem. I heard you'd been found, Mr. Bradley. And right here under our noses. Dan's never going to live that down."

"We all missed it. It took my getting sick to get us to the right place. But he's safe." Helen's gaze lingered on J.B.'s, letting him know how thankful she was. Gracie left to seat another couple coming in, and Helen perused the menu.

They'd been seated less than three minutes when Shells joined them. "Mrs. Bradley." Shells nearly embraced her. "I'm so glad you're here. You must talk to Adam and Dan. Scott is innocent."

"I'm not sure there's anything we can do at this point." Helen paused to introduce J.B. "I have to admit, when I learned that you and Scott had left town and J.B. was missing, I thought for certain Scott and maybe even you were guilty."

"Do you really think I'd kill my own brother? Or marry the

man who did? As I told you before, the real killer—or killers—set him up. Please don't give up on us." Shells' plea extended to J.B. as well. "If I knew what to do or what to look for I'd . . ." Her shoulders rose and fell in an exaggerated sigh. "If I didn't know better, I'd say Adam and Dan are behind all this."

Helen glanced at J.B. He wrote on his pad and handed it to her. *Something to consider. They seemed too eager to put Scott away.*

"Not Adam." Helen shook her head. "I know I've wondered myself, but I just can't see him as a criminal."

People can change, J.B. wrote.

That was true enough, and it had been years since she'd seen him.

"Shells, you said if you didn't know better. What did you mean?"

"Only that Dan wouldn't work with Adam on anything unless he had to. Adam's an outsider. Besides, they hate each other because of me. They both like me and . . . now they hate Scott." She glanced nervously toward the kitchen. "I really need to get back. Please say you'll help us."

"Shells, tell me something," Helen said. "Why did you and Scott run away to get married and why right after the funeral?"

Shells sighed heavily. "That was my idea. I felt so incredibly sad. It was probably not the smartest thing to do, but I needed to do something. I suppose it sounds terribly childish of me. I don't do funerals very well, Mrs. Bradley. There have been so many and . . ."

Helen placed her hand over Shells' trembling one. "It's okay, no need to explain." Shells was impetuous and very young. Running away from grief was something she'd done herself.

J.B. scribbled a message and showed it to Shells. She thanked them and headed for the kitchen.

"What did you tell her?"

J.B. passed the note to Helen. It read, *We'll look into it.*

"We? J.B., you're not in any condition to . . ." Glancing at his note pad, Helen paused.

I can still think.

This was the most animated she'd seen J.B. since the heart

attack. Maybe he needed the challenge of at least puzzling through this crime. "What do you have in mind?"

J.B. grinned. *Let me have a look at your notes.*

"Good idea. Maybe you'll see something I didn't." Helen had written down all she could remember from Isabelle's missing files. She'd read and reread them but couldn't find anything that might have led to her death.

After a leisurely lunch and a short walk on the boardwalk in Long Beach, Helen and J.B. headed back to the bed and breakfast. The outing had exhausted J.B., who opted for a nap. He suggested Helen go to Oysterville and Leadbetter Point without him. He'd rest, then look over her notes.

Helen readily accepted. She had a lot to accomplish, and although she'd have been happy to bring J.B., she also relished her time away. Equipped with snacks and field glasses for bird watching, she set out to finish her research. Helen had explored most of the Peninsula by now and stopped at several places on her way to Oysterville to make certain she had her facts straight. At Nahcotta she visited the Tidelands Interpretive Center at the Washington State Shellfish Laboratory. She and Emily had gone out into the bay one day to dig littlenecks—the nickname for the small clams that restaurants often referred to as steamers. They were delicious steamed in a broth with lime and garlic until they opened, then dipped in butter.

After verifying the rules on limits, she popped into her T-bird again and at Nahcotta turned onto the road leading to the Ark—a five-star restaurant—another interpretive center, and two processing plants dealing primarily with oysters. Helen drove to the end of the dock, parked, and went into the retail store for some smoked salmon.

"Hey, Mrs. Bradley." Bill Carlson sauntered in from the back room, wiping his hands. "How's it going? Heard about your husband. He okay?"

"He's doing better. Thanks. What are you doing over here in the bay?"

Bill shrugged. "We're harvesting oysters today. Won't be long before we'll be out crabbing. Like I told you before—we do a little bit of everything."

Including drug trafficking? Helen wondered but didn't ask. Next thing she knew, she'd be suspecting Emily again. "You two do get around."

"Yep." He gave her a wide grin. "Right now we gotta pick up some littlenecks for Shells. Then we'll head on back to Ilwaco."

"Sounds like you enjoy your work."

"Most of the time. Like everything else there's parts that ain't so good." His grin faded and he lifted his shoulders in a resigned shrug.

"I'm curious, Bill. Isn't the *Klipspringer* rather large for the shallow waters here in the bay? I thought oysters were harvested with a barge."

He smiled. "You're right about that. Got the *Klipspringer* docked up in Bay Center. Made arrangements with a friend up there to use his pleasure craft to run down here for oystering and littlenecking." He rubbed his jaw. "You still working on that guidebook?"

"Almost done with my first draft. I'm researching today."

He nodded. "S'pose you'll be leaving soon, then."

"Hmm. Going home on Sunday. But not before I stay at the lightkeeper's house at North Head. Couldn't resist that. And I'm sure we'll be back. The Peninsula is a wonderful place."

"Be better once we get rid of the druggies. Speaking of which . . . looks like we were wrong about Scott Mandrel. Sure feel bad for Shells."

"Yes, well, there are still a lot of questions."

"Think so?" He leaned against the wall and folded his arms.

Helen swung her bag around to the opposite shoulder. "Shells seems to think he's being framed. She may be right."

"Depends on who you talk to, I guess. Dan and that coastie fellow seem to think there's no question."

"Yes, well, time will tell. I'd better be going." Helen was half-way to her car when she realized she'd forgotten to purchase her fish. She did an about-face and walked back inside. Bill was gone. A man in a stained apron placed a tray of oysters into the deli case.

"Fresh in today," he said. "Can I wrap some up for you?"

"No, but I'll take some smoked salmon. Don't plan on going back to the Bayshore for a while."

"I can wrap them in ice."

Helen shook her head. "Some other time."

Back at her car, Helen leaned against the hood and nibbled on bites of smoked Chinook salmon while watching the activity on the bay. What a wonderful place this was, teeming with fish and wildlife. "When the tide is out, the table is set." Helen couldn't remember who had said that, but it certainly rang true here.

Helen finished her snack, then meandered up the Peninsula, enjoying the distinguished old homes in Oysterville. Many had been refurbished, and most were dated, bringing tourists back in time for a look at what life might have been like in the late 1800s. From Oysterville she headed west, then north on Stackpole Road five miles to Leadbetter Point State Park and Wildlife Sanctuary. While walking north along the shore of Willapa Bay, Helen used her field glasses to closely examine a deer and two fawns. Farther north, she spotted the *Klipspringer*, no doubt headed back to Ilwaco. Not long after, she noted Mike Trenton's *Merry Maid* following some distance behind the Carlson brothers.

They certainly were a diverse lot. She admired that. While some people collapsed with the diminished fishing, others like Mike Trenton and the Carlson brothers dug in their heels and looked for other ways to support themselves. Admirable—so long as what they were doing was legal.

Helen shrugged and turned her thoughts back to the guidebook. This northernmost end of the Long Beach Peninsula would be the final chapter in the book. She could hardly believe she'd done it. And on schedule. Amazing with all the goings on. She felt like celebrating and wondered if Emily and J.B. wanted to as well.

Arriving back at the bed and breakfast, Emily had dinner

waiting. There would be no celebrating unless they did something later. "It's Wednesday, remember. You promised to speak at the writers' group tonight."

"Oh right. Well, tomorrow night, then." Helen didn't want to cancel on the writers' group, since this would be her last opportunity before heading home.

At the meeting Helen shared her writing experiences. How the tragedy of her first husband's death had plunged her into despair and how writing had brought her back. She talked about marketing and finding stories and ideas in everyday life. "In fact," she said, "Isabelle is an excellent example. She was writing a guidebook about the place she'd grown up in and loved. And from what I could tell from her files, she intended to use her research to write more extensively on some topics. She had an article started about salmon fishing and how it's changed over the years. She had another started about how the drug culture's far-reaching effects had infiltrated the Peninsula. And one about pollution. For a while I thought she might be writing about the gunky stuff you sometimes have on the beaches up here."

Several members of the group laughed.

"Newcomers are always thrown by that," an older gentleman said. "Looks a lot like oil or sewage—smells too. But it's actually little organisms the clams feed on."

"So I heard. At any rate, she had the right idea. While researching for one project, bear in mind that it may lead to many other projects as well. Emily, you might want to take over some of Isabelle's ideas."

"Maybe." Emily glanced around the room. "Not sure it's a good idea to resurrect them, though—seeing as one of those things she was writing about might have gotten her killed."

Helen was suddenly in a hurry to get back to the bed and breakfast. She wanted to talk to J.B. about her own notes and to think more thoroughly about Isabelle's article topics. Now that she'd learned more about the Peninsula, those earlier notes might take on new meaning.

She'd left J.B. with a pot of coffee, a printout of her guidebook, and her files. Helen and Emily returned to find papers strewn all over the living-room floor. And no sign of J.B.

Twenty-two

"Good grief!" Emily groaned. "Not again."

"Stay here." Helen ordered. "Call 9-1-1. I'll see if I can find J.B." Just inside the door and to the right Helen spotted three drops of blood on the hardwood floor. And two more just beyond that. The trail of blood led to the kitchen. Helen started to follow, then stopped when she heard a clinking sound.

"Be careful," Emily whispered, lifting a carved walking stick from the umbrella stand beside the door. "Take this—just in case."

Armed with the stick and a prayer, Helen crept forward. She reached the kitchen and heaved a sigh of relief. "Thank goodness. I was afraid . . . what happened?" Helen dropped the stick and ran toward her husband.

He held her with one arm. With the other he held an ice pack to his head. Releasing her, he picked up a pen from the table and wrote, *Doorbell rang. No one there. Went out to look around. Hit from behind.*

"Oh, J.B. Let me see. Are you still bleeding?"

He shook his head. *Just a big lump. I should have seen it coming. Oldest trick in the book.* J.B. looked thoroughly disgusted with himself.

"Did you see who it was?"

Too dark. By the time I came to and got back inside they were gone.

"What about a car?"

No car. At least they didn't pull in.

"Are you sure you're not bleeding?" Helen looked his head over. "There are several drops of blood on the floor."

J.B. pushed the paper and pen aside and spoke quite clearly for one who couldn't open his mouth. "Not mine."

"Then it must belong to whoever attacked you."

There's one way to find out, J.B. wrote.

The sheriff would be along soon. They'd finally have some evidence they could use. Blood—DNA. The long list of suspects could be narrowed down. But what if Dan took the samples and switched them or messed them up? What if he didn't have sophisticated enough equipment and labs? What if Dan was somehow involved?

Helen pulled a plastic sandwich bag from the drawer. Going back to the dining room, she captured one of the blood smears inside the bag and slipped it into her pocket. Tomorrow she'd send it to the FBI office in Portland and have it analyzed.

While waiting for Dan, they took inventory. The only missing items were her manuscript and laptop.

Mischief. A random act. Vandalism. Dan used all three terms to describe the break-in. "You can't go connecting everything that happens down here with Chuck and Isabelle and that stupid guidebook."

"Dan Merritt," Emily scolded. "What a thing to say. You just don't want to admit you're wrong about Scott. With him in jail he couldn't have done this. Which means the killer is still out there."

"I am not wrong about Scott. I got a signed a confession from Kendall that says he killed Chuck Frazier and that Scott paid him to do it. I'm sorry the place got broken into again." He turned to Helen. "And it's too bad about the manuscript. I suspect you have a backup."

"I do. In my bag. Luckily I had the disk with me."

"Good." Dan made a few notes, then he and another deputy gathered evidence and left.

❖   ❖   ❖

"I don't understand it," Helen mused an hour later. A warm

fire crackled in the fireplace. J.B. sat beside her on the sofa, eyes closed, a limp bag of melted ice by his side. Emily had gone up to bed. "There was nothing incriminating in that guidebook. Why steal it?"

J.B.'s eyes drifted open, but he made no attempt to answer her.

"It makes no sense. The only thing stealing my manuscript would do is delay things a little." Helen shifted, leaning her head on her husband's shoulder. "You're tired, and here I am keeping you up with my questions."

J.B. squeezed her hand, then leaned over and brushed his lips against hers. She rose when he did. They embraced and held each other for a long while. She wondered what was going through his mind. How he must be feeling. He had lost so much recently. Would he be able to work through it? J.B. was the first to move away. He glanced at the stairs and back at her as if to say, *Are you coming?*

"You go ahead. I want to clean up our dishes. I'll be up in a few minutes."

He nodded and shuffled to the stairs, looking older and more frail than his fifty-nine years. Helen's heart constricted. She would need to be as strong and encouraging for him as he had often been for her. Strength was something she had little of at the moment.

Hardly daring to think about what lay ahead for them, Helen moved to the rocker and stared into the fire, her mind a jumble of disconnected thoughts. No wonder nothing made sense. She was too scattered, moving in too many directions at once. Caring for J.B. Working on the guidebook. And this odd puzzle of events that wouldn't go away. Though she felt compelled to focus on J.B. and her writing, Helen couldn't let the mystery surrounding the book and the original author go. The more she tried not to think about it, the more it festered and demanded attention.

Suppose the purpose in stealing the manuscript had been to slow her down. Perhaps whoever had done it didn't realize she could run off another copy in a matter of minutes. Or if it came to it, she could simply e-mail the book to her publisher. That could mean they were dealing with a non-computer person. Mike Trenton and the Carlson brothers came to mind. But that was unfair. Just because they made their livelihood fishing didn't mean they hadn't kept up with the latest technology. Still, it was something to keep in mind.

Her gaze shifted to the pile of papers on the table. When Dan left, she and Emily had picked them up. They still lay in a random pile, as disordered as she felt.

Helen had planned to go through them again before making her final revision on the guidebook to make certain she'd incorporated everything—and to look for further clues. "Now's as good a time as any," she murmured. Scooping up the pile, she pulled out the file folders and put them in alphabetical order on the floor in front of her. Each paper, notation, photo, and pamphlet she placed in separate piles on the floor. She couldn't tell right off if anything was missing. It hit her then, perhaps because she'd mentioned it at the writer's meeting. The first break-in—it hadn't been only the information on the guidebook that had been stolen, but Isabelle's articles as well. The first night she'd been there Helen had given them only a cursory glance. She remembered seeing the rough drafts, but she hadn't read them and had no idea what they contained. Could there have been incriminating evidence? Drugs, pollution, fishing. What hadn't the thief wanted her to see?

Ginger pounced on top of the papers, threatening to undo all her hard work.

"Oh no, you don't." Helen unfolded herself from the cramped position she'd been in and scooped the cat into her arms. "You'll have to find something else to play with."

She set Ginger on the floor and rubbed at the sore spots in her knees and lower back. Picking up the files and a fresh legal pad and pen, she went into the kitchen. Ginger followed her in, sat by her empty dish, and meowed.

"Did Emily forget to feed you?" Helen put a cup of water in the microwave, then opened the pantry. After locating the cat food and pouring a scoop in the dish, Helen refilled the water dish. It was then she noticed a brown stain on the counter and another in the sink. Blood?

The intruder had apparently been injured outside or just as he came in. The drops of blood trailed into the kitchen. That meant the thief knew his way around. Had he washed his cut and bandaged it? If so, why not go to the bathroom? Why the kitchen? Because that was where Emily kept her first aid supplies. Using her pencil, she opened the cupboard. The first aid kit was there with the latch undone, hastily put away, no doubt. Emily would have fastened it.

There would be prints, but again, she didn't trust Dan to take them. They could very well be his. He knew the house well. Helen wondered how many of the others did also. Following her suspicions, she opened the cupboard under the sink and pulled out the trash. There, lying right on top, was a wrap from a wide Band-Aid with a smeared bloody print. The find excited her. She'd send it along with the blood sample. Though the one visible print was smudged, there might be at least one good one.

The beeper on the microwave went off. Helen picked out an apple cinnamon spice tea and dunked it in the hot water. Hearing footfalls on the stairs, Helen retrieved another cup, filled it, and set it in the microwave.

"I thought that might be you." She glanced up as J.B. filled the doorway. "Hope my putzing around down here didn't wake you."

He mumbled something and gave her a look she read as *I thought you were coming to bed.*

"I knew I wouldn't be able to sleep, so I decided to arrange my files and . . ." she shrugged. "Now I'm wide awake. Want some tea?"

He nodded, then sat down at the table and wrote, *Find anything?*

"Not in the papers." She told him about he fingerprint she'd found.

Looks like our burglar is not too smart.

"Or in a hurry. You did interrupt him." Helen brought her husband his tea and sat across from him. "I'm glad you came back down. I've been thinking about Isabelle's missing files and trying to remember what was in them. My guess is that whoever has been breaking in has been doing so with the express purpose of making certain I haven't found what Isabelle found. Which makes no sense at all. If there was a question, why not just kill me? They've killed two—maybe three—people already. What's one more?" She rubbed the back of her head, remembering the incident on the bunker. "Of course, it's not as if they didn't try. Someone went through my papers then too."

J.B. frowned and wagged his head from side to side. If he'd spoken, Helen suspected he'd have said something like, *I'll not be hearing any more of that foolish talk.*

"I know. But it seems strange they'd be developing a conscience now." She sighed and, placing her elbow on the table, rested her chin on her fist. "The more I look, the more questions I find."

What sort of questions? his cocked eyebrow implied.

"Like—why had Isabelle put a star in front of Adam's name? Had she been listing suspects and marked those she thought responsible for whatever crime she'd uncovered? I can't imagine Adam being involved in any wrongdoing, but he has changed. Don't you think?"

We all change, he wrote.

"True, but as you pointed out, Adam seems more sullen and disgruntled with life. Bitter. Perhaps his disappointments—his mother dying, losing Shells to Scott—have taken their toll? Still," she went on, "Adam seems more resilient than that."

She paused for a moment, then added, "Then there's Dan. He and Adam are both obsessed about placing the blame on Scott. It doesn't seem possible that both of them would want Scott put away simply because Shells had chosen him over either of them."

More likely they've lost their objectivity, J.B. noted on his pad. *It's easy to do in light of the evidence.*

"I suppose that's true." Isabelle had listed a number of names. Mike Trenton and Hank and Bill Carlson. They were three of many fishermen who hadn't sold out to Scott. Why had

Isabelle mentioned only them? Helen continued bouncing ideas off J.B. until they finished their tea. By then she was more than ready to sleep.

⁜   ⁜   ⁜

The next morning Helen express-mailed the blood sample and Band-Aid wrapper to Tom, then called him to let him know they were on the way.

"I thought that case was closed," Tom said. "That's what Jorgenson told me."

"Yes, well, someone hit J.B. over the head last night and stole my laptop and my manuscript. Mandrel is in jail. The sheriff doesn't think it's connected, but I'm certain it was. That means Mandrel is either innocent or has someone working with him. I need someone from the outside to look at the evidence."

"We'll check them out. But you know if the prints aren't on file . . ."

"Right, but let's not worry about that just yet."

"How's J.B.?" Tom asked.

"Coming along. He's not taking the prospect of retiring well."

"I can imagine. I was afraid something like this might happen."

"What do you mean?"

"I got some of his test results back today. Report shows he has a mild arrhythmia along with high cholesterol and high blood pressure."

Helen rubbed her forehead and leaned against the wall of the phone booth. "Do you think he knew?"

"Maybe. Knowing J.B., he probably figured he could manage it on his own."

"I can't believe he didn't tell me."

"Don't be riding him too hard, Helen. It would be tough for a man like J.B. to admit his health was failing. I have a feeling that's why he didn't want to retire. Maybe needed to prove he still had it."

"That is so stupid."

"True, but I can't fault him. I'd probably do the same myself."

As angry as Helen felt, she thought it best not to confront J.B. just now. He seemed in a much better frame of mind this morning, and she didn't want to hang clouds on a perfectly clear day. J.B. insisted he was feeling much better and wanted to go down to the docks and check on the *Hallie B.* Helen didn't argue, thinking the fresh air would do him good. Besides, how could she argue with a note that said, *I'm needing some time alone.*

After dropping J.B. off at the docks and settling him on the boat, Helen returned to the bed and breakfast, where she used Emily's desktop computer to put in the finishing touches on the guidebook. She printed it out and sent the manuscript, along with a copy of the disk, to her editor. Handing it over to the postal clerk, she heaved a monumental sigh of relief. It wasn't a final draft, and she'd be revising it at least once, but at least she'd gotten through it.

From the post office in Long Beach, she went to Pastimes, picked up two skim milk lattes, and drove to Ilwaco to rendezvous with J.B.

Checking up on me?

Helen's gaze moved from the paper to his eyes, wanting to see if he was amused or annoyed. A smile tugged at his lips, and his blue eyes had that teasing twinkle she'd grown to adore. "Yes, but I missed you too. Brought you an almond latte. Low fat."

They took their drinks to the bridge and sat on the sun deck. The soothing moments brought back memories of their wedding day in the south of France—and of their honeymoon cruise in the Caribbean. She watched J.B. as he wrote a long message on his pad. Why hadn't she seen the warning signs? Had there been any? High blood pressure was often called the silent killer. He'd been more anxious of late, and tired more easily. She'd attributed that to his frustration over retiring. Had it been more?

But no, this thinking was getting her nowhere. Next thing she knew she'd be blaming herself. Best to concentrate on the here and now—on making the necessary changes in their diet and their lifestyle. J.B. had never been as health conscious as she—now would be the time to change that.

The day had been uncharacteristically warm. The sunshine and activity had given J.B. a healthy glow. Definitely an improvement.

He handed her the writing pad. *I've been fooling myself. I thought I could outwit time. Now I see that time will always win.* J.B. basically repeated what Tom had told her, then apologized for not telling her. *I didn't want you and the children fussing over me, telling me what I should do and what I should or shouldn't eat. It was foolish of me to take the boat. I'd been having mild chest pains all day. Would have served me right if I'd had a massive coronary and died.*

Helen swallowed past the lump in her throat. He'd been working on this letter to her for a lot longer than the few minutes she'd been on board. Maybe this was why he'd felt the need to get away. She read on.

I've been doing some serious thinking the last few days. Once I got over being angry with God for letting this happen to me, I realized that I should be thanking Him instead. He's given me a second chance. More time to be with you and to be a grandfather to those lovely grandchildren of ours. At first retirement seemed a nasty word. Now I'll be looking at it as a blessing. At least I'll try. I just hope you won't mind putting up with an old fool for the rest of my days.

Helen brushed the tears aside and let the pad drop to the floor. Words were difficult to come by. His honesty, even if it was late in coming, intensified her love for him. Leaving their chairs, they met halfway and embraced as they had done so many times before. "You're not an old fool," she murmured into his neck. "You're wonderful and sensitive and . . ." She leaned back so she could look him full in the eyes. "No matter what happens—to either of us—we'll work it through together."

He kissed her as deeply and thoroughly as he could with a mouth full of wires, then released her and picked up the pad she'd dropped. He scribbled a message and held it up against his chest. *Now that we've cleared all that up, perhaps you could get lost for a bit longer. I've decided to go back to write my life story and could do with some quiet time.*

Helen gave him a light blow to the shoulder and laughed.

"Just remember that next time *I'm* writing." She reached up and kissed his cheek. "What about dinner? Shall I come get you?"

He shook his head and wrote, *I've plenty of food on board. Think I'll stay the night. Why don't you pick me up tomorrow?*

"Tomorrow? You're really serious about this, aren't you?"

He raised an eyebrow as if to say, *Of course.*

Helen left the *Hallie B* with a spring in her step. J.B. was going to be just fine. She walked past the slips where the *Merry Maid* and the *Klipspringer* were usually docked. A perfect day for fishing. She mentally sent up good wishes for a good catch. Halfway up the dock a shiver ran through her. She paused and glanced around. Though she saw no one, Helen sensed someone was watching her. The premonition followed her to her car, and the uneasy feeling left its residue in her mind like the smelly, grimy algae she'd seen on the sand.

Twenty-three

I'm taking you to dinner tonight," Emily called from the front porch. "And I won't take no for an answer. You'll only be staying here one more night, and besides, I think we should celebrate your getting the guidebook written."

"Sounds great." Helen could think of no good reason to resist. J.B. already had plans, and she did feel like celebrating.

Since it was nearly five, Helen quickly showered and dressed in fresh jeans, a bright pink T-shirt with a tropical fish motif, a matching vest, and her lightweight black jacket. They ended up at Shells' Place. Helen grew suspicious when she and Emily were led away from the main dining area into a back room. A whoop of surprise greeted her. The entire writer's group along with Earl Wilson, Mike Trenton, the Carlson brothers, Adam, Dan, and just about everyone else she'd met during her stay on the Peninsula had showed up. She was surprised to see Earl and made a note to talk to him later.

"I can't believe you guys did this. I don't know what to say."

"You don't have to say anything." Emily nudged her forward. "Just think of it as a celebration for you and Isabelle and the guidebook."

Shells provided them each with a glass of sparkling apple cider, with which they toasted Helen and Isabelle. Helen thought briefly of sending Adam over to the *Hallie B* to invite J.B. but decided against it. He'd seemed intent on writing. Besides, she'd planned a cozy dinner for two the next evening at the Ark in Nahcotta. Better to let him rest.

Dinner consisted of tender chicken breasts topped with cherry sauce—one of Shells' specialties. On the side she'd served cranberry muffins, brown rice with mushrooms, and assorted sautéed vegetables. A scrumptious meal. The dessert was even better—a decadent fudge torte with coffee and tea. The conversations with her table mates, Emily on one side, Joanna Black on the other, related mostly to writing.

"I know you've been busy," Joanna whispered at one point, "but have you given any more thought to who might have killed poor Isabelle? I'd swear on a stack of Bibles it wasn't Scott Mandrel. I still think Dan should go after Mike. He's the most obvious suspect. Remember what I told you about him killing Harry."

"Give it a rest, Jo." Her husband nudged her. "This isn't the time or the place. Besides, the evidence all points to Scott. All we can do is hope his lawyer can get him off."

Before Helen could comment, one of the writers sitting opposite her asked, "What are your plans now that you've finished the guidebook?"

"My husband and I will spend the weekend at North Head, then drive back down the coast to Bay Village. I'm due for a vacation—maybe another cruise. After these last two weeks, J.B. and I could both use some down time. Then I suppose I'll go back to writing travel articles."

"Well, you deserve a rest." Emily pushed her chair back and addressed the group. "Excuse me, everyone, but I have a few words to say, and now's as good a time as any."

Emily waited for the group to settle down, then called Shells in from the kitchen to thank her for the meal. Shells bowed to the applause, then snagged a chair and sat near the door, where she could watch the restaurant and still be part of the gathering.

"As you all know, when I first heard Isabelle's publisher was sending a writer to finish the guidebook, I had my doubts. I truly feared the next one to take over the book was jinxed and that Helen would meet the same kind of fate Isabelle did."

"She almost did," Joanna said. "Let's not forget that incident up at McKenzie Head."

"True enough, but I'm thinking now that Dan may have been right. Maybe it was a vagrant after all. At any rate, the good Lord has laid my fears to rest. As you can see, Helen is alive and kicking."

Emily paused while several of the partyers whistled and applauded, then went on. "I wasn't sure I wanted Isabelle's book finished—especially by an outsider. But the more I got to know Helen, the more I realized that the publisher couldn't have chosen a better person for the job. I'm certain now it's what Isabelle would have wanted. I know I feel better knowing it will soon be in print."

The group agreed and urged Helen to speak. She finally acquiesced, thanking everyone and saying how much she'd enjoyed the project. "Most of all, though, I'm pleased to have made so many new friends. Now that I know how many wonderful things there are to do here, I plan to come back often. And Shells, you can be sure I'll send a lot of people your way. I may even write an article for *Tour and Travel* on the many fine eating establishments here. Yours will top the list."

"Thank you. That's so kind. I only wish you didn't have to go so soon." Shells blinked back tears. Her big brown eyes were filled with so much hurt, Helen wanted to bundle the girl up and take her home. She looked away, wishing she could have done more.

When Helen finished speaking and received the congratulatory cards and well-wishes from those attending, the Blacks, Libby, Mike Trenton, Hank and Bill, and several others said their good-byes and left. She tucked the cards and gifts into her backpack and walked into the main part of the restaurant.

Earl came up behind her. "I heard you say you'd be leaving the Peninsula soon. Wanted to tell you good-bye and wish you good luck on your book."

"Thanks . . . um . . . I have to admit I was surprised to see you here. You didn't come all the way down here for the party, did you?"

"No—not to say that I wouldn't have." Earl winked at her. "But no. I had to come down to finish my inspection and file a report. Hope to head home for the weekend."

Bill was still standing at the cash register talking to Shells. When Helen approached he tossed her a companionable grin. "It's been nice getting to know you, Mrs. Bradley. Too bad you can't stick around and help us find out who's really bringing those drugs in down here."

Shells sighed. "I'm sorry to see you go too. But I guess I already said that. Maybe if you have time over the weekend you and your husband can come for lunch or dinner. I'd like to talk to you again before you leave for good. There has to be something we can do to free Scott."

Dan came up beside them. "I'm sure Helen has better things to do than to help you play detective, Shells. Sooner or later, you'll realize it's a lost cause. Besides, I think we've got the situation pretty well in hand." He straightened and tugged at his belt. As he did, his chest lifted and broadened like a strutting pigeon. "We closed down a meth lab up at Klipsan Beach today—biggest one in the state. Drug use was up all right, but not from stuff coming in from the outside. Thousands of pounds of crank were being made here and shipped upriver to Longview-Kelso and the Portland-Vancouver area."

"Quite a bust." Adam joined them. "J.B.'s the one who figured it out."

"J.B.?" Helen frowned. No wonder he'd been in such good spirits. Why hadn't he told her? One thing for certain, he had some explaining to do.

"He was out on his boat this morning," Adam continued. "Saw some kids hauling coolers down to a couple of cabin cruisers. Nothing out of the ordinary at first, but one of them got greedy. Thought no one was looking, so he opened his cooler and helped himself to a couple bags of something that looked suspiciously like crank."

"Don't tell me J.B. went after them."

Adam chuckled. "You know J.B. better than that. He knows his limitations. Besides, we were after bigger fish. J.B. radioed me and I got hold of Dan. We watched them and let them go about their business. They eventually led us to the houses they'd been using."

Dan clasped Adam's shoulder and grinned. "We expect to make more arrests when the boats make it to their destination upriver."

"That's wonderful." Helen switched the heavy pack from her sore right shoulder to her left. "I'm curious. How does Scott Mandrel figure into it?"

"He doesn't." Shells shoved the cash register drawer closed after giving Adam his change and leaned on the glass counter.

Dan ignored her. "Well, we're not certain yet. We still have Kendall's testimony that Scott was responsible for the bombing and Chuck's death. So far we haven't made a connection to him and the local drug dealings, but we're working on it. I have a feeling he set the whole thing up."

"Why can't you get it through your thick skull that Scott is innocent?" Shells ranted. "You have no real proof. All you've got is the say-so of a drug addict, and he's dead."

Earl, who'd been on the sidelines waiting to pay his bill, jumped to his brother-in-law's defense. "Steve may have had some problems, but he had no reason to lie. If he named Mandrel as the one who hired him to kill Frazier, then that's who did it."

"Right," Shells tossed back. "Someone paid him to frame Scott. Or maybe *he* was running the show—or *you*!"

"Oh, come on." Earl shook his head. "You're crazy—"

"Hey, people," Dan cut them off. "There's no point in arguing. We'll straighten it out eventually." He paused and said, "I sure don't know what you see in that guy, Shells. You deserve so much better."

"Someone like you?" Shells gave him an odd look—one Helen couldn't read. They'd probably been over that ground before.

She stepped back, not wanting to get into the middle of the ongoing debate. It would take weeks to straighten things out and get the testimonies needed to ascertain who had done what to whom and why—if they ever did. Knowing the complexity of some drug operations, she wondered if they would ever find the kingpin or the killer.

"Think they'll ever find out who killed Isabelle?" Emily asked when they'd reached their cars. Helen and Emily had driven separately, as Helen had planned to check in on J.B. and perhaps surprise him by staying the night on the *Hallie B*. That is if he wanted her to.

"I hope so. Isabelle may have stumbled onto the same group J.B. did. Only they stopped her before she could tell Dan."

"It's hard not knowing for sure. Leaves you hanging—like a story without an end."

Helen agreed. It did feel unfinished—as though there needed to be another chapter. "We'll just have to be patient, Emily. Perhaps once the perpetrators are questioned we'll have an answer."

Helen drove the short distance to the boat, wondering what J.B. was really up to. It occurred to her that the missing boat, the heart attack, and everything else may have been an elaborate setup and that J.B. was still working for the FBI. But, no. That was too farfetched even for the FBI. Yet J.B. had wanted the time alone. To do what? Had he accidentally observed the criminal activity, or had he been working undercover the entire time? The idea was ludicrous. J.B.'s jaw was definitely wired shut, certainly not a surgery he'd undergo if he didn't have to. Would he? Or was that fake as well? She shook her head. It was the one thing she hated about undercover work—the deceit. She supposed at times it was necessary—she had even indulged in some of it herself. Still . . . Helen caught her thoughts up short. It did little good to brood about the way Uncle Sam ran covert operations. And it looked like whatever the plan had been, it worked. She'd learn the truth eventually and hoped J.B. had plenty of ink in his pen.

Helen parked in the port parking lot and made her way down to the *Hallie B*.

The moon shone bright again, half what it had been when she'd first come to the Peninsula, but bright nonetheless. It hung over the bay with a brilliance that took her breath away. On her way to the *Hallie B* she passed the *Klipspringer* and the *Merry Maid*. In the stillness both vessels had an eerie quiet about them. Something seemed out of kilter, but she couldn't think what. The *Merry Maid* seemed larger than she remembered. Or did the *Klipspringer* seem smaller? No matter.

She paused a moment. It was odd that Bill and Hank weren't there yet. They'd said they were leaving early for a two-day trip. Maybe not so odd. Earlier in the evening they'd said something to Mike about stopping at one of the local taverns on the way home.

"To each his own," she murmured, eager now to check on J.B. Her sixth sense seemed to be sending out warning signals, and she hoped it wasn't because of J.B. He was supposed to be taking it easy, not spying on criminals.

The lights were out on the *Hallie B*. Could J.B. have gone to bed already? Or was he out solving another crime? It was still early—only nine. Helen climbed aboard and crept to the cabin. It was locked. At the sounds of soft snoring, she released the breath she'd been holding and smiled. Her worries had been for naught. J.B. was safe. She almost wished she had a key, thinking how wonderful it would be to snuggle down beside him. But they hadn't gotten around to making her an extra set of keys yet. Probably just as well. She doubted she'd be able to resist waking him to find out exactly what was going on.

Helen lowered herself onto a deck chair. No wonder J.B. had wanted to stay there. Water lapping at the sides of the boat, lulling him to sleep. The lights of Ilwaco created a halo effect. To the northwest, the town ended almost too abruptly, giving way to a dark, brooding forest. It gave the illusion of isolation. Helen leaned back and watched the moon inch upward. She contemplated walking up to Cape D in the moonlight but decided against it.

She'd need to get back to the bed and breakfast soon or at least call. Emily would be waiting to hear from her. Helen hoisted herself out of the chair. A noise from the port's west entrance claimed her attention. A man carrying a sack of groceries stumbled down the gangplank, fell to his knees, then got back up again. It took a moment for her to recognize him in the dim light. Obviously intoxicated, Mike Trenton stumbled again, this time reaching out to grab a piling. His sack fell. He dove for it, missed, and landed in the water. Helen scrambled off the boat and ran up to help.

Mike's arms slapped at the water. "Help!" he sputtered before going under.

"Take my hand." Helen wrapped an arm around a piling and reached for him. Grabbing his jacket, she hauled him closer, then caught hold of his wrist. He grasped her hand and nearly pulled her in with him.

"Hold still. I've got you," Helen grunted. "I can get you out, but you'll have to help."

"Sure," Mike panted. "Whatcha wan me ta do?" He'd relaxed some, but Helen doubted he'd be much help.

"Grab the dock with your other hand and try to pull yourself up. I'll help you."

Mike grabbed for the wood and missed, practically yanking her arm out of its socket. Pain shot through her. For a moment she thought he may have dislocated her shoulder again. She leaned forward to reduce the pressure. "Mike!" she yelled. "Let go of my hand and hold on to the dock."

"I'm trying." His hand hit the dock, and this time he managed to hold on.

Helen turned at the sound of footsteps.

"What's going on?" Bill ran toward them, his brother not far behind.

"He's drunk. Help me pull him up." Hank and Bill each grabbed one arm and hauled Mike to his feet.

The fall into the cold water should have sobered Mike up some, and maybe it had. But it was too little to notice.

"You think we should take him to the doctor?" Helen asked.

"Naw. He'll be fine once we get him sobered up," Bill said. "Why don't you get his groceries? We'll take him to the *Merry Maid* and get him into some dry clothes."

Reluctantly, Helen picked up the bag Mike had been trying

to carry down. His groceries consisted of a six-pack, a loaf of bread, pork and beans, and some cold cuts. Helen was tempted to pour the alcohol into the bay. If she thought it would alter the course of Mike's life, she'd have done just that. Unfortunately, Mike would have to conquer his problems in his own time and in his own way.

She followed the men and the wet, drippy trail to the *Merry Maid*, then helped Hank and Bill get Mike and his things on board. Once they'd gone into the cabin, Helen went back to the *Hallie B* to collect her pack.

The door to the cabin stood ajar, but the cabin was still dark. Helen moved toward it. J.B. was still lying on the bed. He must have awakened and been in need of some fresh air. Perhaps he was still awake. She slid the door open several inches more and stepped inside.

In the next instant a figure approached from behind. Before she could react, a man clamped a hand over her mouth and dragged her against his hard chest. The muzzle of a gun pressed against her ribs.

Twenty-four

Helen winced as her husband stumbled to the bed, doubled over in pain. "It serves you right, sneaking up on me like that." It had taken her only five seconds to discover the attacker was J.B.—three seconds too late. She'd slammed her heel against his instep, spun around, disarmed him, and cuffed him under the jaw. "What in the world were you doing?"

J.B. groaned and dropped onto the bunk, mumbling something incoherent. What she'd thought was his sleeping form turned out to be pillows.

"Darling, I am sorry. If I'd known." Sympathetic tears sprang to her eyes.

He grabbed the pad and pen lying beside the bed and began writing, then handed it to her.

Not your fault. I heard someone prowling around earlier. Thought maybe one of the kids arrested this afternoon had come back to even the score. Wasn't expecting you.

"Now I feel doubly bad. That prowler was me. Emily and some of the people I've met here threw a party to celebrate my finishing the guidebook. I came by to check on you. You were sleeping, so I decided to go back to the B and B. I was just about to leave when Mike fell in." At his questioning look, she told him about her less-than-heroic rescue efforts. "At any rate, I came back to get my bag and noticed the door was open. Had no idea you were lying in wait." She sat beside him. "I hope I didn't hurt you too badly."

He shook his head and wrapped his arms around her, pulling her snug against him. He murmured something that sounded like, "I'll live."

She asked him then about the roundup of drug dealers and whether or not he'd faked his heart attack.

I wish that were the case, luv, he wrote. *It was by accident I spotted them. Maybe the good Lord knew I needed to crack this one. I was feeling pretty low.*

"Why didn't you tell me when I came by this afternoon?"

He shrugged and wrote, *Didn't want to upset you. Planned to let you know soon enough.*

"You seemed anxious to be rid of me. Were you really planning to write or did you mean to work?"

J.B. produced a separate legal pad with several pages written in longhand.

"So you were writing. May I see it?"

He hid it away in the bedside stand and said, "Not yet."

Helen didn't press him. He'd share them when he was ready.

"Will you stay tonight?" J.B. asked a few minutes later.

"I'd like that, but I'd better not. Emily will be waiting for me. This will be my last night at the bed and breakfast."

"It's just as well. I should try to sleep."

She wove her fingers through his still-dark hair. "Will the color wash out?"

He nodded.

"Good. I like it better natural." She kissed him. "I want my old J.B. back." Her hand dropped to his chest, suddenly aware of how much had changed. Not just his hair but his heart.

Helen didn't meet his eyes, but somehow she knew without looking he was feeling the same.

Making her way back to the car, she began having second thoughts about staying on the boat with J.B. She hadn't meant to convey that she somehow loved him less because of his recent changes or disabilities—if that's what they were.

Helen passed the *Merry Maid* and stopped to observe the merrymaking on board. She momentarily dubbed it the *Merry Men.* Instead of sobering up their friend, Hank and Bill had apparently decided to join him. The three were singing sailing songs and laughing over crude jokes.

"Glad I don't have to be around them when they wake up in the morning," she mused. "Those hangovers can be gruesome."

When she reached the car, Helen had another attack of guilt. Not just guilt, she realized, but a longing. She really did want to be with J.B., snuggled next to him. Though she'd never tell him, she had the strongest urge to protect him. She'd easily overtaken him when he'd sneaked up on her. That would never have happened before the heart attack. He was weak. And what if one of the people he'd turned in did decide to retaliate?

Helen turned back, walked to the pay phone near the entrance to one of the restaurants, and called Emily. "I'm still in Ilwaco," she said, relating how she'd been talking to J.B. and how Mike had fallen into the water. "I'm not sure what to do."

"Why don't you stay on the boat?" Emily said. "Much as I like your company, I'm about to go to bed. Sounds like J.B. could use some comforting about now."

"I think so too, but this will be our last evening together. . . ."

"Nonsense. We can talk tomorrow when you pick up your things. Come for breakfast—bring J.B. if he wants."

Helen glanced toward the *Hallie B*, her spirits suddenly lifted. The lights were still on in the cabin. "Are you sure?"

"Absolutely."

"We'll see you in the morning, then. Or at least I will."

Walking past the *Klipspringer*, Helen was again taken aback by an odd sense that something was not as it should be. She glanced across the way at another fishing boat, the *Dream Fisher*. The boats were nearly the same length, yet different. Her gaze skipped back and forth between the two vessels.

Of course. Why hadn't she seen it before? The *Dream Fisher* rode several feet higher—as it should have with an empty hold. The *Klipspringer* sat low in the water, much like it had the day she'd seen them unloading at the fish processing plant.

Logic told her it wouldn't be full of fish. Even though the hold was cool, the fish were unloaded immediately to assure freshness. And they wouldn't have forgotten. If not fish, then what? Drugs? It seemed unlikely with their attitude toward drugs, but that may have been for show. Of course the hold may contain something legitimate. But what?

Perhaps the craft were simply designed differently, making one ride higher than the other. She shrugged and started toward the *Hallie B*. Hank, Bill, and Mike were still boozing it up. They'd probably be at it for a while. Long enough for her to take a peek into the hold of the *Klipspringer*?

Her curiosity got the best of her. If she didn't look, she'd be awake all night wondering. Helen retraced her steps. When she reached the *Klipspringer* she hurriedly climbed aboard. Once on deck, Helen retrieved the flashlight from her pack and searched for the latch that would open the hold. If she remembered correctly there were two doors, each having a rusty metal ring attached to a rope. Helen found them with no trouble and pulled the aft door up. The opening was about four feet square. A rustic ladder attached to the inside wall let her gain entrance. The hold, though clean looking, had the unpleasant smell of fish and something else. Petroleum? Maybe oil or diesel—not surprising, since the craft ran on diesel fuel.

The hold was smaller than she'd thought, and empty, except for several oil drums in the corner. Too small, she decided. With her flashlight she examined the far wall and realized it was a partition. After breaking a nail and getting a nasty sliver in her hand, Helen gave up on the partition and went back to the drums in the corner.

A cursory examination told her what she'd already begun to suspect. They'd all been concentrating on drugs, but Isabelle had written articles about something else as well. The Carlson brothers did a lot of odd jobs. She suspected dumping toxic waste was one of them. One thing for certain, Adam and Dan needed to know about these barrels right away.

"I don't like it," a husky voice broke through the stillness.

Helen doused the light and backed up against the wall.

"Just shut up and help me." She recognized the second voice as Bill's.

"I wish we'd never hired out to make these drops. We coulda

done okay without the extra money."

"It's too late now," Bill grunted.

"But why Mike? And why us?"

"You heard the boss. It's either him or us."

"Yeah. Heard that a lot lately."

They were on board now—Helen felt the boat shift and heard their shuffling footfalls. Something thudded to the floor. She headed for the drums and ducked behind one, scooting it forward a few inches.

"Put him in the hold for . . . hey, what's the door to the hold doing open?" Bill peered inside the hold. "I told you to keep it closed."

Helen hoped the shadows would hide her as she watched the men. At least she had on a black jacket and jeans. Moonlight reflected off Bill's face, giving his tanned skin a ghoulish look.

"I did close it." Hank came up beside him. "Hey, you don't suppose . . ."

"Cops? Nah. They got no reason to suspect us. You probably left it open when you checked it earlier."

Hank shook his head. "I didn't."

"Well, it don't matter. One of us must have—'course it could have been Mike. Maybe that's how he found out."

"What if it wasn't?" Hank asked.

"You can look around when I hand Mike down to you."

Helen stopped breathing. Her heart hammered so hard against her chest wall, she felt certain it would break a rib.

Hank stepped onto the ladder. "I'll need a light."

"I'll hold one up for you in a minute." Bill groaned as he lifted Trenton's body over the ledge.

Hank, halfway down the ladder, grabbed Mike around the middle, easing him to the floor. Hank jumped down the rest of the way and dragged Mike across the roughhewn floor and leaned him up against the far wall. "Where's the light?"

Bill shined a high-power flashlight into the hold. Helen scrunched lower, peering through the space between drums.

Hank glanced around, then lumbered over to the partition. Removing a three-foot-wide floor-to-ceiling panel, he peered into the other side. More drums. He slid the panel back in place, then climbed back on deck. "Looks okay—nothing's missing. Mighta just been some kids messin' around."

"We'd better hit the sack. I want to head out before dawn."

"Let's have this be the last one, huh, Bill? I don't much like this business."

"Me neither. Never counted on killin' anybody—especially not our best friend." Bill slapped his brother on the shoulder. The door to the hold fell with a heavy thud.

Twenty-five

Helen waited until the footsteps overhead subsided, then eased out of her hiding place and turned on the flashlight. The beam danced over the walls and settled on Mike Trenton— but only for a moment. She swung the beam upward.

"Oh, Lord," Helen mumbled. "Why in the world did you have to give me such an insatiable curiosity? I could at this very moment be snuggled up to the love of my life, and instead I'm in the hold of a fishing boat with a corpse."

That is, if he is a corpse. Helen swung the light back to Mike. He wasn't moving, but his skin didn't have the look of death. She moved closer and knelt down beside him. Reaching forward, she placed her fingers alongside his jaw and took a carotid pulse. He brushed her hand away.

Helen gasped and jerked back. His head lolled to one side. "I guess that answers my question." She grabbed his shoulder and shook him.

"Mike, wake up." Shining the light on his face, she lifted an eyelid. His pupils were pinpoint like Chuck Frazier's had been the night before he'd been killed. While she rubbed his neck and shoulder to arouse him, Helen thought back to the scene on the dock. She'd wondered at the time how he could have gotten plastered so quickly. She suspected it would take a lot of drinks to affect him. They had left the party close to the same time. Had Hank and Bill drugged him? Had they sent him down to his boat alone hoping he'd fall in? Whatever their plans, Helen had most likely altered them.

Perhaps she'd come along for a reason. God did, after all, set people in certain places at certain times. The one thing she did know was that they meant to kill him. What she hadn't figured out yet was why. She suspected it had something to do with the drums in the hold. Like the others, Mike had probably seen or heard too much.

"Either way, you're a dead man unless we can get you out of here." Helen grabbed his legs and pulled him away from the wall, then slipped her arms under his arms in an attempt to get him on his feet. Too heavy. He showed no signs of waking up. She'd never be able to get Mike out of the hold unless he regained consciousness. And he could very well die if he stayed on board.

Still, she couldn't let the urgency of the situation cloud common sense. She'd planned on waiting until she felt certain Hank and Bill were asleep before making her escape. Helen hauled in a deep breath and concentrated on settling down her adrenalized body. This was doable, but she needed her wits about her. She'd climb out of the hold and call for help. Hank and Bill would be arrested and the EMTs would get Mike to the hospital.

After a few minutes of reassuring herself that the bad boys upstairs had gone to bed, Helen climbed the steps and pushed at the door. It moved about a quarter of an inch.

"Come on, open," Helen muttered as she pushed for a third, then a fourth time on the heavy door. Even with her good shoulder against it, the door wouldn't open. The men had either set something heavy on it to restrain Mike, or somehow secured it. Whatever they'd done, she was not likely to get out anytime soon.

Helen descended the ladder. Before sitting down, she checked on Mike again. Still breathing. She wondered how much alcohol he'd consumed and if he'd taken, or been given, something else—like chloral hydrate. And if so, had he ingested enough to kill him? Mike probably weighed fifty pounds more than Chuck had. The fact that he was still alive gave her hope.

Now if she could just keep him that way.

⚜   ⚜   ⚜

The sound and smell of diesel engines awakened her. The *Klipspringer* was moving—a task Helen found nearly impossible. Her joints ached from the numbing cold. Beneath her ear she could hear the steady normal beating of Mike's heart. How her head had ended up on his chest, she wasn't certain. During the night she'd poked, prodded, and talked to Mike in an effort to revive him and hopefully keep him from dying in his sleep. Her efforts had worked so far.

The flashlight lay on the floor beside her, but she didn't reach for it. The batteries had died. Though she'd tried to conserve them, they'd given out the last time she'd checked on Mike and left her in the dark. She sat up and began working the soreness out of her joints.

Helen couldn't see her watch but remembered Bill saying they'd be heading out before daybreak. She wouldn't be missed for hours. J.B. thought she was with Emily. Emily thought she was with J.B. By the time they thought to call one another she and Mike would probably be fish food. Thinking of the containers of toxic waste, she smirked. At least they'd be healthy fish food.

Not that she planned on giving up. Hank and Bill would have a mighty hard time throwing her to the sharks.

"Hey, Mike. Wake up." Helen gave him a shove. He'd no doubt have a hangover, and she didn't even have a cup of coffee to offer him, but she needed him awake and alert. Between the two of them, she felt certain they could overpower the Carlson brothers. She just wasn't sure how.

"Go away," he groaned and rolled over, his head hitting the floor. "Ow, what the. . . ? Where's my pillow? Where am I?"

"You're in the hold of the *Klipspringer*. Courtesy of your drinking buddies. No amenities like pillows—or food, I'm afraid. No lights either. My flashlight batteries died. Your friends are taking us out to sea. And I don't think they plan on bringing us back."

"No, that's not pos . . . they said they were going to quit. O-o-ow."

Helen heard a thud. And another groan. "Mike? Are you okay?"

"Oh, geez, no. I can't . . . my head."

"Just sit still. Take some deep breaths."

"Easy enough for you to say. . . ."

Helen helped him sit up. "I'm going to help you move over to the wall. You can rest your back against it."

"Ouch. Take it easy." When her backside hit the wall, Helen instructed him to scoot back.

Apparently more comfortable, he mumbled a thank-you. "You're . . . that Bradley woman . . . aren't you?" His words were strained and halting.

"What gave me away?"

"Recognized your voice. Wh-what are you doing here?"

Helen explained how the position of the boat in the water had made her suspicious.

"That's what cued me in too. I've been following them. Yesterday I saw them load up the drums over at the dock up at Bay Center."

"Do you know where the drums came from?"

"No. Just a broken-down old truck. License number was caked over with mud, so I couldn't read it."

"How did you get close enough to see what they were doing?"

"High-powered scope. I have a rifle on the boat."

"A rifle . . . the one that killed Harry Bolton."

He was silent for a long moment. "How'd you find out about that?"

"Gossip. Some people think—"

"That it wasn't an accident. I know." He pushed out a heavy sigh. "It was. Haven't gone hunting since. I . . . I swear I didn't know it was him. He was wearing camouflage."

Helen couldn't see his tears but knew they were there by the sudden roughness in his voice. He sniffed. Sorry she had brought up such painful memories, she waited a few minutes, then changed the subject.

"You said the Carlson brothers were supposed to quit. Quit what?"

"I found out what they were doing, and like a jerk I confronted them."

"That wasn't too bright. Especially after what happened to Chuck and Isabelle."

He moaned again. "They didn't kill Chuck—or Isabelle."

"Right, just like they didn't drug you and aren't at this very minute hauling you out to sea to give you a proper burial."

"I can't believe that."

"I heard them, Mike. I'm sorry. When they find out I'm down here with you, they'll try to kill me too."

"Oh man. I trusted them. We've been friends since . . ."

"I know. Since grade school. If it makes you feel any better, I overheard them say they felt bad about it."

Feeling hungry and cold, Helen jumped up and paced back and forth across the floor trying to maintain her balance as the boat picked up speed. "We must be in the river." She gave up and sat back down, hoping the movement of the boat wouldn't make her seasick. "Why didn't you tell Dan when you found out?"

"I couldn't believe Hank and Bill would do anything like that—at least not knowingly. Thought maybe somebody had set them up." Helen heard him shift positions. "Last night when we left the party I told 'em we needed to talk. Thought maybe if I explained it to them, they'd quit. It was working. They told me they didn't know what the stuff was and that the guy that hired him said there wouldn't be any danger to the fish."

"They couldn't possibly be that gullible."

"Guess not. They must have slipped something into my drink when I went to the bathroom. Not long after that I started feeling sick. Stopped to get a couple things at the store and went home."

"And that's when you fell into the water."

"Yeah." He released a deep sigh. "Don't suppose you got any aspirin on you."

"Sorry." Helen folded her arms across her knees and rested her chin on them. "Mike, do you have any idea who Hank and Bill are working for?"

"No. I sort of assumed it was Mandrel."

"I don't think so. He's in jail. And somehow I don't see him doing anything to jeopardize the fishing industry. It's his livelihood. He has seafood plants up and down the coast. I guess I might be able to accept his involvement in drugs, but not dumping toxic waste."

"It might be a waste management business upriver."

"Yes. I've been wondering that myself. Just recently a Portland company got caught dumping into the Willamette River. Earl Wilson told me about another dump in the Cowlitz."

"The guy with the EPA?"

"Hmm. You know, it's odd that Earl's brother-in-law would be carrying the detonator to blow up Chuck's boat. I never really did buy the part about Scott Mandrel hiring him." Helen chewed on her lower lip while her mind fit pieces of the puzzle together. "I think I may know who killed Chuck."

"Who?"

"Earl Wilson. He could easily have hired his brother-in-law. Earl knew how distraught the man was and how desperate. He probably promised to pay him off in drugs. Or maybe he agreed to help him commit suicide. As far as we know, Kendall only had three visitors the day he died. Scott and Shells, and Earl."

"Earl is EPA. He's supposed to protect the environment, not destroy it."

"True. Perhaps I'm wrong. He always seemed like such a nice young man." Helen chewed on her lower lip. "Hank and Bill knew him. He'd gone out with them the day before he chartered out with you. And I saw them together at Shells' Place the day before Chuck was killed."

"Yeah, I remember. Come to think of it, the boys did seem pretty flush that night. Bought drinks for everybody. Said they'd gotten some extra work."

The water was getting choppier. Helen could hear waves slapping against the sides of the boat. She leaned against the wall and took several deep breaths to ward off nausea. Since she hadn't eaten, it wasn't affecting her like it had when she'd gone out on the *Merry Maid*. Still, being below deck was definitely taking its toll. "Think we're crossing the bar?" she asked.

"Feels like it."

"Wonder how far out we're going."

"I'd say twenty miles at least. They'll want to be out of sight."

Helen shuddered. The trip was only just beginning. A surge of sorrow washed over her with the intensity of an ocean wave.

"This could be it, Mike," she said softly. "I'm praying we'll be able to gain the upper hand, but anything could happen."

"I know. They'll probably kill us before they throw us over. I hope they do. Be easier that way."

"Yes, I suppose it would."

Twenty-six

M rs. Bradley," Mike said after a time. "Do you believe in God?"
"Yes. That's the one good thing in all of this. If I do die
today, I'll go to a better place."

"You mean heaven?"

"Hmm."

"How do you know you'll end up there?"

"I believe in what the Bible teaches." Helen closed her eyes.
" 'For God so loved the world he gave his only begotten son. And
whoever believes in Him will not perish but have everlasting
life.' John 3:16. I learned that verse as a child and never forgot
it. My mother always used to say God was the one thing in life
we could be sure of."

"I used to go to church. Took my wife and kids every Sunday.
That was before—before the hunting accident. My life sort of fell
apart after I shot Harry." Mike hesitated, then said. "I . . . I have
a drinking problem. Wife left me a while back. Said I needed to
go in for treatment. Haven't been to church since. I'm a killer
and an alcoholic. Figure God hasn't got much use for me anymore."

"I don't believe that for a minute. God loves you. He always
has and always will. Nothing you do can change that."

"So you think if I tell God I'm sorry for screwing up, He'll
forgive me?"

"Yes."

"How can you be sure? Don't you ever have doubts?"

"I don't know of anyone who doesn't have some doubts. While I believe in God with all my heart, there's a part of me that isn't so sure—a part that wonders if any of it is real. Yet when I think of the alternatives . . ."

"What alternatives?"

"That there is no God—that the world came about as a result of some cosmic fluke. Or if there is a God, He's too high and mighty to care about us. I can't look at the order and the wonders of this planet and the universe and believe that. I guess I've seen enough miracles in my day to confirm to me that we have a God who not only created the universe and whatever lies beyond, but that He cares for each one of us in a personal way."

"Like a father."

"And mother. God is so much more than either." Helen sighed. "It's funny. We're sitting here in the bowels of a boat heading for what could be our final resting place, and I'm not the least bit frightened of dying. At least not at the moment."

"I am."

They continued to sit there in the utter darkness and talk— about their families, about not getting to say good-bye, about death and the life to come. Mike ended up praying and asking God to forgive him and to take care of his family. They prayed together that they might somehow overtake their captors and live.

"You know, Mike, I have a very positive feeling about all of this." Helen could almost feel him smile.

"Yeah. I know what you mean. God must be looking after us. My headache is gone."

"I'm glad."

They sat for a time in silence listening to the steady roar of engines. Faith was a wonderful thing. And Helen intended to cling to every last strand of it to stay alive. She certainly wouldn't give up. That thought brought her back to Isabelle and Chuck.

"Mike?"

"What?"

"You said you didn't think Hank and Bill killed Chuck or Isabelle."

"Yeah. Isabelle was like family to us—you know? Us guys— Chuck, Dan, Hank, Bill, and me did everything together. Isabelle and Emily took us in more than once. They were like our own family. For a while Hank and Bill even stayed with them. They were about fifteen when their parents were killed in a car accident. Um . . . their dad was a fisherman and an alcoholic. Isabelle and Emily helped them hold on to their dad's house and the *Klipspringer* by paying the bills until the boys were able to finish high school and go to work. I suppose it's possible, but I can't see them hurting Isabelle."

"You may be right. Do you remember if Earl was around when Isabelle died?"

"I think he was. He chartered out with me the weekend before. Brought his buddies down then too. Thing is, Hank and Bill wouldn't have taken the job if they thought Earl was responsible for killing Isabelle—or Chuck. They told me they thought their deaths had to do with the drug business."

"There have been a lot of cover-ups. Earl may have killed Chuck and Isabelle and set Scott up to take the blame. He may have used the drug ring as a means to cover up his own activity, then made certain everyone focused on that."

"Maybe, but why? He always seemed sincere about his job and everything."

"Money? We may never know." Her voice rang out in the sudden stillness. The engines had stopped.

Helen scrambled to her feet, her heart racing. "Mike," she whispered, "we'll stand our best chance of getting out of here if we pretend like I'm not here and you're still out of it. Lie very still and make them come down and get you. I'll get behind the barrels. We'll surprise them."

"What do you plan to do?"

Helen didn't get a chance to answer. The door to the hold opened as she found the drums and slipped in behind them. Bill peered down into the hold, shining a light on Mike. Mike looked like a rag doll, head forward, arms hanging at his sides, legs slightly apart. "He's still out. Either that or he's already dead. You'll have to go down and carry him up."

"Why me?" Hank whined. "This was your idea. I wanted to dope him up and throw him off the docks."

"Come on, bro. You're stronger than I am. Besides, I have to radio in that we're ready."

Grumbling, Hank backed down the ladder into the hold. He headed straight for Mike. "Hate doing this, old buddy."

Mike bounced to his feet and thrust a fist into Hank's gut. "Maybe you won't have to."

"What the—" Hank doubled over, letting out a long string of expletives. He came at Mike, smashing him against the wall. Helen crept up behind Hank and tapped him on the shoulder. He spun around, his eyes wide with shock. Before he could recover, Helen delivered a sharp kick to his knee-cap then jabbed a fist to his trachea. He buckled and slumped to the floor.

"Let's go." Helen helped Mike to his feet and climbed up on deck. Mike was still on the ladder when Bill came out of the cabin.

"How'd you—" Bill stammered.

"Bill, I'm glad you're here," Helen gasped. "Hank's been hurt."

"No way . . ." Bill bent over the hold and before he could catch on, Helen stepped behind him and shoved him in.

"Quick," she shouted to Mike. "Close the hatch."

Mike did, latching it in place. He grinned up at her. "Wow, you're good."

"I've had a lot of practice."

Mike climbed up to the fly-bridge, started the engines, and radioed in to the Coast Guard station. "They'll meet us at the dock," he yelled down to her.

Helen nodded and gave him a thumbs-up sign. They'd done it. Now all that remained was to have Dan pick up Earl Wilson for questioning. She wondered if he really worked for the EPA. Like Mike had said, that was the one hitch. Earl had seemed sincere. She was usually able to read people quite well. Was she losing her touch?

They'd only gone a short distance when Mike yelled for her to join him. When she got up on the fly-bridge, he pointed to a boat in the distance. "I'm not positive, but I think that's the *Merry Maid*."

"How can you tell?" she yelled over the sound of the engines.

"Been sailing her for years. See if you can find me a pair of binoculars. Might be some in the forward cabin."

Helen found a pair on the berths near the bow. The cabin was in as big a mess as Hank's and Bill's lives. She felt sorry for them in a way. From what Mike had said, they'd had a hard life. No excuse for what they were doing, but it helped her understand their desperation. She passed the ice box on her way out, stopped, and went back to it, snagging a couple of sodas and apples. She also grabbed a bag of unopened chips from the counter.

Helen brought the binoculars topside and handed them to Mike. She set an apple and drink on the console for him, then opened the chips.

"Thanks." He squinted at the boat on the horizon, then raised the glasses. "It's the *Merry Maid* all right."

"Can you see who's piloting her?"

"No." He handed the glasses to Helen. "Take a look. I'll head toward her."

"That might not be a good idea. I have a hunch it might be whoever Hank and Bill were working for." Helen lifted the binoculars and nearly made herself sick looking at the high swells. She strongly suspected Hank and Bill's boss had arranged to meet with the *Klipspringer*. Perhaps they'd planned on staging Mike's death. He'd be found on his own boat, a victim of drug and alcohol overdose. That way they'd never have to contend with a body washing ashore.

Helen found the boat and focused in on it. The driver was piloting from the fly-bridge, but she couldn't quite make out who it was. Not Earl, she realized. He was much taller. This person was no bigger than a child and had dark hair. She closed her eyes and hung the glasses around her neck. *Shells?*

Helen shook her head in disbelief. She hadn't even suspected . . . no, that wasn't quite true. There had been a time—when Shells had disappeared with Scott. Taking a bite of her apple, Helen turned back to tell Mike.

"There has to be an explanation." Mike ran a hand through his thick hair. "She couldn't possibly be involved. Even if she was, she's a woman . . ."

Helen lifted an eyebrow. "Shells is a strong woman. We've seen that in the way she's put together her restaurant. She's determined. Besides, she apparently isn't working alone. She must have hired Hank and Bill to do her dirty work for her. And Kendall. Maybe she and Scott were together on it."

"I'll grant you she's tough, but to kill her own brother?" He shook his head. "I don't think so."

"I guess we'll find out soon enough, won't we?" The boats continued toward each other until only a few feet of ocean separated them. Shells idled the engines, letting the *Merry Maid* drift closer. The expression on her face was hard.

"What are you doing on my boat?" Mike hollered over to her.

"I heard you might be in trouble. Came out to see if I could help." Shells jumped onto the aft deck. "Quick, toss me a line and help me tie the boats together."

"No way," Mike yelled. "It's too dangerous."

"Don't be silly. The water's calm as glass. Besides, I'm coming aboard one way or another, Mike. Would you rather I let your craft float free?"

"What makes you think I'll let you get close enough to climb aboard?"

Shells lifted the lid on the bench in front of her and pulled out Mike's rifle. "If you don't, I'll blow a hole clean through her and the *Klipspringer.*"

"You wouldn't! You'd die in the process."

"Ha. I'll have the dinghy. Your choice." She pointed the barrel down.

Mike swore and tossed her a line, which she attached to one of the cleats on the *Merry Maid.* Mike helped her secure the boats together until they were separated only by the fenders.

Helen shuddered. Mike was right. Tying the boats together was a dangerous thing to do. She and J.B. had stopped to help a boater in trouble—rough water, wind blowing. Boats don't rock together, she and J.B. had discovered. One bobs up, the other down. The pressure on the cleats and lines had pulled one of their cleats out.

"That's better," Shells said.

"How'd you know I'd be out here?" Mike asked. Helen had to give him credit. With all he'd been through, he was acting as though the situation were as everyday as washing clothes.

"I finally figured out who was framing Scott." She made no move to set down the rifle. "I came down to the docks last night to talk to you and saw Hank and Bill take you on board the *Klipspringer*. I was afraid they might dump you, so I went back to your boat and followed them out this morning."

"You expect me to believe that?"

"I don't care what you believe, Mike. It's true."

"Why didn't you go to the police?" Helen asked.

"With what? My suspicions? I didn't know what was going on. I thought maybe I'd find out more by following them." She tipped her head to one side.

"Not a smart thing to do," Helen said. Though her face looked strangely innocent, Shells had a cold, calculating look in her eyes. Helen remembered seeing it before and had mistaken it for determination.

"What are you doing here, Mrs. Bradley? Don't tell me Hank and Bill got you too."

"Almost. I'm not that easy to get rid of."

"Where are they?" Shells scanned the deck of the *Klipspringer*.

"In the hold. Which is where you're going." Mike advanced on her and made it as far as the railing.

Shells raised the rifle and fired.

"Mike, don't!" Helen's warning came too late. Mike teetered on the rail, then fell back on deck. The shell from the 30.06 tore a hole in his side. He dropped to his knees, writhing in pain.

Helen started toward him.

"Hold it. Make one move and you're next."

Helen lifted her hands and backed away. "He's bleeding. At least let me put pressure on it."

"For what? He's going to die anyway. All of you are." A large swell lifted one boat, then the other, causing the line to shudder and the fenders to groan. Shells pressed her knees against the bench for balance.

Helen stumbled, catching herself on the ladder leading to the bridge. "You won't get away with this."

"Of course I will. Don't you see? Hank, Bill, and Mike were dumping toxic waste. We confronted them and they were going to kill us. I managed to get to the gun. But I was too late to save you. You'd already been killed. I'll be the only survivor. After a while I'll get over my grief and Adam and I—"

"Adam? Surely he doesn't have anything to do with this."

"Of course not. But he loves me. He'll believe anything I say."

"Then why—what about Scott?"

"Oh, I'll feel terrible about him, but no one will blame me for divorcing him. Poor Scott will be convicted as a drug smuggler. Even as we speak the boys are naming him as the big gun." Her smile came far too easy, and Helen couldn't help but wonder how it had happened. How a sweet little girl could have grown up to become so sinister.

"You were behind the drug dealing too?"

"Been doing that for years. Small scale until recently. It takes a lot of money to run a restaurant—and my training wasn't cheap." Shells lowered the lid on the bench and replaced the cushions, then knelt on them.

Helen shook her head. "What about your brother, Shells— and Isabelle? Did you kill them as well?"

"Oh, I didn't kill them. Steve Kendall did that. He loved me too, you know."

"But you hired him. Just like you hired Hank and Bill to kill Mike." Helen shook her head. "How could you, Shells? Especially Chuck."

"That was unfortunate. But what else could I do?" Shell's small voice held a hint of remorse. "I slipped him the chloral hydrate, hoping he'd give up his stupid idea of investigating on his own. If I'd let him follow Hank and Bill, he'd have found out what they were doing and turned them in. They would have told Dan it was me who hired them. I couldn't take the chance, so I had Steve plant the bomb."

"Why, Shells?"

"I told you. Money." Shells shrugged. "Enough with the questions. Open the hatch and let my bungling buddies out."

"I'm not sure I can," Helen said. "It's awfully heavy."

"Do it."

"I can't. Last night after they left Mike and me down there, I couldn't budge it. If you want it open you'll have to help me."

"Try."

Helen hooked a hand around the ring and pulled, not bothering to loosen the bolt that locked it in place. She grunted and strained for several seconds, then collapsed on her knees. "I can't."

For a moment Helen didn't think Shells would fall for the bait. In disgust, Shells shifted the rifle to her left hand. Using her right, she steadied herself on the railing and crossed over to the *Klipspringer*.

Before Shells could raise the rifle again, Helen charged her. The blow knocked Shells off balance. The rifle flew over the railing and into the water. Shells caught herself and lunged forward, ramming a fist into Helen's face, clipping her jaw and nose. Pain rocked Helen. When she staggered back, Shells dove on top of her. Helen grabbed her wrists before she could deliver another blow.

"You might as well give up. You're as good as dead."

"I don't think so." Helen could feel a trail of blood dripping from her nose.

A huge swell caught them broadside. Shells toppled over. Helen turned loose of her arm and hammered a fist into Shells' face.

Shells screamed. Helen twisted Shells around and pulled her arm up sharp behind her back. Shells jabbed an elbow into Helen's ribs. Helen loosened her hold and Shells spun away. They were face-to-face now, Helen bent and ready for another attack. Shells, more determined than ever, had the look of a bull ready to charge. As she did, Helen dropped to the floor, caught

Shells in the stomach with both feet, and propelled her up and over the railing.

Shells' scream was silenced as she disappeared into the icy gray water. When she emerged, her anger turned to cries for help. Holding her stomach, Helen tossed Shells a life ring. When she was certain Shells had hold of it, she turned back to Mike.

"You're not going to leave me out here, are you?" Shells' tone was that of a child.

"It would serve you right."

"That's—that's murder."

"No kidding." Helen had no intention of letting her die. Not that she didn't deserve it. Helen would take much more satisfaction in seeing Shells pay for her crimes in prison.

Mike's wound didn't appear life threatening, but he'd lost a lot of blood. She ran to the cabin, secured a sheet and pillow, then returned topside.

"Help me! Please! Don't let me die. I'm freezing."

"In a minute." Helen tore a side strip off the sheet and created a makeshift pressure dressing by wrapping it around him several times. "Hang in there, Mike. You're going to be all right."

Before hauling Shells in, Helen found a rope. She sincerely doubted Shells would put up a fight, but she wasn't taking any chances. She hauled Shells up. Once she had Shells on deck, Helen quickly secured her wrists to the railing.

Helen then brought all the blankets she could find from the cabin and used one to cover Mike and the others to wrap around Shells. She was chattering now, tears spilling down her face. Helen felt like crying too. Her arms and legs were turning to rubber.

"You can't give up now," she told herself as she climbed up on the bridge. "You're almost there."

Helen radioed in and gave the Coast Guard a brief accounting of what had happened. But she was unable to give a location.

"Listen carefully, ma'am," the radio operator commanded. "You'll need to activate the EPIRB."

"The what?" Helen could hear the hysteria in her voice and gripped the wheel to calm herself.

"Emergency Position Initiating Radio Beacon. It's an orange cylinder about five inches in diameter and two feet long with an antenna. Should be one located outside the cabin. To activate it, pull it out of the bracket and turn it upside down, then set it back in. It'll automatically start transmitting a radio signal and we'll find you. I've already alerted the fleet. We'll find you within the hour. Just stand by."

Helen replaced the radio. Panic slithered through her like a dozen tiny snakes. She shivered and hauled in a deep breath. "You've been in rough spots before," she reminded herself. *True,* she argued against the voice of hope. *But you've never been lost at sea.* She found the EPIRB, handily right where the radio operator had said it would be. After turning it upside down, she returned it to the bracket.

Stand by.

Helen returned to Mike to check his vital signs. Stable.

The dense fog swirled around them. Ocean and sky melted together without so much as a line of separation. The calm seas Shells had mentioned earlier had grown rough with enormous swells. With every swell the boats rose and fell, like two brutal enemies in a tug of war they strained at the lines, groaning and screaming with each tug.

Stand by.

Helen felt certain the Coast Guard would find them, but an hour was a long time and she doubted very much the vessels could remain side by side without breaking up.

"God," she whispered, "I can't believe you've brought me this far just to let me die." Helen bit into her lip and took a deep breath. One wrong move and she could be crushed between the boats or thrown into the sea, but she saw no other option. If she didn't separate the craft, the *Klipspringer* and its passengers along with the *Merry Maid* would end up another fatality in the Grave-yard of the Pacific.

Twenty-seven

Helen stood at the window, gazing out past the North Head Lighthouse to the narrow line of white clouds on the horizon. From their second-floor bedroom she had a spectacular view of the water. The sky was a robin's egg blue. The ocean, with its rows of whitecaps, looked almost serene now. It was hard to imagine it as having been as miserably gray and menacing as it had been only two days earlier. That had been Friday. Today was Sunday.

Helen breathed in the warm homey scent of her Earl Grey tea and took a long sip. Her mouth still hurt from where Shells had delivered a strong right, but other than that and a few bruises on various body parts, she'd fared quite well. Mike was doing fine—back to work already.

Dan and Adam were still in shock at discovering their lovely Shells was a cold-blooded killer and that she had used them and Scott as well as Kendall and the Carlson brothers to get her way.

And Shells. Helen sighed. She'd be all right physically, but mentally . . . the ordeal had sent her into a psychotic break. Helen guessed she had some type of personality disorder. The psychiatrist wouldn't say. There would have to be some in-depth testing before they'd know for certain.

Helen heard J.B. get out of bed and walk toward her. She felt his presence behind her.

He placed his hands on her shoulders and nuzzled the back of her neck. "You're up early, luv." His jaw was still wired shut, but he was able to speak with much less pain now. Most things were clear enough to understand, but for longer sentences he still relied on his pad and pen.

"Couldn't sleep."

"Nightmares again?" He wrapped his arms around her.

She leaned back against him, thankful for his support. "No." The night before she'd awakened in a cold sweat. Reliving the terror of drowning at sea. She hadn't, of course. Helen had activated Mike's radio beacon and separated the boats, then piloted the *Klipspringer* just far enough away to put a safe distance between the two vessels. True to their word, the Coast Guard found them fifty minutes later.

It's over now, Helen reminded herself. While the dread of narrowly escaping death still lingered, what bothered Helen even more had been the surprised look in Shells' eyes when Dan arrested her.

"I keep thinking about Shells and wondering what happened in her life to cause her to turn to criminal activity. She seems to have no conscience. I have a hard time understanding how she could have been so charming on the one hand and so cold and calculating on the other."

"It's always hard to understand how people can be driven to do such abominable things."

"I'm sure her mental illness contributed to it. And the fact that she was abandoned as a child."

"Well, she's definitely psychotic."

That was true enough. Shells had tried to talk Adam into posting bail and leaving town with her. When he turned away in disgust, she'd tried to proposition Dan. "I'm amazed she went so long without anyone noticing."

J.B. moved away and came back with pad in hand.

Many of our most devious and ruthless killers are also among the most clever. Ted Bundy. Diane Downs.

Helen turned her gaze from J.B.'s pad to the view outside the window. "At least we have evidence to prosecute." The blood she and Dan had collected pointed directly to Shells. Helen's laptop and manuscript had been found in Shells' bedroom, as had Isabelle's files. Why Shells had taken them was still a puzzle. Helen suspected, Shells, in her paranoia, wanted to be certain they contained no clue as to her illegal activities.

Dan had gotten signed confessions from Hank and Bill saying Shells had contracted them to dump the barrels twenty to thirty miles off shore. She'd made a deal with a company upriver to dispose of the waste. What Shells hadn't done herself, she'd hired out.

"Want to stay here another day or two?" J.B. asked.

Helen smiled up at him. "No. I'm more than ready to go home."

"Good." J.B.'s loving gaze lingered on her bruised face. He trailed his forefinger along her jaw, then looked away to write another message. *I'm glad we'll be going home together.*

"Hmm. Me too." Not wanting J.B. to pilot the *Hallie B* down the coast alone, she'd made arrangements with Adam, Mike, and Dan to take her car to Bay Village. Adam would drive, and Mike and Dan would follow in Dan's car. The three would return home after a few days R and R in Lincoln City. She glanced at her watch. "We'd better pack. I want to stop and see Emily before we leave."

"And Scott," J.B. reminded.

Helen nodded. Scott was free now, but devastated. Shells had set him up to take the blame for everything. J.B. had taken the young man under his wing and had promised to check in on him before going home.

⁕   ⁕   ⁕

The next morning, they picked up their two weeks' worth of mail at the Bay Village post office and began sorting through it.

J. B. snatched up one of the letters and hurriedly tore it open. Whatever was in it must have been good news because he jumped to his feet, hauled her up into his arms, and said something akin to "It's been accepted."

"Jason Bradley!" Helen exclaimed when he calmed down and let her read it. "Why didn't you tell me what you were up to?"

237

"Wanted to surprise you." Then he wrote, *I wasn't certain I could pull it off. Sent a proposal to an agent several weeks ago. I've been wondering what direction I should go. I guess now I have my answer.*

J.B.'s answer had come in the form of a book contract offering a hefty advance for a novel based on a portion of his life story, called *Spy Games.*

Helen was thrilled. Her dream man finally had something to occupy his time. They spent the next few hours celebrating and making plans to build an addition onto the house for their two offices. They would both have their own space.

Acknowledgments

A special thank-you to the U.S. Coast Guard at Cape Disappointment, Vancouver Police Department, Clark County Medical Examiner's office, and to Michael Curtis, Judy Frandsen, John and Deana Hughes, Jan Bono, Margo Power, and Birdie Etchison for their advice and expertise.

Red Sky in Mourning is a work of fiction, as are all the characters. However, many of the places such as Cape Disappointment, Fort Canby, the Lewis and Clark Interpretive Center, Bubba's Pizza, 42nd Street Cafe, The Ark, Colleen's Creations, Sweet Williams, and many others are very real and as wonderful as I've described. The Bayshore Bed and Breakfast is not real, but was based on an equally magnificent bed and breakfast called Caswell's on the Bay.